THE EXILES

When Harry Brandon sets out to delve into
the history of the Selways, he is seeking more
than a family background. He is searching for
himself.

THE EXILES

by

LYNN FOSTER

LONDON

HODDER & STOUGHTON

AUTHOR'S NOTE

Although *The Exiles* is based on the television cycle of the same name which was transmitted by the B.B.C., I was anxious, in writing it, not simply to transfer to the printed page material which was originally intended for the visual medium. Therefore, a good deal that was contained in the television plays has been omitted, and a good deal more has been added. The television series was planned as four separate plays, each one complete in itself. In this book I have redesigned the material to fit within the framework of one general theme.

The general background of this book is based on historical fact, but the story is completely fictional.

There are no such people as the Selways, the Spencers, the Camerons, and the Dooleys. There are no such places as Billabirra, Cameron's Crossing, or Woollaby.

While the author does not pretend that there is no such place as Sydney, she insists that there is no such beach as Harry Brandon's beach. There is no such person as Harry Brandon. In particular, there is no such person as Edward Selway.

CHAPTER ONE

THE trouble was that daffodils didn't mean a thing.
I tried to concentrate, to make a picture. "See it in your mind's eye," Old Pye had said. I couldn't. Rory Moran's voice droned on. Daffodils. The others were nudging each other and nodding towards Pye and giggling. He had his eyes closed and he was smiling. He could see the daffodils all right.

The temperature was well over a hundred and rising. From my desk I could see the heat haze rising off the playground, and I could hear the locusts. We'd been told they weren't locusts, of course. "They're cicadas," Pye insisted. And we said, "Yes, sir," and went on calling them locusts. Greengrocers, and Yellow Mondays, and Snowy Bakers, and Black Princes, and Double Drummers. It sounded as though the Moreton Bay Figs had started to sing. Rory was chanting to the end: "And then my heart with pleasure fills, and dances with the daffodils."

Rory sat down and the others straightened their backs and looked expectant. Pye came out of the Lake District and opened his eyes.

"Could you see them?" he asked.

Everyone, except me, looked smug and chanted, "Oh yes, sir."

Pye looked at me. "You weren't paying attention, Brandon."

"I was listening, sir."

"Poetry is speaking painting," he said.

I started to think about that.

"Stop staring out of the window, Brandon."

I looked at him, but went on thinking about what he'd just said.

Pye made a speech about Wordsworth, and the Lake poets, and spring . . . the English spring. He was off again with that funny look he'd get when he talked about England. Then suddenly he realised that the class was laughing at him, so he took it out on me.

"Use your imagination!" he said to me. "Learn it by heart tonight, and don't just learn it parrot fashion. Think about it while you're learning!" Then he got up and said, "Lunch!" and stalked out.

The others looked at me, grinning, and began to push each other about as they made for the door.

I was the stranger, the unaccepted. My mother had been ill and someone had given her a cottage for the summer so that she could recuperate and finish the book she was writing, so a term in a bush school was my share of her travail.

I followed them out on to the verandah, and we went round to the shady side. Rory and Ted Hill were fighting at the water-tank, splashing water into the mug, then taking mouthfuls and squirting it out at each other. Old Pye suddenly put his head round the end of the verandah and called, "Don't waste water!" So they stopped.

I opened my lunch. Egg sandwiches. Mother had wrapped them in lettuce leaves to keep them fresh, but it was too hot to eat them. Rory came and sat on the edge of the verandah near me. He had bare feet and I envied him. My mother had drawn the line at bare feet for school. There was always a smell of sour milk about Rory. His father had a dairy, and Rory helped with the milking before he came to school, and he looked after the pigs, too. He was beautiful, Rory was. All black hair and blue eyes. But he smelt of sour milk and pigs. He took the newspaper off his sandwiches. I knew what kind of sandwiches they were going to be, but I watched him just the same. Dripping and golden syrup. His sandwiches were always dripping and golden syrup. The dripping had soaked into the bottom slice, and the syrup into the top. Rory's lunch always made me sick, but I always watched him open it. His teeth bit into the mess, and as he chewed the dripping and golden syrup began to ooze down his chin, and he put his tongue out and licked it off. That was my time for feeling sick, so, as my stomach heaved, I got up and went over to the water-tank. The water was warm and there was a tadpole in the mug.

Ted Hill called out, "Don't you want your lunch, Harry?"

I said I didn't, so Ted and his sister, Margie, ate it.

After the sandwiches were gone, they let me play rounders with them for a while, but it was too hot to go on for long, so then we just sat on the verandah till it was time for afternoon school.

All the afternoon I felt guilty about Pye. He kept looking at me the way people look at you more in sorrow than in anger. I felt guilty about his damned daffodils.

After school, the others went along the road to the township, but I cut along a bush track because our cottage was up on the headland above the bay. At night we'd sit on the verandah and look down and we could see all the lights of the township, and sometimes, when there was a storm blowing, the tide would come so far in, and the breakers would crash so hard, that we'd wait for the next one to come racing in and crash on top of all those lights. It never did.

Walking along the bush track I was thinking about daffodils, but I was keeping an eye open for snakes. Sometimes they came out on to the white sand of the track to sun themselves. It didn't do to get absent-minded and step on one. The bush was still. Up on the headland there'd be a breeze, but down here the bush didn't have the energy to rustle. I was thinking about what Pye had said about spring. "The miracle of spring," he'd said. "Black trees turning green, horse chestnuts flowering, crocuses, daffodils, bluebells, primroses." I started to think about spring. "Use your imagination, Brandon." This track in spring. Wet underfoot because of the July rains, the smell of boronia, all the different kinds of wattle. "Not wattle," Pye was always saying. "It's acacia. Not wattle." But we went on calling it wattle. The bush both sides of the track would be yellow with wattle, so many different kinds, you couldn't count. Yellow. The colour of daffodils. But not daffodils. Use your imagination. I tried to imagine what the bush would be like if it weren't evergreen. What if it lost its leaves? I wandered lonely as a cloud. What would it feel like to be a cloud? What would it feel like to walk beside the lake, beneath the trees? All right. I was walking beneath the trees, along the margin of a bay. But it was different. They were different trees, and it was a different bay. Use your imagination.

When I got home, I couldn't hear the typewriter, so I knew my mother had either stopped work, or was wrestling with something that wouldn't come right. I stuck my head round the door, and she looked through me. That meant she was wrestling. So I went to the kitchen and had a glass of milk and some bread and jam and began to learn "The Daffodils". I decided the best thing was to learn it first and think about it afterwards. I wandered lonely as a cloud.

I'd learned as far as "tossing their heads in sprightly dance" when Mother came out. "Sorry, darling, I'd just struck a bad patch," she said, and kissed me. "Don't eat too much bread and jam," she said. "Mr. Harrison sent up a great parcel of black bream. We'll have them for tea."

"You know," I said, "it must be hard for Mr. Pye to live in Australia. It must be rather like living with the heathen." It had suddenly occurred to me that the more-in-sorrow-than-in-anger look Pye had been giving me all the afternoon was a kind of missionary-gone-wrong look.

My mother looked surprised. "Must it? Why?"

"Calling cicadas locusts, and acacia wattle."

"Who does?"

"I do. We all do. And not knowing about daffodils."

"What do you mean? You've seen plenty of daffodils."

"Not stretching in never-ending line along the margin of the bay. And spring. It must be hard for him to live in a country where there isn't any spring."

"Of course there's spring."

"Mr. Pye says there isn't. Mr. Pye says the bush stays the same all the year round."

"But that's absurd! The bush doesn't . . ."

I had to be patient with her. "I know it doesn't, but Mr. Pye says it does."

My mother was always careful not to undermine my confidence in my teachers, so she didn't say anything, but I could see that she was thinking around. She picked up the book to give herself time. I decided to throw something else in to help her out.

"Mr. Pye says that poetry is speaking painting."

She was reading the poem.

"Mr. Pye says . . ."

"Mr. Pye didn't say it first. Plutarch did. 'Simonides calls painting silent poetry, and poetry speaking painting'."

"You just said Plutarch said it."

"Plutarch said, 'Simonides calls . . .'"

But it didn't really matter. I had a sense of anticlimax. It was the only thing Pye had ever said that was worth thinking about, and now it turned out that he hadn't said it first. My mother was still reading the poem. Suddenly, she looked up and smiled and said, "My mother always called them daffydowndillies."

I had to tread carefully. She never talked about her parents. Sometimes a thing like this would slip out, and then she'd change the subject quickly. I pretended I hadn't heard, so more came slipping out.

"I remember, when I was a little girl, my father used to talk about the spring in England."

I didn't dare to ask a question, and I went on pretending I wasn't listening. The tail of one of the black bream was sticking out of the parcel on the table. I pushed it in, and then the head stuck out the other end. It was quite a decent-sized bream.

Once, at school in Sydney, I'd gone home to play with a boy in my class. He had a grandmother, and she gave us strawberry shortcake. I was very impressed, and afterwards I told this boy, whose name I can't remember, that I also had once had a grandmother, and a grandfather too, but that they had died in the flu epidemic after the war, so I couldn't remember them. Then the boy had asked, "What about your other grandmother and grandfather?"

"Other?"

"Everyone has two lots."

The ones who'd died had been my father's parents. That was the first time it had ever occurred to me that my mother had parents, too. I couldn't wait to get home to ask her about them.

She was peeling potatoes, that time.

"Are my other grandmother and grandfather dead, too?" I asked her.

She stopped peeling and looked at me.

"Not the ones who died of flu. The others," I said.

She said, "I hope not, Harry. I hope not."

"Where are they then?"

That was the first time she changed the subject. She began to talk about what we were going to have for dinner. That was the time I learned to tread carefully. But, as I've said, since then there were times when things would slip out, and I'd just let them slip.

There was more slipping now.

"They used to talk about how homesick they were, even after thirty years," she said. Then she smiled. "They were like Mr. Pye. They thought the bush never changed."

I was so surprised by the word homesick that I forgot to tread carefully. "Homesick?"

"For England."

"Were they English?"

"My father was. My mother was Irish."

I was longing to ask where they were, but I thought it better to dodge round a little.

"Did you come from England with them?"

"No. I was born here." She smiled again. "My father and mother met in Sydney. He came here to prospect for gold."

Then suddenly she saw the bream's head sticking out of the parcel. "Those fish!" she said. "I should have taken them out of the paper ages ago! See if there's any ice in the ice-chest." Then she began to bustle about, looking busy.

I've forgotten things that happened five years ago, and it's strange how vividly I remember that day when I was eleven years old. I'd started off with daffodils, and I'd ended up with the Selways. That was the beginning of my obsession with the Selways. Maybe it was the word "daffydowndillies" that had caught me, maybe it was "gold", maybe it was "homesick". I think it must, after all, have been "homesick", because I know that from then on I found myself surprising Mr. Pye by my understanding and compassion. He mistook both emotions for insolence, of course, and I had a bad time for the rest of my term at his school.

Anyway, there I was. Harry Brandon, Australian. Aged eleven. It said on the flyleaf of my Warner and Marten's *Groundwork of British History*:

> Harry Brandon,
> 232 Moreton Street,
> Randwick,
> Sydney,
> New South Wales,
> Australia,
> The Southern Hemisphere,
> The World,
> The Universe.

I was the grandson of Jack Selway of England. That's all I knew.

CHAPTER TWO

M Y mother's name was Eleanor Selway before she
married my father. She came to Sydney in 1902 from
somewhere in the country. One day a thing came slipping out
about when she was a little girl in the country, and I didn't
tread carefully enough. I asked her where, in the country,
she'd lived. She shied away, mumbling something about
"near a little township called Cameron's Crossing", then she
changed the subject.

I got out my atlas that night while I was supposed to be
doing my homework, divided the map of New South Wales
into inch squares, and searched each square. There was no
sign of a place called Cameron's Crossing.

My mother is, or was, a journalist and novelist, but she's
never written anything very distinguished. The thing about
her is that she never tried to pretend, either to me or to herself, that she was a good writer. "I'm too lazy," She
used to say. Once she said, "I had a grandfather who
talked all the words out of himself before he had time to put
them on paper. My trouble is that I think the words out of
me before I can be bothered putting them on paper."

Lazy or not, she made a good living in the old days. She
sold a lot of stories, and she did free-lance journalism,
and she wrote several books. The books were all about
people who had unhappy love affairs.

She'd been in Sydney ten years when she married my
father. He was a newspaper cartoonist, and he also did book
illustrations. There was one little book of poems he illus-
trated with some exquisite woodcuts. I don't remember
him at all. He went to the war a couple of months after I was

born in 1915, and he was killed at Beersheba in 1917. In my mother's bedroom there was a photograph of him in his Light Horse uniform, the slouched hat turned up at the side, and the feather jaunty as hell.

"It was taken in Cairo," my mother said, "the leave before he was killed."

"What was he like?" I asked.

She smiled and said, "Mad." I knew by the smile that she had liked the way my father was mad.

It was quite a long time before I began to feel that my mother and I were oddly lacking in family ties. My father had been an only child, so, after his parents died, there were no Brandon relations. I must have been about seven when the strawberry shortcake episode brought a couple of grandparents named Selway into my life. Then the next Selway I discovered was an uncle.

Half-way through my first year at primary school I resolved to change my name. There was a local character who was known as Flash 'Arry because he always wore morning dress and a grey topper. The front of his shoes were cut out, and he wore no socks, neither did he wear a shirt under his dove-grey vest. In winter he'd put a newspaper over his chest to keep the cold out. His profession was concerned with the gathering of cigarette and cigar butts, and he smelt like a very ripe gorgonzola. I think it must have been this smell that made me revolt when they began to call me Flash 'Arry at school. I stormed home to my mother and announced that, since my real name was Henry, I wished to be called by it in future.

I hadn't expected her to be so passionately opposed to the change. She sounded almost angry when she said, "I don't want to call you Henry!" Then she must have realised that I was both astonished and puzzled by this totally unexpected vehemence, because she made a wry face that I knew was meant to be an apology, and said in the mock-angry voice that I was used to, "What a ruffian you look since you became a schoolboy. Go and wash those filthy hands, and do your hair. And must your socks always droop round your ankles?" I turned to go to the bathroom, hopping as I pulled my socks up, and as I got to the door she said very quietly, "Harry." I stopped and waited; it seemed a long time before she went on, "Your Uncle Henry was killed at Gallipoli. I saw his name in the casualty list the day after you were born. That's why you were christened Henry, and it's why I'd rather call you Harry."

I can't remember that it occurred to me to wonder why my mother had had to learn about her brother's death from a published casualty list. I didn't pursue the subject of changing my name.

I've always envied those people who know from early childhood just exactly what they are going to do with their lives . . . the infant prodigies who compose sonatas at the age of three, the ones who write poems at eight. I once met an Englishman who had kept a dossier of every book he'd ever read, complete with his impressions of them. He said he'd never doubted that he would be a writer himself. When he showed me the dossier, I thought with some dismay of the hotchpotch I'd have made of a like review of my reading habits. *Gem* and *Magnet* first. Then Hopalong Cassidy all mixed up with Stevenson and Conan Doyle and Edgar Wallace. Bulldog Drummond and Sexton Blake. Dickens and Ethel M. Dell. Scott and Oppenheim. Shakespeare and . . . Well, anyway, I'm not a writer, so there would have been no point in the dossier.

I always got bad marks for art at primary school. We used to draw a square, or an oblong, or a circle, and then put a flat wash on it, and then add a design. My flat washes were always messy. They were either too wet, or too dry, or too streaky. All the colours always ran into all the other colours, and my paint-box was always a shocking mess. I had a passion for yellow, so that the yellow compartment was always empty, and I'd have to borrow from the boy sitting next to me.

Working with crayons I was no better. The teacher would put a shiny red apple on the desk and tell us to draw it, and the others would all turn in shiny red apples with neat high-lights. My apples were always a bit on the skew, the high-lights never had nice clear-cut edges, and the colour was always a bit muddy because I wouldn't be sensible and stick to just plain red.

One day we were taken to the Art Gallery and lined up in front of an enormous canvas called "The Widower". Our teacher said that this was a painting with great emotion in it, and that when we could share the emotion we would be able to appreciate the artist. As far as I can remember, The Widower was sitting at a kitchen table looking very despond-ent indeed, while about his feet played a great many Vic-torian children. In a bunk attached to the wall, the lady, who must have been his late wife, was lying stiff and cold.

The only emotion I gathered from it was a feeling of sur-prise that the lady had chosen to die in the kitchen.

My lack of appreciation of The Widower was a great sorrow to me, because up till then I'd been cherishing a notion that, although I was no good with flat washes and crayons, I might be all right if someone gave me some oil paints.

My mother's literary friends were always patting me on the head and asking me what I was going to be when I grew up, but I said I didn't know, and that brought great tutting and shaking of heads. Visions of a wasted life stretching far, far into the future.

By the time I left school, I still didn't know what I was going to do with my life. I passed my Leaving Certificate in 1931, and that was no year for anyone to be leaving school. The Depression had taken some time to migrate to the Southern Hemisphere, but by 1931 it was well into its stride. It hit my mother rather badly because the newspapers stopped buying free-lance stuff. There had been some talk of my going on to the University, but I couldn't quite see my-self letting Mother support me for another three or four years. I expected opposition from her when I told her I was going to get myself a job, and I was surprised when she glumly agreed. That was the first time I realised how badly things were going for her.

When the Leaving results came out, and I found I'd got

B

quite a good pass, I was convinced that Sydney was full of
employers just waiting to welcome me. I'd decided that an
architect's office would be the best thing. Who knew? I
might turn out to be a draughtsman. But the day after the
results were announced no architects were advertising for
juniors, so I thought I might work temporarily for an im-
porting firm who stated in the *Sydney Morning Herald* that
they wanted a clean, intelligent, well-educated, and trustworthy boy.

I bowled along thinking about all the exotic commodities
with which I should soon be associated, and how nice it
would be to bring home a weekly pay packet. I found that
two hundred clean, intelligent, and trustworthy boys had
got there ahead of me. They, also, had got their Leaving
results yesterday.

During the next three months I got to know most of them
quite intimately, because we all turned up for every job that
was advertised. The extraordinary thing was that, although
at least one boy must have got the job we all turned up for,
our numbers never dwindled. Indeed they got larger. There
must have been about three hundred of us by the time future
employers were warned by their business associates that we
were a hungry-looking and noisy-sounding lot. From then
on most of the advertisers asked us to apply by letter. I wrote
innumerable letters. Occasionally I'd be short-listed, and
I'd go along with high hopes, only to find ten or twelve
familiar faces waiting with me in the outer office.

As time went on, and the clean, intelligent, etc. boys
swelled in numbers, the Positions Vacant columns in the
Herald got shorter and shorter.

Friends of my mother's began to insist that the only thing
was influence. Though, at first, she was unwilling to listen
to them, in the end she gave in, and they all began flapping
about suggesting that I go and see George So-and-so, or
Fred Something-else. I went to see them all. Dozens of
them. They all shook their heads, and some of them said
that if things got any worse they'd have to put off half the
present staff. One said that if I were a trained book-keeper

he could wangle me a temporary job in the accounts department while the junior had a fortnight's holiday; it didn't
seem worth while to spend a year learning book-keeping to
get a job for a fortnight. Others said to come back and see
them later because they were sure that prosperity was just
around the corner.

It was a politician who had caught on to the idea that
prosperity was just around the corner. He'd been in politics
for a long time: Federal politics. No doubt he'd been beaver-
ing away down in Canberra for years, doing his best to be a
good back bencher, but it wasn't until he gave the nation his
personal assurance that prosperity was just around the corner
that he sprang into prominence. The Press boys, to a man,
were delighted and astonished by the profundity, the
sagacity, the eloquence of this pronouncement. Such was its
success that the orator began to like the sound of it himself.
He never missed an opportunity to repeat it; and the Press,
with renewed appreciation, faithfully reported each occasion.
After a while, the orator's name became a household word.
We, the *hoi polloi*, called him Old Prosperity. His real name
was Edward Selway.

I said to my mother, "This Edward Selway. Is he any
relation of yours?"

I expected, at the most, to hear that he was a distant
cousin. I was astounded when she nodded and said, "He's
my brother."

Another brother.

Misinterpreting my surprise, she looked alarmed and said
quickly, "Harry, you're not thinking of asking him to help
you with a job! I won't allow that!"

I burst out laughing. "Him! I wouldn't want to work for
anybody that was a friend of that ass!"

My mother smiled and said, "He isn't an ass. He's a very
earnest and conscientious man."

He was also the best joke that had hit us since the Depression started, but I didn't argue with her.

While the Sheep Show was on that year, Sydney was full
of large, very sunburned characters in big hats. My mother

stayed in the house and got on with the novel she was writing, and although she had several business appointments in town, she cancelled them all.

I came home one night to find her sitting in the kitchen crying her eyes out. She hadn't heard me coming, and, when I opened the door, she jumped up and disappeared into her bedroom. The evening paper was lying on the table, and when I picked it up, the first thing I saw was a picture of the largest, smuggest ram I've ever seen in my life. The caption said that he was the blue ribbon winner at the Show and that he came from Billabirra Station, near Woollaby. I couldn't see why a picture of a ram should make my mother cry, so I concluded that she must have had bad news about some job she'd been hoping for.

A couple of months later I picked up a magazine that someone had left in the tram. In it there was an interview with Old Prosperity. He told of his early struggles to gain recognition. "My struggles were not financial," he was reported as saying. "Indeed, I owe a great debt of gratitude to my father, who, although completely in disagreement with my choice of politics as a career, helped me to gain my first foothold on the ladder of success. My father, of course, is Mr. Jack Selway, owner of Billabirra Sheep Station, near Woollaby. In being determined to pursue my own choice of career, I was only following in the footsteps of my father, who, although the scion of a wealthy Yorkshire family, chose to come to Australia in search of adventure, and who became one of our country's most glorious pioneers . . . a true Jason who found his Golden Fleece."

It went on for several pages after that, but I was feeling too sick to go on with it. At any other time my nausea might have been caused by the journalese, but this was the sickness of rage. Now I knew why she was crying over the blasted ram! While this scion of a wealthy Yorkshire family, this Jason, was lavishing all his care on a great, fat, smug ram, his daughter was sitting banging away at a typewriter wondering whether it was going to earn enough to pay the rent next week.

I was still raging when I got home, and I stamped into my mother's room to tell her what I'd just read; to have it all out with her. I found her sitting there at the typewriter looking very pleased with herself.

"Hullo, darling. Any luck?"

"The job was already filled when I got there."

"Never mind. I've just got a series to do. Six articles. Isn't that wonderful?"

She looked gayer than I'd seen her for months, so I didn't have the heart to say anything about Mr. Jack Selway.

CHAPTER THREE

MANY years later, just a few months ago, as a matter of fact, I ran into a friend of mine in London. He was having a very bad time of it. Over a drink he said glumly: "You know, you think you've reached rock bottom. You tell yourself that this is as low as you can get, that things can't possibly get any worse. And then all of a sudden, they're worse."

Well, that's what happened back in 1932. Things had been bad enough in 1931, but in 1932 all of a sudden they were worse.

Uncle Edward Selway was still piping away in Canberra that prosperity was just around the corner, but the acid enjoyment of that joke was becoming stale with repetition. As I remember it, the Federal Government didn't mean as much in those days as it was to come to mean during the War and afterwards. Back in the thirties we all seemed to be much more concerned with the activities of the various State Governments. At any rate, New South Wales had its work cut out keeping up with the doings of its Premier, J. T. Lang. Jack Lang had us all in a lather of sweat wondering what he was going to do next. We were only slightly comforted by the slogans which told us: "Lang is right," "Lang is greater than Lenin."

By 1932 I had stopped thinking of myself as a prospective office boy. Any job that came along meant at least a few shillings. I loaded packages for twelve hours a day in the dispatch depot of a department store during the summer sale. The overtime came in handy. For three weeks I stood over an evil-smelling vat in a floor-polish factory. Occasionally I'd find someone who needed a boy to do odd jobs for a couple of days.

I wasn't working the day they opened the Sydney Harbour Bridge. It was a gala day, even though the powers that be were in a blue funk in case there should be rioting by the unemployed. They needn't have worried, of course, because the unemployed were just as anxious as anyone else to have a free day out. There were flags flying, and bands playing, and school-kids marching, and everyone was in holiday mood and hoping for some fun. It turned out that we got more fun than we'd expected, because that was the first time we saw a real, live Blackshirt.

The solemn moment came when the Premier who was right and greater than Lenin stepped forward to cut the tape and open the Bridge; but, before he could raise the scissors, there was a great commotion as a comic-opera posse, on horseback and wearing black shirts, charged in front of the official party and cut the tape with their swords. The bridge was rescued from dishonour, and was proudly opened in the name of Fascism! We learned afterwards that the black-shirted gentry called themselves the New Guard. It gave us something to laugh about for quite a long time.

In 1932 my mother said one evening, "Harry, I think we'd better move."

She'd been doing very little work lately. Nobody was buying locally-written stuff because they could get all the syndicated material they wanted from England and America for next to nothing. Monthlies and weeklies, which had once provided a short-story market, were disappearing one by one. Nobody was either publishing or buying books any longer.

I asked, "Where'll we move to?"

"I saw a flat today, in Paddington. It's much cheaper than this one."

I didn't much like the sound of Paddington, but I said, "Good. Much closer to town. I'll be able to walk instead of paying tram fares."

She fiddled with her teacup and said, "There's only one bedroom. Will you mind sleeping in the sitting-room?"

As though I minded where I slept.

We moved to Paddington the next week, and when we saw the filth of the place we both put on a great act of unconcern and said we'd have it ship-shape in no time. We piled all our furniture and belongings in the kitchen while we scrubbed the bedroom from floor to ceiling, and then we moved everything into the bedroom while we went to work on the kitchen. A friend of my mother's popped in during the afternoon, ostensibly to help us, but all she did was drink innumerable cups of tea and exclaim at intervals, "My dear, did you know the chain in the toilet's broken?" And, "My dear, what about that stove! You'll have to take it to pieces and boil it!" And, "Darling, I don't want to worry you, but you'll have to keep an eye on that crack in the wall! If it gets any bigger . . ."

We went on working round her.

She did manage to get some reaction from us late in the afternoon, when she suddenly turned dramatically, teapot poised, and said, "My dear. Bugs."

My mother nearly had a fit. "Where?"

"Oh, I haven't seen any, but the place is sure to be full of them."

Having at last managed to shatter our grim cheerfulness, she went off happily leaving us to do the washing-up. We spent the rest of the afternoon and evening peering suspiciously at walls and skirting boards, and scratching ourselves surreptitiously.

The previous tenant had left the sitting-room piled high with old rubbish, but, by midnight, we were both too tired to do anything about that. So I put my bed up in the middle of the mess, and, leaving Mother sitting on the edge of her bed peering anxiously at the walls, I flopped into a sleep from which a regiment of bugs couldn't have wakened me. We never did see any bugs, but we had a battle royal with the cockroaches in the kitchen. During all the years we lived in Paddington we never let up on those cockroaches, but it was like fighting the Chinese. For every one killed, half a dozen more moved up into the front line.

I woke up on the first morning in the new flat, looked at the pile of debris, and, cursing the previous tenant, I hauled myself out of bed wondering whether the neighbours would object if I dumped the lot into the back yard and made a bonfire. I began raking around to see whether or not the stuff was burnable. It turned out to be mostly old canvases; a couple of them were completed, but most of them were no more than rough sketches. They were pretty horrific, and I wondered if we'd got this flat because our predecessor had been carted off to a lunatic asylum. Whether he was mad or not, he couldn't have been short of cash to have been able to afford to waste canvases like that. One corner of the room was a mess of old tubes of paint and brushes. One of the canvases had no more than a squiggle right in the middle of it, so I set it up on the easel, cleaned a couple of the brushes as well as I could, and started to paint the street the way it looked from the window, working round the squiggle, as I thought, pretty neatly.

I was working away in my pyjamas when my mother came in and said, "Harry, what on earth are you doing?"

I showed her my view of the street with the early morning sun working its way round the corner at the grocer's shop. She examined it for a long time, and said, "It's pretty awful, isn't it?" I said, "Of course it is. I've never painted anything before." Then she said, "There wasn't a single bug last night," and I said I was relieved to hear it. Se we went to the kitchen to have breakfast.

I didn't have a bonfire in the back yard. I stacked all the canvases and stuff in a corner and scrubbed the sitting-room: by that night we were settled in.

There were some pretty tough characters living round our way, but there was a fellow who lived next door who didn't look so bad. One day I went out and helped him to mend a puncture in his bike tyre. After we'd finished, he said, "I'm goin' down to the beach for a swim. Come, why don't you?" I told him it was too hot. I didn't mind the walk down the hill, but coming back up it would be murder in this heat. He said, "Me brother's away cherry picking. You can have

his bike for a loan of." So I went and got my towel and costume, and had his brother's bike for a loan of, and we went
down to the beach. Going up the hill wasn't too bad on the
bike, because we just hung on to the back of the tram and let
it pull us up, and then we coasted down.

On the beach everyone knew everyone else, and they all
inquired after my new friend's work prospects, and then went
on to ask about his two brothers and his father. When told
that they'd all gone fruit picking, there was a good deal of
earnest discussion as to whether the picking game was worth
a candle, and there were stories told about how you humped
your bluey for days to get somewhere only to find all the
fruit had been picked weeks ago.

There was a big chap with enormous shoulders, narrow
hips, and a head about as big as a good-sized orange. His
name, I found out later, was Briggard, but they all called
him Big 'Ead. Big 'Ead appeared to be a natural leader. He
took charge of everything and nobody minded at all. He
said to me, "What's your job?"

I told him I was out of work.

He looked at me as though I were dotty. "I know you're
out of work. Who isn't? What would your job be if there
was a job to be at?"

Without any hesitation at all, I said, "I'm going to be a
painter." It was the first time it had ever occurred to me
that I was going to be a painter, and I wanted to bite my
tongue out for having let it occur to me at that particular
moment, because I expected everyone to roar with laughter.
They didn't though. They all looked very solemn, and Big
'Ead said, "Any of youse that hear of any painting job going,
you tell me and I'll tell young 'Arry." Then he added to
me, "You better join the Club, 'Arry."

Never were the beaches of Sydney better manned than
they were during the thirties. The Surf Clubs found no
difficulty in getting volunteer life-saving patrols. We were
all there, even when we weren't on patrol. The fashionable
colour was Depression Tan.

We'd go down to the beach, and be there as the sun began

to come up over the horizon. The flags would be set to show people where it was safe to swim that day, and then we'd put up the rope patrol enclosure. After a while, whoever it was that was due to buy the *Herald* that day would come down to the beach with the paper neatly folded. Then a couple of chaps would keep an eye on the early morning surfers and watch for sharks, while Big 'Ead went through the Positions Vacant and the Situations Vacant. He'd say: "'Ere, Fred, they want an experienced waiter at the Grand. Op it." So Fred would hop it to get dressed and be at the Grand by breakfast time.

I don't think it occurred to any of us that we'd have saved ourselves a lot of time and trouble if we'd bought the paper on the street corner near home and gone through the advertisements for ourselves. It wasn't just that your turn to buy the paper only came round once in about thirty weekdays; though it was obvious that you were thus saved twenty-nine pennies. It was that there was something comforting in being one of a mob. When there wasn't anything in that morning's paper that was worth your going after, you weren't left cooling your heels all by yourself waiting for tomorrow's paper. You, along with twenty or thirty others, said, "Might as well have a swim." There was an added advantage to the beach rendezvous. You got to hear about the local jobs that weren't advertised.

"'Ere, young 'Arry. Mr. Baker up in Russell Street wants someone to whitewash 'is storeroom. You're a painter. 'Op it!" Big 'Ead said to me one morning.

"Don't you want the job?" I asked.

Big 'Ead looked disgusted. "'E doesn't want to pay a man's wages. Says a kid can do it. 'Op it!"

I got a lot of odd jobs because they didn't want to pay a man's wages.

Sometimes someone would come down to the beach with a small packet of Capstans. The packet would be opened, and each cigarette carefully halved. If there were more than twenty of us there, the young ones would have to go without.

The sisters of some of the boys would start arriving during the morning, and they'd bring their girl friends, and the girl friends would bring other girl friends, and we'd all hold our hips in and stick our chests out and show off a bit.

The relationship between the girls and the boys was a determinedly sexless one. Nobody dared to get serious about a girl, because you couldn't expect a girl to go steady with a chap who couldn't even afford to take her to the pictures. Sex, itself, was definitely out, because nobody could risk getting a girl into trouble.

It wasn't only the illegitimate birth-rate that fell. Nobody was having babies just then. As a matter of fact nobody was doing anything very much. Everything was at a standstill. Half-finished buildings stood deserted, and there would be a "Work Suspended" sign on the gate. No hospitals were built, no schools, no maintenance was done on roads or public works. By 1933 a third of the working population of the country were unemployed. Even the odd jobs were scarce then.

Uncle Edward Selway made a speech at the Town Hall and said that prosperity was just around the corner.

I read in the paper one night that Mr. and Mrs. Luke Selway had been at Randwick Races that day, and would be entertaining friends at their hotel that evening. During the Sheep Show I read that Mr. Jack Selway and Mr. Jonathon Selway had been present that day to see their stud ram judged champion.

There was one regular job I had about that time which I've forgotten to mention. Every Saturday morning I'd deliver the meat for the local butcher. He didn't really need a delivery boy, so I never got paid in cash, but every Saturday I'd take an armful of white butcher's paper, and what I didn't use for sketching I'd glue up and pin on to stretchers.

I did a lot of painting that winter. My mother never commented, but one day she came into the sitting-room with an elderly gentleman in tow. He looked prim and maidenly. She said, "Harry, this is Mr. Manning. He's going to give you lessons."

Mr. Manning carefully inspected everything I'd done, and said, "You might as well save your energies. You can't paint." Then he took off his coat and began the first lesson.

Mr. Manning and I fought with glorious ferocity for a whole year. We argued and shouted at each other, and sloshed paint about, and he kept screaming, "You can't paint! I tell you you just can't paint!" And I screamed back, not quite so high-pitched, that I was bloody well going to paint! In between the shouting and sloshing I learned a lot from Mr. Manning. "Look," he kept shouting, "I can only teach you the things not to do! I'm a lousy painter myself! I can only teach you not to be as lousy as I am."

In the summer I'd go down to the beach for the early morning briefing, and if there was no job to go after, or if I didn't have to do a patrol, I'd get on the bike of the brother of the boy next door (he was away fruit picking again) and, with all my gear strapped on the handlebars, I'd go off somewhere and paint.

I could never get what I wanted. I'd see it all just the way it was going to end up on canvas; I'd go to work, and when it was finished it was nothing more than a prissy-looking bit of rock, or cliff, or stretch of scrub that had nothing to do with any kind of reality.

If I'd had any knowledge of art, of course, I'd have been frightened off. If I'd been brought up within cooee of the Tate or the Louvre I would never have had the audacity to start.

If there hadn't been a depression; if I'd started work as an office boy in 1931, or if I'd become a bank clerk and worked my way up to general manager, or head cashier; if the devil hadn't pushed a paint brush into idle hands, if . . . well, anyway, I've got the grace to blush every time I go into the Tate.

Another thing that happened in 1933 was that I met Jan.

CHAPTER FOUR

FIVE of the boys in the Surf Club had a dance band. Every now and then they'd get a job playing for a social or a local hop, and occasionally the pianist and the sax player would be engaged for some twenty-first birthday party, but their big night was the Surf Club Dance. That was their one sure date of the year, and they'd put on their sky-blue suits and become very professional, pretending they didn't know the rest of us from Adam, while they played "I'm Dancing With Tears In My Eyes".

The Club Dance was an event, and we'd all get dressed up in our best, with our shoes polished, and our collars stiffened so that they stuck into our sunburned necks giving us hell until the heat began to make them wilt.

All the girls would line up on one side of the room, and the boys on the other, pretending to ignore each other. The joke that never got stale was: "Hullo. I didn't know you with your clothes on."

Sometimes, if someone had had a job that week, he'd bring a half-crown bottle of the kind of rum known as "rot gut". He'd hide it under the Club house, and during the evening his friends would make elaborate exits, and come back ten minutes later smelling of peppermints or musk.

There was a big, sandy-haired chap called Bobby who was very popular with everyone. On the beach the boys all liked him because he was a good swimmer and won the Junior Surf Championship for the Club. The girls liked him because he looked very handsome in his costume, was burned a nice even mahogany, and his blond hair stood straight up on his head. Apart from that he was always very polite and was careful to divide his attention equally among them.

Well, this was his first Surf Club Dance, and he arrived late. You could see all the girls watching the door, waiting for Bobby.

It was the first time any of us had seen him wearing anything except swimming costume, and it was a shock when he did appear. It wasn't just that his suit didn't fit. It was that it looked as though he'd just been caught in a heavy downpour. When he came in we all looked out to see if it had started to rain, but it hadn't. It turned out later that he'd decided to wash his suit because it was the only one he had and it was a bit grubby. Of course it hadn't dried in time. He'd tried to iron it with a very hot iron to get it dry, and it was a good two inches above his shoe tops. Well, we could have laughed that off if it hadn't been for his hair. We were used to the sandy mop standing straight up, and there he was with it all smarmed neatly down, and carefully parted. It was several shades darker than usual.

The shock was greatest for the girls, of course.

Bobby was very glum at first, and kept trying to hide himself behind a row of chaps near the wall, but then somebody took him down under the Club house, and he came back smelling of peppermint and he looked much more cheerful. He started asking the girls to dance, one by one, being careful never to dance with the same girl twice. Except for Jan. He asked Jan twice and then a third time, and everyone sat up and took notice.

Janet Wright was the sister of one of the older Club members. She'd been coming down to the beach all the season, but her brother, Bill, was a fierce duenna. He announced to all and sundry that anyone who started mucking about with his sister would get his block knocked off. I'd had my eye on Jan for quite a while, and had been working out schemes by which I could both make some progress with her and avoid having my block knocked off. But I didn't have the courage to ask her to dance because I was such a bad dancer.

When Bobby danced the third time with Jan, we all began

to look at Bill out of the corners of our eyes. He watched
them for a while, then he turned to Big 'Ead and said, "Poor
bastard. Something's got to make up for that suit."
Then Bill and Big 'Ead made a trip down under the Club
house.

That dance ended, and Bobby went over to have a word
with the band. I saw Jan look quickly round the room. Her
eyes lighted on me, and stayed there. She wasn't smiling or
anything. She was just looking at me. I strolled over, and
she said out of the corner of her mouth, "Harry, ask me to
dance."

I said, "I'm a terrible dancer." Then Jan said, "I'd love
to, Harry." The band began to play "The Pagan Love
Song", and the next second I was dancing with Jan. Bobby
came back from the bandstand, and tapped me on the
shoulder and said, very politely, "Mine, I think, young
Harry," and Jan said, "No. I told you, Bobby. Harry asked
me for this one ages ago."

Bobby looked very odd. It was a very hot night, and we
were all wilting, but Bobby had rivulets of dark brown
sweat coursing down from his hairline on to his neck. I'd
never seen anyone sweat dark brown before.

Bobby smiled with his beautiful white teeth just to show
that he didn't hold it against me, and bowed and went off to
find another girl to dance with.

Jan said, "Harry, did you notice the smell?"

"Smell?"

She looked after Bobby in a rather troubled way, and
said, "I thought I was going to be sick." I didn't know what
the blazes she was talking about. Bobby had been in the surf
all day, so he couldn't smell that badly, and at least his suit
was clean.

Half-way through the next dance, the girl who was dancing
with Bobby excused herself and bolted for the door. Then
the line of girls against the wall seemed to break up, and in
no time they were all dancing with their brothers. Bobby,
looking hurt and puzzled, was without a partner for quite a
long time.

The arrangement suited me, because I went on dancing with Jan, and I was just starting to get the hang of the two-step when Bill and Big 'Ead came back. I saw Bill look at me, so I put on my most innocent expression, and held Jan a bit farther away from me.

Bobby, without a partner, and trying to look as though it were by choice, strolled across to join Bill and Big 'Ead for a bit of male conversation. They chatted for a while, and I saw Big 'Ead looking closely at Bobby's dark brown sweat. Then, just as Jan and I were dancing past them, I saw him lean over and sniff. He stepped back and said, "Gawd struth, Bobby, you don't 'alf pong!"

Bobby wasn't angry. He simply stood there, puzzled. "Pong?"

Big 'Ead turned to Bill. "Take a sniff," he said.

Bill leant over and took a sniff. "Jesus!"

Big 'Ead considered Bobby for a while. "What did you wash your suit in?"

Bobby went on looking puzzled and said, "Water! What do you think?" Then he took his handkerchief out of his pocket and mopped the sweat off his face because he was embarrassed. The handkerchief had turned dark brown.

"What's that?" Big 'Ead demanded to know. He leant over and smelt the handkerchief. "Struth!" More dark rivulets were already beginning to course down Bobby's face. Big 'Ead examined them more closely. "'Ere, what've you got on your hair?" he asked.

Bobby shuffled uncomfortably for a minute, and then he burst out, "Well, where was I going to get the money to buy flaming hair oil?"

Bill said, "Now don't get off your bike. We just asked."

Bobby said, "Well, someone told me dripping made good hair grease."

Bill and Big 'Ead howled together—"Dripping!"

And Bobby burst out again, "Well, how the hell did I know my mother'd burned the joint last Sunday!"

Bill and Big 'Ead grabbed Bobby, and Big 'Ead said, "Come on, mate," and they disappeared.

c

Jan began to laugh. "Dripping. Very stale. Full of onions. Harry, you should have smelt it."

I laughed too, and held Jan a lot closer now that Bill was out of the way. I thought about all the months I'd known her and been scared to say much to her, and look what I'd been missing.

After a while, Bill and Big 'Ead and Bobby came back, and Bobby's hair was very blond and sticking straight up all over his head again. They'd undressed him and put him under the shower and scrubbed him with Lifebuoy soap. Bobby was quite good-humoured about it all, and said it was all very well for them that had hair oil, and that what with the sun and the salt water, his head was like a paddock full of dry grass. Everyone else said it was a good thing the shower had been had before supper-time, or nobody would have been able to eat a thing. Bobby said that if they really liked the smell of Lifebuoy with their sandwiches and coffee who was he to argue.

The blissful evening ended when Bill came over to me, and said, "Here, young Harry!" I stiffened and waited for my block to be knocked off, but Bill said, "I promised to take Marion home. You live round our way. Would you see young Jan home for me?"

So that was how Jan became my girl friend, and from then on, I'd have done a cross-country run to Bourke if Bobby had asked me to.

Not that Jan and I went in for what Bill called "mucking about". At first we only saw each other on the beach, and there we carefully observed the law against pairing off. Sometimes we'd go into the surf together, but that didn't give much chance for conversation, especially if there was a good surf running and the shoots were coming fast. Then we'd lie on the beach and sunbake. If it could be managed without causing any comment, we'd stretch out on the sand together and talk. If not, we'd just occasionally look up and smile at each other over a mass of bodies. We often went home from the beach together, but Bill was always there too, lacking only a mantilla.

Then Jan got a job in a solicitor's office, and there was
great excitement. After that she didn't come to the beach
any more during the week, so I started painting again, and,
late in the afternoon, I'd pack up my gear and make for the
tram stop so I could be there to meet her on her way home.

It was wonderful being with Jan. She was never bossy or
proprietorial. She never wanted to know where I'd been, or
with whom. She took the news that I was going to be a
painter very well, and started to read all the books she could
find about painters and painting.

After a while we stopped going down to the beach every
week-end, because we were bored with pretending that we
didn't want to be together. So we'd pack some sandwiches
and my painting gear and go off somewhere by ourselves.
I'd paint and Jan would read. One day she looked up from
the book and said, "You won't go mad and cut your ear off
or anything, will you?"

I didn't know what she meant, but I said I wouldn't.

Sometimes, round about six o'clock on Saturdays, when
the dance-band boys were finally convinced that nobody was
going to need their services that night, the word would go
round that there'd be a hop at the Club house.

These dances, apart from an occasional trip to the pictures
in the shilling seats, were the only entertainment we ever had.
Not that it would have occurred to us to go to the theatre
even if we'd had the money. The arrival of the new-fangled
talking pictures, coupled with the depression, had thrown
panic into the hearts of the theatre owners, and they'd sold
out to the enemy. My mother used to talk about the days
when you had the choice of twelve theatres to go to in Sydney, but they were all picture houses by the early thirties.
All except one. Whenever you inquired what was playing
there it turned out to be *Maid of the Mountains*.

At first I hated not being able to take Jan around to places
that involved the spending of money, but in the end she convinced me that she didn't mind, so it wasn't so bad.

Both Jan's brothers were out of work, and her father, who
had a job with the railways, was laid off one week in every

three, so the thirty-eight shillings a week that she earned as
a shorthand typist came in very handy at home.

My mother liked Jan, and I got on well with her family.
Bill finally faced facts and abandoned the role of duenna
with a last dark warning about mucking about.

Altogether, things wouldn't have been so bad if it hadn't
been for my mother. If you can think of anything more
soul-destroying than being six feet tall, strong as a horse,
going on for twenty, and almost entirely dependent on your
mother, I'd like to be told about it. Not that she ever cared.
We managed, but God knows how, to pay the rent and eat;
and when I got a job every now and then and brought home
a pay packet, she'd carry on as though I'd done something
clever.

I never saw any reported doings of the Selways these days.
I'd stopped, long ago, being bitter about them, but I couldn't
stop being curious. Sometimes, when Mother and I would
be talking about nothing in particular, I'd neatly work the
conversation round to childhood memories, and I'd sneak
in a question about her childhood. She never allowed herself to be caught. She'd shut up like a clam.

I can't think why I was so obsessed with the Selways.
After all, most people spend their lives trying to avoid their
relations. I think perhaps it was that in 1934 one couldn't
believe in a future, so that it became terribly important at
least to believe in a past.

CHAPTER FIVE

I GOT a job at the Showground at Easter in 1935. I was a barker at the Royal Show. There was a chap who did lightning charcoal sketches of people in the crowd for half a crown a time. He was dying of throat cancer and couldn't do his own spruiking, so I'd stand up there and yell myself hoarse, and he'd do his stuff, and I'd get sixpence out of every half-crown. I liked him, but he looked so ill that I was terrified he was going to die right there in front of me in the middle of a drawing. He lasted a week, then one day a boy came and told me that Dad had been taken off to the hospital.

So I drew a big hoarding that said: "The Great Harry Brandon! Australia's Leading Caricaturist!" and I did my own spruiking while I sketched. I wasn't very good at it. People paid over their half-crowns expecting something they could put on the piano. The usual comment when I handed over my work of art was, "Struth! He makes a man look like a flaming emu, and then he has the gall to charge half a dollar for it!"

In the end I had only one surefire sale. Uncle Edward Selway was back in the news again, because the Commonwealth Government were talking about a New Deal, and Uncle Edward had added a footnote to the effect that prosperity was just around the corner. So the crowd didn't mind if I made Uncle Edward look like an emu, or a shark, or a pig standing with his front feet in a trough, or even a pompous-looking stud ram wearing a blue ribbon.

I sold quite a lot of Uncle Edward.

One day, though, the going was hard. They must have

spent all their money before they came to me. There were half a dozen people standing round, and I was talking my head off at them, when I noticed a young chap standing on the edge of the crowd. A boy from the bush. I could tell them a mile off. I put on my best sales talk for him, but he only grinned and shook his head. So I fell back on Uncle Edward. That did the trick. When I informed the crowd that I was about to give them Mr. Edward Selway, and that furthermore I was going to give him to them for only half a crown, they all jeered back that they wouldn't have him as a gift. This was the usual backchat, but the bush boy looked anxious and called out, "I'll buy it!" as though he were afraid I might be put off.

I did Uncle Edward as a stud ram. When I handed him over, the bush boy looked at him for a long time and then roared with laughter. He laughed for so long that the crowd became alarmed and moved on to the Bearded Lady.

I was holding out my hand for my half-crown. Since I seemed to have entertained him so well, I was sorry that I hadn't asked five bob. "You're obviously an admirer of Mr. Selway," I said.

He handed over the two and six, and then carefully folded the sketch and put it in his pocket, saying, "I can't wait for the family to see this."

"They also are admirers of Mr. Selway?" When talking to customers I always put on my poshest voice just to show that the one I used for spruiking was an act.

He grinned and said, "Well, I don't know so much about that. You see, Ted Selway happens to be my uncle."

I was just about to launch into the funny little patter routine I'd worked up about Old Prosperity, and what the bush boy had said didn't sink in for a moment. Then I did a double take. "Your uncle!"

He shrugged and said, "Don't blame me."

"But he's my uncle, too," I said.

"Yours!"

"Is your name Selway then?"

He nodded. "Yes. David. But who are you?" He looked up at the hoarding behind me.

"My mother's name was Selway," I said. "Eleanor."

He looked at me in an awed way and then said quietly, "You're Aunt Nell's son?"

That was when I began to regret having let myself be surprised into telling him who I was. All I'd been thinking about was that at last I'd found a real live Selway. Now it could be that things were going to be difficult. It could be that this live Selway wasn't going to want to have anything to do with his Aunt Nell's son. It could be that I was going to have to belt his ears off just to make up for that bloody pampered ram. And I didn't want to have to do that because I rather liked the look of him.

He looked at me for a long time, and then he said, "Just wait till I tell the family I've found Aunt Nell." He really looked pleased about it. "Ever since I was a kid," he said, "they've been talking about how wonderful it'll be when they find Nell. Whenever any of them come to Sydney, they walk round the streets peering into faces hoping to meet her."

He still sounded awed. I felt an idiotic sense of relief. It wasn't their fault then. I don't know why the hell it mattered.

"Where is she?" he asked.

I began to panic a bit. "Look," I said, "don't go rushing off to fetch them. I think I ought to warn my mother . . ."

"Oh, they're not in Sydney," he said.

That was a relief.

"I came down by myself to have a look at a new tractor my father's thinking of buying." He looked at my sketching gear and then around to see if I had any customers. I hadn't, so he said, "Do you have to go on with this show of yours? I'd like to buy you a drink."

I answered, "I'll pack up for the day. It isn't often you meet a wealthy cousin from the bush."

He frowned and said, "You can forget the wealthy part."

"I can?"

He looked gloomy. "What with wool down to eightpence a pound . . ." He trailed off as though that were sufficient explanation.

I shook my head sadly. Those poor Selways. Wool down to eightpence a pound. Those poor Selways on the breadline.

We went off to have a drink, and my cousin David told me all about the privations the Selways were suffering. His mother and father had put off their usual Easter trip to town for the Show and the Randwick Meeting. His sister had cancelled her proposed trip to Europe, and had decided to get married quietly to one of the Parkers of Woollaby instead. I didn't know who the hell the Parkers of Woollaby were, but that sounded like a dreadful privation to me. As for David himself, he'd been hoping for a new car this Easter, but with things so bad, he had agreed to make do with the old one.

I don't want to give the impression that he was whining about all this. He was simply giving me the family news. He'd lived with these dreadful economies for so long that he took them for granted.

I had an evil idea. I said that as soon as we'd finished this drink, he'd better come home with me and meet Mother. He agreed at once, so I let him buy two bottles of beer and we set off.

He insisted on getting a taxi and that killed me. Fancy the neighbours seeing me rolling home in a taxi.

When we got to our street, I saw that the neighbours had done me proud. They were all sitting on their doorsteps, or hanging out of their upstairs windows, chatting and exchanging the news of the day, and Mrs. Maloney from Number Four was as drunk as a duchess and twice as haughty as she bowed very low to me and reminded me that I was taking her to the opera that night. The taxi caused a sensation. The street sounded like a gum tree full of cockatoos.

David was looking round trying not to show how horrified he was. The house we lived in was the only big one in the street. It looked pretty dingy, but you could see that he was relieved that at least his Aunt Nell lived in a big house.

Going in the front door, I explained that the house was cut up into flats, and, as we lived on the ground floor, I took him round through the back yard into our kitchen.

That did it. He stood at the kitchen door, gaping.

"I'm sorry I can't take you into the sitting-room," I said. "It happens to be where I work and sleep and you can't get into it for canvases." I murdered two cockroaches that were fighting a battle to the death on the kitchen table.

He stopped gaping, walked over to the sink and dumped the two bottles of beer on the draining board. Then he swung round in a fury. "Why has your mother never been in touch with the family?" he asked. "There's no need for you to live like this!"

"Oh, come now," I said. "With all those economies you wouldn't have wanted two more mouths to feed."

"You bastard!" he said, and I forgave him for everything. "You let me go drooling on! You let me . . ."

I said, "Go on. Hop it! It was a bad joke that didn't come off. I find I'm not laughing. Go back to your hotel before Mother gets home."

I'd known, of course, that Mother was out when I'd invited him home. Now I wanted him to go quickly, just in case she should come back early.

He was standing looking at me, puzzled, when, to my horror, I heard the front door opening. She had come back early. Then I felt terribly ashamed of the mischief I'd made.

"Look," I said, "I'm sorry. Do me a favour, will you? Hop out the back door the way we came in. I'll talk to my mother and . . ."

My only hope was that she would go straight into her bedroom to take her coat and hat off. But she didn't. David was still standing there looking puzzled when she came into the kitchen gingerly carrying a brown-paper bag.

"I swear I'll never buy tomatoes from those Oxford Street barrows again," she said as she came in. "I told him I wanted him to give me nice firm ones from the front, and I

could have sworn he did. It's sleight of hand, of course."
Then she saw David, and thinking he was some friend I'd
brought home, she put on her best welcoming manner.

I was feeling such a heel that I wanted to bolt, but I knew
I had to get this over and done with as soon as possible. "I
seem to have found a relation," I said, and I couldn't help
sounding churlish, because there didn't appear to be any
way of doing it gently.

My mother's welcoming smile vanished and she stood
staring at David. I felt sorry for him too, because he was so
embarrassed. After a bit he went over to her and put his
hands on her shoulders and kissed her on the cheek and said
gently, "It's wonderful to meet you at last, Aunt Nell."

She went on staring at him for a while, and then asked,
"Who are you?"

He said, "I'm David. David Selway."

I was the onlooker, the one who'd created the mess, and
all I could do was stand back and let them fight their way out
of it.

My mother said, "I wonder if you'll excuse me? I must go
and take my coat and hat off, I . . ." and she went to the door,
stopped and turned round. "I'm making a fool of myself,
aren't I?" She smiled at me, but I was feeling too miserable
to smile back. She came back to the table and asked me,
"Where did you meet?"

David answered for me. "At the Showground."

She was in a panic for a moment. "Is everyone down for
the Show?"

David said that he was the only one who'd come down
this year.

My mother looked relieved, and, to give herself time,
turned and smiled at me again. I was able to force a feeble
grin. Then suddenly she said to David, "I used to wonder
what I'd do if I ran slap bang into one of them. Then, about
ten years ago, I looked in the mirror and knew they wouldn't
recognise me, anyhow."

David said, "Grandma and Grandfather have never
stopped looking for you."

That distressed her so much that I felt I had to take a hand. I tried to sound as apologetic as I felt. "Dave," I said, "be a sport and go back to your hotel. I'll get in touch with you before you go home." I turned to Mother. "This is all my fault. A stupid joke that went sour."

David said, "I carried two bottles of beer all the way from the Showground."

My mother, who had been frowning at me, obviously trying to fathom what the joke was that had gone sour, turned back to him and smiled. "Is your throat dry too?"

David nodded.

She said, "I was forgetting it's just as bad for you as it is for me."

I went and got some glasses and David poured the beer. My mother said she only wanted half a glass to soften her throat up, so he took her at her word, and then filled his own glass and mine.

Mother sipped her beer for a moment, and then she said to him, "So you're my nephew?"

David nodded again. "Luke's son."

She looked surprised. "Luke's son!" She smiled. "Dear Luke."

Then, to my astonishment, she sat down at the table, leaned across to David, and began eagerly to bombard him with questions. How was Luke? How was Jonathon? And then a lot of names I'd never heard before. The Camerons. David Spencer. Snowy. She was enjoying herself. Suddenly she looked ten years younger.

I wasn't feeling quite so miserable about it all now. It seemed that I hadn't made such a mess of things after all.

They went on talking about people I'd never heard of. I knew there were two questions she was keeping till last. In the end they came out as one question. "And Father and Mother?" She held her breath till after David had said, "Oh, they're still going strong. Grandfather still insists on working, although there are plenty of us to take over for him. Grandma still spends all her life in the kitchen."

After that Mother thought she might have the other half glass of beer because she was thirstier than she'd thought. While she was drinking it David said, "You're going to find big changes when you get back, Aunt Nell." She stopped drinking for a moment, but he didn't notice. "Wait till you see Cameron's Crossing. It's quite a big township now."

She put the glass down and said, "Really? It was just a pub and general store when I left."

"You wait till you see what Mick's done to it."

"Mick Dooley's still there?"

"He owns the whole of Cameron's Crossing and all the land back to the foothills. He says he's going to make it into a big town some day."

I was like a dog being taken for a walk by two people too intent on their own promenade to stop and give it time to sniff round in likely places. There was a faltering here, though. There was time to sniff here. Mick Dooley.

Then they were moving on again, and I had to go with them.

David asked, "Aunt Nell, how soon can you be ready to come home with me?"

Mother put her glass down, suddenly looked very efficient, put on the air of one who deplores all this sitting about drinking, and said, "I must go and take my things off."

But David got up and asked, "Can I telephone them and say we're coming home on the night train?"

Mother looked as outraged as if he had put an improper suggestion to her. "Of course you can't!" she said. "I'm not coming home with you!" Then she went to the door, and said again, "Of course you can't!" Then she went out.

It was all very phoney, that air of outrage, like a bad actress misreading the author's intentions.

David looked miserable and said, "Have I said the wrong thing?"

I stopped being the onlooker. "You can't expect her to go meekly off home with you after thirty years," I said.

"Why did she leave in the first place?" he asked.

Now that was something I'd been hoping he'd be able to
tell me, but I didn't admit it. I just shrugged and tried to
look as though it was none of my business.

David began wandering round the kitchen appearing to
examine everything as though he were about to offer me a
price for it. I knew, though, that he wasn't even registering
what he was looking at. He was trying to think of some way
to break through into our lives.

I liked him. He'd handled the meeting with Mother very
well. It couldn't have been easy meeting someone who'd
been a legend all his life. He looked like a hearty sheep man,
but he had a sort of gentleness too . . . a strength of gentleness. He'd nudged Mother along so quietly and firmly that,
in the end, the only way she'd been able to shy away from
him was by putting on a bogus act.

Now he began to nudge me. The start of the break-
through.

He wanted to know about my father, and I told him.
Then he wanted to know about Mother and I told him that
too.

He said, "The family aren't completely illiterate. They
can read. I'm wondering how it was they never saw her
name on anything she wrote."

I explained that she'd never used her own name.

"What about you?" he asked. "Do you do that . . . cari-
cature stuff for a living?"

I said that I was a painter and couldn't help letting it
sound a bit aggressive. I waited for that expression people put
on when you say you're an artist, the one they keep otherwise for mentally defective children. I waited for him to
look around the kitchen again with a "so-that-explains-it"
smile, a "they-live-like-this-because-he's-too-lazy-to-get-off-
his-backside-and-do-a-day's-work" smile.

But he didn't smile at all. He didn't look round the
kitchen. He didn't bat an eyelid. He said, "I don't suppose
people have the money to buy pictures these days."

"They wouldn't buy mine even if they had the money."

He grinned and asked, "Are they as bad as that?"

"Terrible," I said.

I didn't mean it, of course. I was just opening a conversational door that would lead me into a thesis I'd been working on lately, having to do with the frustrations of living in a country that was an artistic desert. I'd kept it tucked away in readiness for an audience, and my cousin David looked a very likely victim.

The modest, self-deprecation of that "terrible" would give me the right to speak on behalf of all those who were so much better than I, would exonerate me from any suggestion that I was playing for sympathy, would put the case for the neglected artist who . . .

He took the wind out of my sails by saying, "You'd better stop being terrible, Harry. You'd better start making money. You'll never be a good artist in Australia until you make money at it."

I felt cheated.

He went on, "You must remember that you're living in a country where the national heroes are a dead racehorse named Phar Lap and a cricketer named Bradman."

I did Mother's act of shying away into the phoney. "I won't have a word said against the Don," I said.

He grinned. "For that matter I won't have a word said against Phar Lap. I won a tenner on him in his last Cup."

All those brilliant and cutting observations I'd been going to make! Wasted!

I said, "I've never met an arty crafty sheep man before."

He said, "I've never met an artist before."

Well, it was no use crying over spilt milk. I cheered up a bit. "You can consider yourself a patron, "I said. "You paid half a dollar for Uncle Edward."

That brought his mind back to the family, and my mother. He began to tell me that I must persuade her to come home with him at once, and I began to tell him that nobody on earth could persuade my mother to do anything she didn't want to do, but somewhere along the line the conversation got tangled up, and I finished up announcing that I was going to give a party. "It's time you came out of the wool-shed, and met some city types," I announced.

He forgot to be tactful and said that if there was going to be a party he'd pay for it.

"Listen, son," I said, "don't come the rich relation on me. Remember the price of wool."

He grinned and looked embarrassed and said, "Break it down, Harry."

"When I give a party," I said, "I pay for it."

He said, "I'm buying the beer anyway."

"Beer! Are you kidding? We can't afford beer!"

"What do we drink then?"

"A very pleasant beverage known as Depression Nectar. We buy a quart of plonk . . ."

"Plonk?"

"Oh, you ignorant sheep cocky. Plonk is the very best château bottled red wine at two bob a quart."

"We call it sheep wash."

"We buy a quart of plonk for two bob, and a pound of prunes for sixpence, and we put it all in a saucepan with some cloves and any other odds and ends that happen to be lying around, and then we boil it up. When it's cold it's Depression Nectar."

"I'll tell you what," he said. "You do me another Uncle Ted and then, instead of my giving you half a crown for it, I'll buy the plonk and the prunes."

"The trouble with you," I said, "is that you want to go down in history as the geezer that first encouraged Harry Brandon's great talent. If you will insist on throwing your money around, you can buy a billy of fried rice at the Chows'."

The invitations for the party were no problem. I just let Big 'Ead know, and he organised everything. I could see them all forming fours down on the beach while Big 'Ead gave them their orders.

My mother was no problem either. She said she wanted to think, so she'd better go to the pictures.

I went round to Jan's place and left a note, then we did the shopping, then we cooked the nectar. By this time all the neighbours knew the Brandons were having a party, and word had gone round that I'd picked a triple at Randwick, the Races being the only source of money with which our street was acquainted.

CHAPTER SIX

Everyone said the party was a great success from the word "go". Bobby's suit had never looked the same since it was washed, but at least it was dry that night. David got on well with everyone, and Big 'Ead came over to me and said, "He'll do. Your cousin from Woop Woop, he'll do, young Harry." Big 'Ead was watching his aitches that night. He only dropped them on the beach. It was something to do with not being a cissy. If you dropped your aitches nobody could possibly call you a cissy.

Jan was late, and I was impatient. She was my *pièce de résistance*. I might be a layabout who couldn't get himself a decent job, but at least I could prove to my bush cousin that when it came to girls, I was as smart as paint. I just couldn't wait to show Jan off to him.

When she came, I could see at once that he was impressed, and I couldn't have been more pleased.

Oh, I was the clever boy all right! Roll up, roll up, ladies and gentlemen, and see the Great Harry Brandon, Australia's Leading Cartoonist! Come and watch him hand his girl over to his cousin! Look at the plate, ladies and gentlemen, you wouldn't know it from gold!

Jan tried to avoid being pushed on to the plate. She kept coming to me and putting her arm through mine, and talking to me: I kept sending her back to David.

I'd never given a party before. It went to my head. I was its very life and soul. I was brilliantly gay and witty. I did my Showground spiel for them. Then I did impersonations of various types of employers interviewing various types of prospective employees. Then I did the rent collector trying

D

to catch up with the inhabitants of our street. I had them in stitches.

It was about one o'clock in the morning when I looked across and saw Jan and David sitting in a corner. He had her hand in his, and they were just looking at each other. Not saying a word. Just looking at each other. Bobby was talking to someone behind me: "What hope have you got?" I heard him say.

The party broke up a little while later, and everyone went home. Jan and I helped David to find a taxi, and they were very polite and off-hand when they parted. As I took Jan home, I twisted the knife round a bit and talked about David, but she seemed to prefer talking about what I'd done at the Showground that day.

David stayed in Sydney for a week trying to persuade my mother to go back home with him. Whenever Jan knew he was going to be in the flat, she made some excuse to keep away. If they did meet by accident, they were so elaborately unconcerned with each other that I was afraid my mother would notice. Luckily, she was fighting a battle of her own, so she didn't realise what was going on.

It's difficult to go on an emotional spree when you've nothing definite to be emotional about, but I certainly did my best to make life hell for myself that week. I kept telling myself that (a) just seeing two people holding hands at a party didn't mean they'd fallen finally and irrevocably in love, that (b) since Jan's behaviour to me was no different from what it had always been, it was obvious that she still preferred me, that (c) if Jan had fallen for David it was my own damned silly fault for having taken her so much for granted, that (d) . . . well, anyway, by the time I got to (z) I was right back where I'd started; knowing with a ghastly sort of instinct that he had nudged her into being in love with him, and that they both hated themselves for it.

The trouble was that I felt hate should have been my prerogative.

I was the onlooker again, the disengaged, the twelfth man

sitting in the pavilion. By the end of the week, when I knew
that David was going home, I was sitting there with my pads
on, waiting for someone to get hurt so that I'd be called into
the game. Then play stopped, fizzled out. Complete anticlimax. David came one night to say good-bye. Jan dropped
in just as he was leaving, and they said good-bye like two
people who'd met casually at a party the other night. Then
David left and went home. That's all there was to it. The
next day everything had fallen back into the old routine. The
Easter Show finished the following week-end, so I did a lot
more painting, and Jan would come in the evenings and sit
there while I worked. There were dozens of times when I
wanted to tell her what it meant to me to have her there, but
I thought she might think I'd gone potty, so I just talked,
instead, about what the two of us would do when I became
a famous artist.

Two days after David left Sydney my mother received two
letters by the morning post, and she went away by herself to
read them. I hadn't made any attempt to interfere in her
decision about going back with David. I knew she'd come
round to talking to me about it in her own good time, but
until then I had to mind my own business. She came back to
the kitchen where I was having my breakfast, and she looked
quite cheerful. A cockroach peered coyly from under the
sink, so she dispatched it and spent five minutes searching
around for its relatives and friends, and then, out of the blue,
she said, "I'd like you to see Billabirra. We'll go there sometime for a holiday."

I said I thought that would be a good idea.

She said, "I've just had letters from Mother and Father."

I was too old a hand to rush things. I just sat there, a
question mark eating toast.

She said, "It's all so silly now that I look back on it."

I did my best not to look interested and said, "It is?"

"The way I left home, I mean. Great drama. There was
no need for it."

I ventured a small comment. "I suppose there seemed to
be need for it at the time."

She smiled. "I thought so. I was too big for my boots, of course. Jealousy came into it too."

"Jealousy?"

I was saying to myself, 'Go slow. Take it easy. Don't rush things.'

Mother said, "Everybody seemed so concerned with which university this brother or that brother would go to. Nobody even suggested that I might like to go to a University."

"Which Universities did they go to?" I asked.

"Ted went to Sydney. Luke to Cambridge."

Luke to Cambridge. That explained a lot about David. "Did you want so much to go to a university then?"

She laughed, and thought for a moment before answering: "I don't know what I wanted, really. All I knew about life was what I'd read in books."

I looked round the kitchen and said, "You certainly chose the hard way to learn, lady. This ain't in books."

She laughed again, and didn't look as though she wanted to change the subject yet, so I ventured another question. "Is that why you left home? Because you didn't know what you wanted?"

She put her head on one side and considered me for a moment. Then she said, "I thought I was the heroine in a melodrama. It turned out that I only had a bit part."

Well, I could make whatever I liked of that. Whatever I did make of it just wasn't sense. Her father, though, that Jason who'd found his Golden Fleece. I wanted to be able to make something of him. And her mother. What parts had they had in this melodrama? I tried to imagine Edwardian parents threshing about, being Edwardian. It wouldn't work, because I couldn't imagine what the plot was. I started out by a circuitous route. "I read somewhere," I remarked, keeping it casual, "that your father was a Yorkshireman."

She nodded.

Scion of a wealthy Yorkshire family, it had said in the magazine. What did that make him? The black sheep of the family? Sent to the colonies in disgrace, was he? Cut off without a bob, was he? A remittance man, perhaps?

My mother seemed to register what I'd just said. "Where did you read about him?" she asked.

"Some magazine interview with Old Prosperity."

She laughed and said, "Oh, Ted!" Then she began to talk about Ted as a small boy, how he'd always been a kind of politician from the time he'd first learned to talk. But it wasn't Ted I wanted to hear about then. He would keep. He could come later. I wanted to start at the beginning. I decided to take a chance and plunge in head first. "Tell me about Jason," I said.

She looked startled. "Jason?"

I'd been calling him Jason in my own mind for so long that I'd forgotten she didn't know about it. I explained to her about the interview with Uncle Edward. She laughed for quite a long time, and then asked, "Did the interview say how much Father loathed his Golden Fleece?" I told her that I hadn't finished reading it, but that I certainly hadn't had the impression it would go on to say anything of the sort. Since she seemed to be so much in the mood, I ventured another question. "What about this wealthy Yorkshire family business? Was he a remittance man?" That amused her even more than the bit about the Golden Fleece. "His father was a farmer," she said. I found myself feeling relieved that he wasn't a remittance man.

"Why did he come to Australia?"

"Because he had the gold bug."

"The gold bug?"

"I wouldn't be a bit surprised if he's still talking about finding gold one day." She sat down at the table and took the piece of toast I'd left, and began to eat it dry. "He was a wool classer or something like that in a warehouse in Bradford. Come to think of it, I suppose he was too young to be a wool classer. He was only eighteen." I pushed the butter over to her, but she didn't notice it. "He loathed wool; the feel of it, and the smell of it." She was smiling. "The number of times I've heard him jeering about the pocket handkerchief paddocks his father had in Yorkshire; and the tiny flock. Thinking about it now, I'm sure he only jeered when he was most homesick." She considered her piece of dry toast for quite a while, and then she went on, "It's funny, isn't it? He's instinctively a sheep man. Even in the early days it seemed that he just couldn't go wrong with sheep; and yet he's always hated them. He didn't want to be a farmer, so he went into the wool warehouse, but that didn't satisfy him either, because he still wasn't far enough away from sheep."

I said, "He picked a fine place to come to if he wanted to get away from sheep."

"I told you that he came here for gold. While he was in the warehouse, he read somewhere about a German who had discovered a slab of gold in New South Wales. If I remember rightly, the slab was supposed to have been seven feet high and worth twenty-five thousand pounds." She laughed, and added, "So Father came to New South Wales to find a slab of gold eight feet high."

"When did he come?"

"He landed in 1875."

"A bit late for gold. The big pickings, I mean."

"He didn't know that, of course."

"He was eighteen?"

"Yes."

I was trying to imagine him. A Yorkshireman. Eighteen. Coming to what must have seemed to him to be the ends of the earth.

My mother suddenly got up from the table and put down the remains of the piece of toast. 'This,' I thought, 'is where the subject gets changed.' But, to my surprise, she didn't sweep into her efficient act and start clearing away the breakfast things. She stood there and looked at me for a moment and then said, "I feel very guilty to have deprived you of Billabirra all these years."

"You haven't deprived me of anything," I said.

"Oh, I'm not talking about the money part of it. It's the place, Billabirra itself."

"What's Billabirra like?"

"The homestead, you mean?"

"The whole place."

"It's a big station. Even bigger, David tells me, than when I knew it." She thought for a while, and I kept quiet. "When I first knew it, it was very small. No more than a couple of thousand acres. We lived in the old homestead down on the river flat. It was no more than a bark humpy, really. Mother and Father built it themselves. It was just one room to start with, and then Father added a room every time a new baby arrived. I can remember it perfectly, although I was only about four when the new homestead was built up on the hill."

"What you haven't explained," I said, "is what your father was doing raising sheep when he hated the sight of them."

With every question I'd asked, I'd been waiting for the brush-off. This one was going to be it, I was sure. But it turned out that this was an unusual morning, because my mother said, "I once started to write a book about them. About my mother and father, I mean. I didn't ever finish it. It's no more than a blueprint for a book, really. You'd better read it. At least it will give you the facts."

You could have knocked me down with a feather.

She went out of the kitchen, and came back later with a manila folder. There was a typescript in it. She put it on the table. Then came the efficient act I'd been waiting for. She began to bang crockery about and said, "Come on. Are you going to take all day with your breakfast?"

I picked up the folder, and stretched myself and yawned and said I was going to have a shower, and she said it was about time too, and she had no patience with all this sitting about, wasting a morning. So I put the folder in the sitting-room, and then I went and had my shower. But I was in and out of it in no time at all because I was itching to get at the typescript.

CHAPTER SEVEN

I SPENT the rest of the morning reading.

My mother had been right when she'd said that what she'd written was only a blueprint for a book. The story was there, but the people weren't. There were two straw dolls called Jack and Polly Selway, and I didn't believe in them for a minute. Now I've already said that my mother wasn't a very good writer, and thinking back on it, I suppose it sounded a bit patronising. The fact of the matter is that I wouldn't have known that she wasn't a good writer if she hadn't said so herself. Reading this typescript, though, I knew that the trouble with it was nothing to do with good or bad writing. I remembered how she'd said, years ago, that the reason why she wasn't any good as a writer was because she thought all the ideas out of herself before she had time to put them on paper. It seemed to me that while she was writing this narrative, she'd been afraid to think at all. She simply wrote down facts.

And the facts were too fantastic to be swallowed even by someone as thirsty for information as I was.

If she'd written a romanticised story of pioneer struggles, I'd have taken the whole thing with a grain of salt, and thought it was a damned good yarn. As it was, it was both frustrating and disturbing because I couldn't tell from the narrative whether my grandparents were utterly stupid, or foolhardy to the point of megalomania.

She began at the beginning with an eighteen-year-old Yorkshireman named Jack Selway stepping off the clipper at Circular Quay on the morning of June 1st, 1875.

I wanted to know what he felt like, what he was thinking, what his impressions were of this place that was the end of the earth. All I learned was that he was the owner of the clothes he stood up in, another suit in the box that still had to be unloaded from the ship, some underwear, a gold watch and chain, and ninety-three pounds in sovereigns in a money-belt. He had come to look for gold.

He was befriended by a man named George Russell. No mention of how they met or where they met. Russell took Jack to the house of a rich wool exporter named Matthew Cayley. It was in Cayley's house that Jack met Polly Durant, the daughter of an Irish journalist. What did Polly look like? How long had she been in Australia? What was she doing in the Cayley house?

Jack and Polly fell in love. Just that. I stopped reading for a moment to try to fill in the background for myself. Love among the antimacassars. A leisurely, rather coy Victorian courtship. Then the next sentence came right up from the page and hit me in the face. It was: "They were married on June 14th, 1875."

Married!

Exactly two weeks after stepping ashore in Sydney, Jack Selway was married to Polly Durant. Even in crude colonial society such haste must have seemed a trifle injudicious.

The next sentence was even more puzzling. "Jack had selected three hundred and twenty acres of land in a river valley in the north-west. It was country that hadn't yet been surveyed. It had recently been thrown open by the Crown for selection at one pound an acre." Selecting unsurveyed land meant that you went down to the Land Commissioner's Office, and he showed you a map, and you put your finger on it and said, "I'll have that bit," and then some time later you found yourself out in the bush, and the bit you'd bought turned out to be a stretch of thick scrub where it was likely no white man had ever been before. You either cleared it and lived on it and survived, or you put your tail between your legs and went back to where you'd come from. It could be that you didn't even live to arrive there in the first place.

The year 1875 would have been the difficult time for land-hungry immigrants, because by then the Government had stopped carrying on like drunken sailors ashore with a year's pay in their pockets. In the early years it was an embarrassment of riches. There they were with a great continent to give away, and you only had to arrive in Sydney looking wistful, and the next thing you were the owner of a parcel of land with convict labour thrown in.

By the 1840's the riches began to dwindle a bit when famine at home sent shiploads of hungry Britons to a place where, it was rumoured, they could eat. They wanted land.

In 1850 came the beginning of the gold rush. It took a lot of the prospectors a very short time to find that if you wanted gold, you had to dig for it, so they decided to settle for a nice bit of land. It was now that the generous Government's face became very red indeed; because it didn't have any more land to give away: not land that anyone knew anything about. Of course there was the country on the other side of the mountains, goodness knew how many thousands of square miles of it. But who on earth wanted to go west of the mountains? Explorers, certainly, had been out there and had mapped most of it. Some of them hadn't lived to bring their maps back.

Still, if people wanted land . . .

The Government shrugged its shoulders and decided to throw the whole, vast, unknown shooting match open to those who were prepared to pay for it. You bought unseen, and if you bought a pig in a poke, it was more than likely that you wouldn't live to complain. You could only buy three hundred and twenty acres. That was so you couldn't become too wealthy, too influential. Enough land to keep you alive, but not enough to make you too big for your boots. Some of the recipients of earlier generosity were already too powerful for comfort.

To get back to Jack Selway.

He'd bought his permitted three hundred and twenty acres. According to the narrative, he only had to pay five shillings per acre deposit; the rest could be paid off more or less when he felt like it. (The Land Commissioner blushing with shame, no doubt, knowing that when Mr. Selway arrived to take up his selection, the chances were that it would be three hundred and twenty acres of desert.)

What I couldn't understand was why Jack Selway was buying land at all. He didn't want to be a farmer. He hated sheep. He wanted to dig for gold. Yet here he was paying out eighty of his ninety-three pounds for a piece of land. The next sentence cleared up the mystery. Jack had heard that there was a gold strike in this river valley, and had decided that he'd be in a better position than the other prospectors if he owned the land out of which he was going to dig his eight-foot slab of gold. Foolhardy but understandable.

Just the same, my mother surely didn't expect me to believe that he intended to take up this selection! He was eighteen. He'd been in the colony a couple of weeks. In all probability he hadn't had time to venture into the wilds of the Sydney suburbs. How on earth did he think he was going to make a journey of hundreds of miles through unknown country? What about his wife? They'd only just got married. How could he contemplate leaving her in Sydney while he . . .

I turned over a page of the typescript, and discovered that my mother not only expected me to believe her story, but she stated as fact that on the day of their marriage Jack and Polly Selway set out from Sydney to take up their selection. Jack and Polly! She went with him!

I didn't believe it.

I put the typescript down and went to look for her. She wasn't in her room and she wasn't in the kitchen. I yelled, "Mum!" and muffled sounds came out of the bathroom. She was washing her hair.

I went back to the typescript, and learned that two days after leaving Sydney, the Selways arrived in Bathurst. Well, that was all right. Nothing very difficult about that. Bathurst was quite a big place by then. A lot of people must have been travelling between Sydney and Bathurst. The crossing of the mountains wouldn't have been the hazardous journey of a few years earlier.

I got out my history book, and looked up dates. By 1875 there would have been a railway to Mount Victoria on the top of the mountains. Then the Cobb and Co. coach did the rest of the journey down the other side of the range on to the western plains.

Then the facts got out of hand again. My mother asserted that after spending one night in Bathurst, the Selways set out on their journey north. Just like that. Like saying they hopped on a bus.

They travelled by dray. No comfortable covered wagon. Just an open dray. They took with them a few sheep, some cattle, riding horses, and pack horses. They were accompanied by a bushman named Bill Harper. I found myself feeling slightly less alarmed when I read that. At least they had someone to show them the way. Then it turned out that this Harper didn't know the way, and they kept getting lost. Every time I turned over a page, I expected to find that they'd turned back. But they didn't. They arrived in their river valley three months later, and because it was spring they had no time to build themselves a place to live in. They had to set to work at once to clear the land and sow the seed that was going to keep them alive next year.

It was either super-human or sub-human, I couldn't tell which.

I contented myself with the thought that I didn't believe a word of it, and went out to look for Mother again. I bumped into her in the hall with a towel wrapped round her head.

"You've got the dates mixed up," I said. "You say he left Sydney two weeks after he got here from England."

"That's right," she said. "Exactly two weeks to the day."

"Are you sure it wasn't the next year, when he'd had time to get acclimatised?"

"Quite sure. My brother, Jonathon, was born the next year. They were already settled on the selection by then."

"You don't give any indication of what they were like," I said. My voice boomeranged back at me, sounding very governessy. Somewhere from the past I heard an echo of another voice using the same tone and saying, "Use your imag-

ination, Brandon." I didn't have time to think about that
then, though. "If I knew what they were like, perhaps it
wouldn't be so hard to believe," I added.

She frowned and put her head on one side as she always
did when she was thinking, and the towel turban came un-
ravelled. She took quite a long time to fix it again.

" I know what you mean," she said. "That's why I never
finished the book. I began to write it about ten years ago.
By that time I hadn't seen them for twenty years, and they'd
become hazy in my mind. I couldn't remember what they
were like, and I didn't want to turn them into a couple of
fictional characters."

I knew she was lying. Whatever else had happened, her
parents certainly hadn't become hazy in her mind.

"I still say you've got the dates wrong," I said. "To make
a journey like that, they'd have needed to be used to the
climate, they'd have needed at least a few months of roughing
it to . . ."

"Don't you think it more likely," she asked, "that if my
father had been here longer, if he had had the vaguest idea
of what he was faced with, he'd have thought twice about
starting out?"

"But what about those friends in Sydney. Cayley and
Russell. Surely they told him!"

She smiled and said, "The trouble with you is that you're
one of those revolting people who always read the last page
of a book first to see whether you're going to like it or not.
Go and finish reading."

I started to go back to the sitting-room, and she called
after me: "Have you still got your school history book?"

I said I had, and that I'd just been looking up dates in it.

"You'd better read what it says about the squatter-
selector controversy."

"But . . ."

"I'll catch my death of cold standing round in a draught
with my hair wet," she said, and disappeared into her bedroom.

I looked up "squatter" in the index.

Nowadays the word "squatter" in Australia is synonymous with wealth. It stands for all those noughts on the end of the yearly wool cheque.

But in the old days it was a dirty word. It meant that you were an outlaw. It meant that the Crown hadn't given you or sold you land. It meant that you'd just collected together a mob of sheep, and you'd gone up-country until you'd found a likely-looking pasture, and there you'd squatted.

The Crown pretended not to know about you for quite a while. After all, you were on unsurveyed land that nobody else wanted, and what's more you were growing wool. You were coming in from the backblocks every year with great bullock drays loaded with the stuff, and wool was the backbone of the colony's economy.

Then came the land panic and all those immigrants wanting a few acres. The Land Commissioner now permitted himself to remember you and how illegal you were, so he thought it would be a good idea if you handed over that free sheep run of yours to people who were prepared to pay for it. You, of course, raised hell. If you could write, you wrote reams of letters. If you couldn't write, you went to Sydney and put your X on a protest any solicitor was prepared to write for you for a sovereign. In the end, those drayloads of wool of yours did the trick, and a compromise was reached. You were allowed to lease your run for a certain period. During that period you had the pre-emptive right to buy all or any part of the land you controlled at the Crown price of one pound an acre. What you hadn't bought by the time your lease was up, the Crown could throw open to selectors.

You'd won your fight. You weren't illegal now. You probably had a lease of fourteen years, and you were paying good rent for it. Why bother buying? After all, you were a long way out. It wasn't likely that those poor miserable selectors grovelling for their few acres would have either the guts or the nouse to come this far. Just out from the Old Country most of them. New chums. Even if, by some stroke of ill-luck, one of them happened to select part of your run, it was most unlikely that he'd ever find his way here. You were sitting pretty.

The way Professor Scott explained it all in the book, it was much more complicated than this, of course, but I only wanted the general picture.

I went back to my mother's narrative, prepared to find Jack Selway about to do battle with the local squatter. I turned over a page, and there it was.

The squatter's name was Andy Cameron, and he came to life right there on the page. A huge red-headed and bearded Scot. At least, his hair turned out later to be red. The first time he appeared he was so dirty it was impossible to tell what colour either he or his hair were. He ran his sheep on a million acres. He lived in a humpy, along with his dogs, and the only furnishings were a packing-case and a pile of sheep-skins on which he and the dogs slept. You could smell the humpy half a mile away when there was a good breeze blowing, my mother wrote.

I was beginning to get interested. There was Andy Cameron ranting and raving, calling Jack a land stealer. There was Jack, as innocent as you please, not having the vaguest idea what all the fuss was about because he'd never even heard of the word squatter. There was Polly indignantly insisting that they were not land stealers, and they had the papers to prove it.

And then, right in the middle of a sentence, the story stopped.

The sentence was: There was a niggling little thought trying to push its way into Jack's brain, and . . .

I turned over the page, and there was just a blank sheet of paper.

I went looking for my mother and found her in the kitchen by the radiator drying her hair.

"Where's the rest of it?" I asked. "What you gave me only goes up to where Andy Cameron arrived."

"That's all there is," she said. "I didn't get any further."

She looked very vague and put on that air of rising above the whole thing that she always resorted to when she was feeling guilty about something.

There was nothing for me to do but laugh. "You are the limit," I said. "I thought I was getting the whole story."

She looked indignant. "You said you wanted to know about the beginning!"

"Well, what happened afterwards? Did they stay on the selection?"

"They're still at Billabirra, aren't they?"

"Was the selection the beginning of Billabirra, then?"

"Of course it was."

I did a silly thing then. I was too sure of myself. "What happened when you left Billabirra?"

She did her old act of shying away. She didn't change the subject. She deliberately misread the question. She said, "I came to Sydney."

I didn't dare to say, 'I meant before you left home, you idiot,' so I played her along a bit until I could find my way back. "Did you start writing straight away?"

She said, "I'd already sold a couple of short stories to the *Bulletin*. That was a help."

"Already? Before you left home?"

She nodded.

This looked like my way back. "I'll bet you left home because you were an unappreciated genius. I'll bet you made up your mind never to return until you'd made fame and fortune."

My mother laughed. "Don't be silly," she said. "Genius is taken for granted by the Selways. We're all geniuses. If I'd gone home and announced that I'd just won the Nobel Prize for Literature, my mother would have said, 'Have you, dear? That's my father you get that from, now I want you to run down to the dairy and fetch the cream.' And my father would have said, 'There now, our Nell's written another little story.'"

She did the accents well. The Irish mother, the Yorkshire

father. They came alive for a minute. Maybe I was prepared to believe, after all, that they'd done that fantastic
journey back in 1875.

Just then there was a knock on the back door, and Jan
came in, and I lost interest in the Selways because I was so
glad to see her.

CHAPTER EIGHT

I GOT a job the following week. Things were beginning to look up a bit. The rusty wheels were beginning very slowly to turn, and you'd see an occasional building going up, or a house being painted, or a road being mended. Positions and Situations Vacant were starting to appear again in the *Herald*. They all wanted boys straight from school, of course. Once it had been, "Sorry, son, you're too young." Now it was, "Sorry. We want boys leaving school so that we can train them."

We were getting into our twenties.

Anyway, I got this job road-mending, and I came home one night feeling dead tired. The pick was finding muscles I didn't know I'd had. It was Friday, and I was looking forward to the weekend. I was thinking that if I could un-stiffen myself by Sunday, Jan and I could go somewhere and I could paint.

When I walked into the kitchen, my mother said, "Darling, I want you to run down to the grocer's before they close." She sounded exactly like her own imitation of her mother. "I want you to get a large tin of that cockroach powder."

I didn't want to run down to the grocers, so I said, "Oh, Mum, you know that stuff doesn't do any good."

"It scares them away for a few days. Just as long as we can keep them scared away till after Sunday."

"Sunday?"

"My mother's coming to Sydney. On the Saturday night train." Her expression dared me to comment, so I just shrugged as though the arrival of this unknown, straw-doll grandmother was an everyday occurrence, and then went down to the grocer's.

The cockroaches took the hint. By Sunday morning there wasn't a sign of one, but my mother didn't trust them. She peered and prodded about and moved things and shook more powder around and said once, "If one puts in an appearance while she's here, I'll die."

The amount of scouring and moving we did on Saturday did my seized-up muscles a power of good.

When we'd first moved into the flat and my mother had warned me that I'd have to sleep in the sitting-room, she'd intended that I should simply sleep there on the divan at night, and that by day all traces of my occupation would be whipped out of sight. She'd reckoned, of course, without the painting gear. As it was, the sitting-room furniture was all piled in one corner, and I was spread all over the place. I did see, though, that this wouldn't do for my grandmother. So we moved all my gear out, and we dusted and polished, and we put the sitting-room stuff where it ought to be, and you wouldn't have known it by the time we were finished with it.

Jan came to help us. It was she who remembered to polish the front door-knob.

On Sunday morning my mother and I were sitting up all dressed in our best waiting for the sound of the taxi so that I could go out and meet it, when there was an awful hulla-baloo next door. We went out to the kitchen, because hullabaloos in our street were always interesting and we could hear better from the kitchen. It seemed that Mr. Mulligan, who was supposed to have been at Mass, had just arrived home very drunk indeed, and the whole street was so intrigued to know where he'd managed to find a drink, let alone get drunk, on a Sunday, that it was like a flock of cockatoos again.

That was how we came to miss the noise of the taxi arriving.

The first thing we knew there was a knock on the back door. The back door. The kitchen door. The front door-knob all polished, the sitting-room all waiting, and some idiot had directed my grandmother to the back door. Out through the back yard, over the rusting bedstead, under the clothes lines, round the rubbish tins, to the kitchen door.

I opened the door, and there she was. My mother was standing near the kitchen table, having had one last, anguished look round for cockroaches. My grandmother stood at the door. We all seemed to stand still for ages.

Between the kitchen table and the kitchen door were thirty years.

Then my grandmother said, "Nell Selway, you're a fool!" And my mother said, "I know, Mother. I know."

The thirty years were bridged.

My mother came to the door, and they put their arms round each other, and they both cried. I just stood there. I was the onlooker again.

My grandmother must once have been very beautiful. Indeed, she still was, with the kind of beauty that isn't afraid of or ashamed of age.

Then they both blew their noses, and my grandmother said, "I should have had a new hat. This one's years old. Couldn't buy a new one on Sunday, though. Do I look a frightful old bushwhacker?"

My mother said, "You look wonderful. It's so good to see you."

The old lady put on the voice that sounded like my mother's imitation of her. "If you hadn't been so stubborn, you could have seen me weeks ago in my own home. In your own home." Then she sat down firmly at the kitchen table and said she was dying for a cup of tea. My mother began to say she was sorry she'd come to the back door, and wouldn't she rather go into the sitting-room, and . . .

The old girl sniffed and said, "Since when have I been too good to go into a kitchen? Though I can't imagine how you do your preserves and jams and baking in that stove!"

She turned to the stove and clapped eyes on me, because I'd gone there to put the kettle on. She studied me for a long time, and then she said, "Nell Selway, I'm so angry with you

I can scarcely speak. To think I've had another grandson all these years and I didn't know!"

My mother was embarrassed because she'd forgotten about me, and she began to stammer out a silly-sounding formal introduction. I kissed the old lady, and then she began to cry again and was furious with herself. "It wasn't going to be a bit like this at all. I planned it all on the train. Such a nasty journey on the train. It was so hot I thought I'd suffocate, and then when we got to Central this morning, there was a wind cold enough to cut you to pieces." Then she blew her nose again, and patted my hand and said, "Harry," and she smiled.

I've never in my life seen anything quite like that smile.

She turned to my mother. "He's like Jack," she said.

"Oh, no," my mother protested. "He isn't in the least like Father."

"He is. Inside. Like Jack." Then she smiled at me again, and I was head over heels in love. How was I to know I was repeating history?

My mother asked whether she'd come to Sydney alone, and she said David had brought her, but had thought it better not to come to the flat with her. He had put her in a taxi and would meet her back at the hotel.

David was back in Sydney. Little alarm bells started tingling round inside me, but I gave myself the luxury of ignoring them. I was wallowing in being in love.

Thinking back on it now, that afternoon has a crazy sort of Dali quality. Nobody said what they were really thinking. Everybody said the first things that came into their heads. It was like hanging watches on a hall stand. I was the fish's eye down in the left-hand corner. I was the one that was in love with his grandmother.

By the next day the fantastic quality had gone, and we were all relaxed with each other. While I went to work, they went out on a shopping spree because my grandmother said that was why she'd come to Sydney. First of all a new hat.

When I got home that night, there she was sitting up in the kitchen in her new hat. She had red spots on her cheeks and

her eyes were very bright. I thought it was the excitement of
the new hat.

The argument began that night. I went to have a shower
and to change, and when I got back to the kitchen, there she
was still wearing her hat, saying, "Of course you're coming
home with me. Your father's expecting us. We'll go on Friday."

My mother said, "You can't expect me simply to walk
back into the house and take things up again after thirty
years! Too much has happened!"

My grandmother said, "You don't imagine it's just a
matter of picking up where you left off, do you? Do you
think we've stayed the same? Do you think we've just gone
placidly along doing nothing except grow up and grow old?
Oh my goodness, no! Sure, you'd be amazed at the number
of skeletons our family's stowed away in cupboards during
the last thirty years."

I could see she wasn't used to being argued with, this one.
But she'd met her match in my mother. Suddenly I knew
why my mother had been afraid to put her on paper. It
couldn't be done. There was simply no way of doing justice
to her. If you tried to put that bossiness down on paper, you
ended up with the stock matriarch. If you tried to describe
the smile, you were reduced to clichés. There weren't the
words to describe the quality that radiated from her. Perhaps
a poet could do it, if he were an earthy enough poet.

The argument went on, punctuated by shopping expedi-
tions, all the week. My mother kept saying, "I've made my
own life, and I must live it the way I've made it."

My grandmother kept saying, "Now, Nell, I want you
to be sensible!"

We didn't see much of David. He didn't come to the
flat. When we went to the hotel for dinner on Tuesday night,
though, he seemed glad to see us, and explained to me on the
quiet that, having had a taste of his Aunt Nell's stubborness,
he'd thought it better to let Grandma cope with it alone.

I didn't see much of Jan either. It was my fault, because I
didn't try to get in touch with her. I was too busy twisting
myself round Polly Selway's little finger.

I remember wondering one night, just before I fell asleep, whether it was to keep out of range of that little finger that my mother had left home. I had said to her as she was going off to bed, "Mum, why don't you go back to Billabirra?" and she'd answered, "I've got to make it clear that I want to do things in my own way, Harry."

On the Wednesday I had a stroke of luck. Things got a bit confused on the road. We'd come to a corner, and the foreman didn't know whether we were supposed to go round it, or on up the hill to the intersection. It was so long since a road had been mended that everyone was out of practice when it came to making decisions. The upshot was that we got the afternoon off on half pay while they sorted things out at the Council Chambers. Some of the blokes began to winge, but I got away quick smart. I knew my grandmother was coming to lunch.

I found my mother alone in the kitchen looking worried.

"She's not coming," she said. "David rang and left a message down at the grocer's. I've only just got it. I'd better go to the hotel."

"What's wrong?"

"The message said there's nothing to worry about. She just has a slight cold, and he's persuaded her to stay in bed for the day."

"Well," I said, "she did say on Sunday that she thought she was getting a cold. Much the best thing to stay in bed."

My mother didn't look at all comforted. "You don't know her," she said. "The only time I've ever known her to stay in bed was when my brother Henry was born." Then she looked surprised as well as worried. "Do you know she's never had a day's illness in her life?"

I said, "Mum, will you let me go to the hotel and see her?"

She looked even more surprised. "Would you like to?"

"I've never had a real chance to talk to her."

My mother relaxed and laughed. "You and your talking."

I cleaned myself up and got ready to go, and as I was leaving, my mother still laughing, said, "Now don't go and wear her out with your old questions."

"I won't, if she's as good as you are at side-stepping answers," I said.

"If she's really ill," my mother said, side-stepping like mad, "come back at once and get me."

I promised I would, and went off to catch the tram.

David met me at the hotel, and wasn't at all gloomy, and said there was nothing wrong with her except a bit of a cold and the after-effects of an orgy of shopping, and he took me up to her room.

She wasn't in bed at all. She was fully dressed with her new hat on.

"Grandma," he said, "you promised you'd stay in bed!"

You could see he and the little finger were on good terms.

"Bed!" she said. "Beds are for sleeping in. I'm not tired. Harry, love, how nice that you've come to see me."

I explained about the road, and she was enchanted and said she'd like to go and see it, and then she turned to David and asked, "Weren't you going to have lunch with that tractor man?"

David said he'd just been about to phone the tractor man and cancel the lunch when I'd appeared, so my grandmother said there was no need for him to cancel it now, because she had me to look after her.

So David, with some reluctance, went off to keep his lunch date, and looking after him as he went out of the door, she said, "He's unhappy about something. I love him very dearly and he tells me things as a rule, but he won't tell me what he's unhappy about."

I thought it was just possible that I might have cleared up the mystery, but I couldn't be sure.

"What kind of day is it?" she asked.

"Beautiful," I said. "Cool autumn breeze, warm autumn sun. Not a cloud in the sky."

"Do you want to sit in that stuffy dining-room and eat three courses?" she asked.

I said I didn't particularly.

"What this cold of mine needs is some sun," she said.

"I've spent too much time indoors since I've been in Sydney. Let's buy some sandwiches and fruit and go and eat them in the public gardens."

The public gardens. That had me flummoxed.

"Of course!" she said. "They're called the Botanical Gardens now, aren't they? When I lived in Sydney they were the public gardens."

So we bought some food and we went to the Botanical Gardens.

It was one of those days you dream about years later if you happen to be fog-bound in a London winter, or sweltering in a New York summer. There'd been a short sharp shower of rain in the night, and the gardens looked as though someone had been at them with the scrubbing brush. The harbour had brought out all the family diamonds for the occasion, and the effect was a bit ostentatious and dazzling, but we weren't in the mood to worry about good taste.

I started to lead her down across the lawn to the wall at the water's edge, but she veered off towards the chrysanthemums. She seemed to be looking for something, so I let her have her head.

We went along a path, and then we came back along the same path. Then suddenly she seemed to find what she was looking for, and she took a narrow turning that wound round through the dahlia beds. Eventually we came to a seat in a cul-de-sac. By some miracle the seat was empty.

"It's the same one," she said.

"The same one?"

"Imagine it being here still after all these years." She went and looked more closely at the seat. It was pretty battered and needed a coat of paint. "It might not be the same seat, but it's the same place." She looked around. "I think there were rose bushes then. Not dahlias. Yes. I remember now. Rose bushes. One or two of them were still flowering although it was June." She laughed. "Poor Jack. It took him such a long time to get used to midwinter in June."

Years of dealing with my mother made me cautious. I had

to take things gently. So I sat down and opened the packet of sandwiches.

I needn't have worried. Polly Selway wanted to talk. Just try and stop her.

"You're so like him, Harry," she said. "Not to look at, of course. He's stocky. Not nearly as tall as you, but the jaw's the same. Stubborn. Your mother has it, too. She gets her stubbornness from her father, you know."

I wanted to laugh, but didn't dare to, so I gave her a sandwich.

In the end I ate most of the sandwiches. She didn't feel very much like eating, she said, because she'd had a big breakfast. She did eat some of the fruit.

"Is this where you used to come with him?" I asked.

"Only once," she said. "The time he asked me to marry him."

"How long had you known him?"

"A week. The day we came here, though, was the first time we ever really talked."

"And he asked you to marry him."

"There was so little time, you see. No time for any of the conventional things."

"When did you fall in love with him?"

"The first time I saw him. He looked so ridiculous, I couldn't help falling in love with him."

"Ridiculous?"

She laughed. "Very self-important. There he was standing there in his best Bradford suit, with his jaw stuck out, all feet and hands, trying to look like a very devil of a fellow. I knew he was scared stiff and I loved him for trying so hard not to show it."

The other straw doll was beginning to come to life now.

"Tell me what he was like," I said.

She put her head on one side the way my mother does. "You know," she said.

"I want you to tell me."

She began to talk, then, about how he'd read of the slab of gold, and how he'd made up his mind to emigrate, how, after months of argument with his family, he'd finally got his way and sailed from Liverpool. "All he thought of was gold," she said. "He expected to find Sydney full of miners and blackfellows. He was disgusted when he found it full of wool wagons."

From where we were sitting we could see Macquarie Street. In the thirties it still looked much as it must have looked when Jack Selway saw it for the first time. You only had to ignore one or two new buildings. This was the beginning of the beautiful city an ex-convict architect had planned to build on the shores of the harbour. But that was back in the leisurely time before men became greedy. It was back in the time when exiles were concerned only with creating graciousness in a wilderness. It hadn't occurred to them yet that there was money to be made. By the time Jack arrived, the city beyond Macquarie Street must already have begun to look like the provincial Englishman's dream of Home. A Manchester brought to the South Seas. The exiles making things look homey for newer exiles.

"Those wool wagons!" my grandmother said.

Enormous teams of straining bullocks, and the bullockies' language making the air blue.

"The dust," she said, "and the mud they churned up when it rained."

"How long had you been in Sydney when he arrived?"

"Five years. I was twelve when we left Ireland. There were five other children younger than I was. There was the night in Dublin when my father came into the room where we were all sleeping, and he told us we had to get up and get dressed quickly. It's all hazy after that. Some neighbours hid us while the soldiers searched our house, and then, the next day, we were smuggled on to a little boat that took us to Queenstown, and that night we sailed for Australia."

This was the grandfather my mother had told me about. The one who was a poet.

"What had he done?" I asked.

Polly smiled. "Oh, that one! Talk the leg off an iron pot, he would. Talk, talk, talk! You never heard such a man for

talking! In Ireland at that time it didn't do to talk too
much."

"He became a journalist here, didn't he?"

"Not at first. Not when we first got here. That came
later. At first we were close to starving. There wasn't much
room for a talking and writing man in Sydney at that time.
Later on, four years later, he got a job on a Melbourne newspaper, and took the family away there."

"You stayed in Sydney?"

"I was happy at the Cayleys, and I was earning my keep."

"Earning?"

"Hasn't your mother told you about it, then?"

I thought I ought to explain that my mother had been
reluctant to give me much family history. Before Polly had
time to register her disapproval, I hastily added that talking
about the family always made Mother miserable. That side-
tracked us for a while as Polly delivered a homily on the
stupidity of children who ran away from home.

Though I was all ears, I didn't want to be side-tracked, so
I didn't give her the chance to go on for very long. Back to
the beginning.

"How did you earn your keep?"

"There was Mrs. Cayley. A dear soul, she was. A gentlewoman. Though what a gentlewoman was doing married
to a ruffian like Cayley, I'll never understand. It was said
that he was an ex-convict. I always found him kind, mind
you. My father warned me that he was a scoundrel, and
didn't want me to stay there once they'd all moved away to
Melbourne. But I . . ." She stopped and looked at me again,
and said, "Fancy now! If I'd gone off to Melbourne with
them none of it would have happened!"

She had a coughing fit then, and I began to worry about
letting her talk too much. I tried to persuade her to go back
to the hotel, but she said she'd come out for some sun, and
she meant to get it. It was warm and we were out of the
wind, so I thought she was right about the sun doing her
cold good.

"Mrs. Cayley," she said, "was what you call nowadays

a dipsomaniac. In my day we said she didn't enjoy good health. It was my job to ward off visitors when she was having a bad day, and keep an eye on her the rest of the time. You know it's amazing the places that nice woman found to hide bottles!''

"You were seventeen," I said.

"Oh," she said, "a girl wasn't as young as all that at seventeen in my day. In any case, I was very fond of her. She always treated me as one of the family. That was how I came to meet Jack. If I hadn't been one of the family, I wouldn't have come into the drawing-room that day and seen him standing there with his jaw stuck out. He'd been brought to the house by Cayley's business partner, a man named George Russell. There was a plausible rogue for you. Jack was just off the ship. Russell had helped him to find lodgings and then brought him to the Cayleys'. It all seemed to be such a great kindness at the time."

The way I'm writing this down it seems that she just sat there and talked without stopping, but it wasn't like that at all. She'd say something, and then she'd stop and think about it for a while. Sometimes she'd look slightly astonished, as though it couldn't possibly have been to Polly Selway that all this had happened.

I was well trained, though. I didn't try to push myself into any of the pauses.

CHAPTER NINE

IT would be absurd for me to try to pretend that, after all these years, I remember everything she said that afternoon. Her exact words, I mean. Every now and then, I can see her face and I can hear her voice, and the very words come back to me, but there's a lot to be filled in in between.

About Jack she said, "I don't want you to think he was a stupid man. I said I fell in love with him because he looked ridiculous, but he had the nicest possible way of looking ridiculous. It's not likely I'd have fallen in love with him if he'd been stupid, is it?"

I said I couldn't think of anything less likely, and she smiled and patted my hand, and said, "That's right, Harry. Butter me up. David learned in his cradle that he could do anything with me if he buttered me up enough. I'm a very vain old woman."

She wasn't an old woman, though. She was seventeen. And I was sitting in the public gardens with her amongst the roses, and I was ridiculous in the nicest possible way, but I wasn't stupid.

"Lots of much older and more experienced men would have been taken in just as Jack was," she said. "It was my fault more than his because my father had warned me that Matthew Cayley was a scoundrel. I should have been prepared. I suppose you'd say we were both fair game because we were still young enough to believe that anyone who was kind was also honest."

There was no limit to the kindness of George Russell and Matthew Cayley.

Russell seeing Jack come ashore from the clipper, a cocky

lad from the North Country with money in his money-belt;
a lamb all ready for the shearing. Easy enough to start a conversation. One kind word all that's needed. Russell helping
him to find lodgings, and then taking him to Cayley's house.
Matt Cayley, a wealthy wool exporter; and, to a Bradford
man, who can be more respectable than a wool exporter?
Jack standing there in his best Bradford suit, his money-
belt round him, his jaw stuck out, waiting for Polly to come
into the room and fall in love with him. Russell and Cayley
talking about sheep, about wool. That's where the money is,
Cully! Jack announcing that it's gold he's come for, and the
other two roaring with laughter. Gold! There's no money
in gold these days! Jack telling them about the agent who
came aboard the clipper as she docked this morning. This
agent had been full of a story about a man who had ridden
into Sydney only the other day with his saddle-bags stuffed
with nuggets as big as your fist. Cayley and Russell sobering
up, reassessing their man; giving him rope. Well, of course,
there is gold about. But it's a chancy business. The safe
thing is wool. You can't go wrong in New South Wales with
wool. Still, if it's gold Jack's set his heart on . . .

Polly came into the room somewhere here. And Jack saw
her for the first time, and she smiled.

All during the next week Russell and Cayley went on being
kind. Always anxious to help newcomers to find their feet.
Colonial hospitality, you know. Since it was gold he wanted,
Cayley introduced Jack to a lot of tough characters who'd
been on the gold fields. The salt of the earth, Matt said they
were. They were delighted to give the new chum all the information he wanted about the diggings, the kind of equipment he'd need, the type of life he must be prepared to lead.
It was heady stuff. Jack was already carrying his eight-foot
slab to lay it at Polly Durant's feet.

All that week, Cayley's kindness warming him, colonial
hospitality enveloping him, Jack was meeting Polly in the
hall, seeing her across the room, watching her on the stairs,
but there was not a word that could be said to her until the
day they met in the public gardens.

Polly only had an hour. Mrs. Cayley was showing nesting signs. That meant a hidden store somewhere. That meant a bout coming on; so Polly couldn't leave her for long.

In the gardens a brief hour, and no time for a slow build-up to intimacy. No time for conventional courtship. No time for coy doubts and shy withdrawings. The two of them holding hands on a garden seat, plunging right bang into the middle of being in love.

He was worried in case his money wouldn't last out. He couldn't afford to cool his heels in Sydney. He had to get to the goldfields. Would she wait for him? A year. No more. In a year he'd be back in Sydney with his fortune made. Then they'd be married and away home on the first ship. Polly said she'd wait.

It was half-way through Jack's second week in Sydney that he heard about the gold strike. He and George Russell were together in Bridge Street when they met a friend of Russell's who passed on the information in the strictest confidence. Jack couldn't believe his luck. A new diggings! Cayley looked grave when he heard about it. Lord love us, that was out in the back country!

Cayley knew his man by now. A bit of opposition would make that jaw set all the firmer.

The back country was no place for a new chum to go! You'd have to be an old hand with years of experience in the bush to get within cooee of the valley where that gold was! The jaw did set firmer. Cayley was on safe ground.

Now wait a minute, though. Cayley had just remembered something. Hadn't the Land Commissioner sent out a public notice only a few days ago announcing that a big tract of outback country was being thrown open for selection? Now where had Cayley put that notice? In his desk, very likely. Yes, here it was in the top drawer. And wonder of wonders! There was the valley of the gold strike plumb in the middle of the Land Commissioners' map! Well, of course this settled it. This made everything simple. Jack's course, was perfectly straightforward. If he was going to be fool-hardy enough to go west, at least his friends would be comforted by the knowledge that he had safeguarded himself.

Safeguarded himself? Jack hadn't quite got the point.

George Russell patiently explained that it was quite possible Jack would make that long journey into the never-never only to find on arrival that other prospectors had beaten him to it. After all, there must be hundreds of prospectors starting out from Bathurst at this very minute. Cayley amended it to thousands. He remembered what it was like on the mountain road after the strike at Lambing Flat. You couldn't move for prospectors. It would be a pity to go all that way only to find that the whole valley had been staked out. No, there was only one thing for it! Jack must buy a bit of the valley for himself. Then, when he got there, any prospector who had beaten him to it could be told to go to hell.

Jack didn't want to buy land. It wasn't that he smelt a rat. He just didn't want to own land.

The memory of my grandmother's voice takes over here.

"That's when it became my fault. I persuaded him to buy the selection. I should have known something was wrong, but all I was thinking about was being with Jack. If he'd gone to some mining camp, I couldn't have gone with him, you understand. But with our own bit of land, and him to have all the time in the world to look for gold, and me to grow a few little things to eat, and the two of us together . . . Oh, only the dear Lord knows the way I was seeing that bit of land in my mind!"

A neat little green field with the soft Irish light on it, and the mist rising in the evening, and a man coming in tired for his supper.

Jack gave in in the end and kind Russell and kind Cayley made all the arrangements. The news that Polly was going to marry Jack and go with him was received with astonishment and joy, but there was no time for celebration because the arrangements had to be made so quickly. Already those gold-hungry prospectors would be on their way. Besides,

F

with only thirteen of his ninety-three pounds left, Jack couldn't afford to stay in Sydney.

Polly had a little money saved up. That would help to buy provisions and equipment. Then Mrs. Cayley, recovering from her bout, and almost sober, was moved to give them a cheque for a wedding present.

My grandmother's voice again: "I'll swear Mrs. Cayley wasn't in the plot. I'm certain she didn't know what those two were up to."

The cheque bought them a dray and supplies enough to last them a year. Cayley and Russell, not to be outdone in generosity, added their wedding present of a small flock of sheep and some cattle.

The mention of sheep set Jack back on his heels, but Cayley told him it was better to have food on the hoof than to have to live for months on salt meat. Then George Russell remembered Bill Harper. Jack and Polly would need someone to guide them to their selection. They'd never find their way alone. Bill was the very man! An expert bushman, and by an odd coincidence, he happened to be, at that moment, in Bathurst. There was nothing to it. Cayley would write to Bill by tomorrow's mail, and tell him to have everything waiting for them in Bathurst . . . supplies, sleeping tent, dray horses, stock.

Polly wrote to her father in Melbourne that she was about to get married, and he wired back that he was delighted and that there was a letter following. If Michael Durant had known that his daughter was going to be married and miles away from Sydney within two days, he would have hurried up his investigations into this selection idea of Cayley's. As it was, he took his time, and on the day his letter arrived at the Cayley house, warning his daughter that she and her husband must on no account fall in with the plan, Polly and Jack Selway were already married and in Bathurst.

My grandmother: "How they must have laughed when they opened Papa's letter and read it."

The Selways were already exhausted by the time they got to Bathurst. The trip up the mountains in the little train had been hazardous but exciting, the trip down the other side of the mountains had been terrifying. They'd spent the night at Mount Victoria, and then, the next morning, before sunrise, they'd started down in the big American coach. They hadn't expected the descent to be so steep, nor the road to be so bad.

My grandmother: "There we were in a wide coach on a narrow road that was full of potholes and fallen tree trunks. On one side was a precipice rising upwards, on the other another precipice going sheer down, we didn't know how far, because the valley was filled with mist. It seemed, in places, that there were no more than a couple of inches between the wheels of the coach and the edge of the valley. It only needed a shying horse or a broken wheel to send us all spinning down." I remember that she laughed then, and added, "There was one passenger who kept telling us about the number of coaches that had overturned on that road, and the number of people who'd been killed. Oh, we were glad to get to Bathurst, I can tell you."

They had expected to spend a few days in Bathurst, but obviously Cayley was taking no chances. They were met by the bushman, Harper, who informed them that he had everything ready for them, and that they must be prepared to pull out the next day.

My grandmother again: "Oh, he was a hateful man. Surly. Evil. Our hearts went down into our boots when we met him. There was nothing we could do, of course. It wasn't likely that we'd be able to find anyone else to guide us at such short notice, and besides, he'd already been paid part of his wages. I'm certain the next months wouldn't have been so bad if it hadn't been for Harper."

The first week was easy going. The weather was fine, and there was a rough track for them to follow through the bush. Jack and Polly led the small procession in the dray, with the horses hitched behind them. Harper followed droving the cattle and sheep. Polly and Jack took it in turns to ride beside the dray, accustoming themselves each day to longer hours in the saddle. In the evenings they stopped at some place where there was grass for the animals and water for themselves. The first job was to hobble the horses, then they built their camp-fire and cooked their evening meal.

On the first evening Harper, with ill grace, showed Jack how to set the billy to boil for tea, then he brought a tin dish and some flour and baking soda and showed Polly how to make tomorrow's damper, for they'd seen the end of bread for a very long time.

In the months that followed, Harper never once spoke to them except to grunt some direction to Jack.

My grandmother: "The first night we expected him to come and join us at our camp-fire, but when we suggested it he walked away, built a fire of his own, and just sat there, watching us. Always watching us. Hating us. Until in the end it seemed that that hate was all round us."

During that first wonderful week, though, even Harper's hate couldn't depress them as they sat by their camp-fire in the evening eating salt meat followed by damper and treacle, and washing it all down with black, sweet tea that tasted of gum leaves. It was all such a great adventure that first week, that Polly and Jack laughed to think of those soft city folk who had warned them that the going would be hard.

There was a tent in the dray, but they never used it because they preferred to sleep in the open. They'd even brought a mattress with them from Sydney, but that, too, stayed in the dray. Jack would gather ferns and bracken and make a bed for Polly beside the fire, and she would lie and look at the glittering, frosty stars while Jack shared four-hour shifts with Harper watching the animals to make sure they didn't stray, and the only sounds in the night were the tinkling of the horse-bells and the croaking of the frogs in a near-by creek.

After the first week, Jack was impatient to get on. The stock made travelling slow, and he cursed the stupidity of the sheep and their complete indifference to the importance of time. He suggested to Harper that he and Polly should push ahead with the dray and horses, but Harper only grunted and told him not to be a bloody fool. Although Jack was angry at the time, by the second week he had to admit to himself that Harper had been right, because the rough track they'd been following dwindled off into thick scrub, and now there was no indication of the way they must go.

In the third week the great adventure turned into back-breaking work. They had to make their way through thick scrub and over uneven ground; they had to chop a way through for the dray, and a dozen times a day its wheels sank into holes or fouled against boulders; there were times when the dray had to be unloaded, dragged out of its difficulties and reloaded. And all the time the despised sheep pushed on unconcerned, cropping at each stop, managing without difficulty to get through country that was impossible for the dray.

They came to a river, and it was deep and fast flowing. They wasted three days while Harper rode out to find a place where it could be forded. And then they got over just in time, because on the following morning it began to rain, and even the shallow place where they'd crossed became a raging torrent.

It rained without ceasing for a week. Not gentle rain, but a heavy, continual downpour. Dried creek beds became impassable rivers, and solid-looking ground turned to bog under the wheels of the dray. They were soaked to the skin in the first ten minutes of the downpour and they stayed wet for the entire week. It was impossible to make a fire at night because the wood was wet and the rain doused any spark of flame they managed to start. Jack tried to pitch the tent for Polly, but the ground was so wet that it was just as bad inside the tent as outside it. In the end he rigged up a tarpaulin and they sheltered under the dray.

Harper remained unperturbed. There had to be rain, he said. This was the time of year for it. If it didn't rain now there'd be a drought in the summer. He wrapped himself in his sodden blanket, and made a hole for his hip in the wet earth, and went to sleep with his head on his saddle. The sheep huddled together and bleated mournfully, but they never stopped cropping.

Then, one morning they were wakened by the sun, and by midday they were dried out and warm, and the bush round them seemed suddenly to become alive with birds and small, scurrying animals. They saw a pink cloud rise, screeching, out of the big gums ahead of them. Cockatoos. Harper shot into the middle of the cloud, and that night they had their first change of diet from salt meat. They surprised a mob of kangaroos feeding near a waterhole, and for the next week they cooked kangaroo meat each night.

But the enchantment of the first week had gone, and now it was just plain drudgery by day, and the consciousness of Harper's watching, hating, by night.

Polly's dream of a little bit of soft, green Irish land had turned into a nightmare. She dreamed, again and again, that the bush around them was Harper, hating them. Lean, hard, ugly, evil, and hating.

But they were half-way there. It was too late to turn back.

While my grandmother had been talking, I'd been thinking about a picture I wanted to paint. No wonder I'd never been able to get things right on canvas. All those prissy landscapes! The trouble was that I'd choose a bit of country and I'd watch it, and then I'd try to paint it. What I had to get was not me watching it, but it watching me. It watching me, and telling me to hell with me, it didn't intend to give me an inch.

Her voice brought me to the surface.

"I'm dying for a cup of tea," she said.

I looked at my watch and realised that we'd been sitting there for two hours.

"I'll take you back to the hotel," I said.

"Isn't there somewhere here that we can get a cup of tea?"

"Yes, there's a tea place over there."

"Let's go there, then."

We got up from the seat, and she put her arm through mine, and said, "This was a good idea. The sun's made me feel better already. My cold's quite gone."

She did look better too. Her face and her eyes were glowing. I was thinking how clever I was to have effected the cure.

The Great Harry Brandon. If you haven't got a foot for putting in it, just borrow one of Brandon's. He's got a million of 'em.

CHAPTER TEN

I've never seen anyone drink as much tea as my grandmother did that afternoon. When debility overcame the first pot, she called for another, and then a third.

"The kettle's always on at home," she said, and asked the waitress to make it strong. Then she looked at me and repeated, "Home," and didn't say anything for quite a while.

"I was just thinking," she said at last.

I said I knew she was.

She patted my hand and said, "You're a good listener, Harry."

I wanted to tell her that I'd been in training for this for a long time, but I didn't interrupt because she was thinking again.

After a while she said, "I was just thinking how long it took us to get round to calling Billabirra 'home'."

I waited for the next bit, knowing she didn't expect me to say anything.

"Years and years," she said. "Home, you understand, was England, Ireland, London. Neither of us had ever been to London, yet we called it Home. Jack would talk about how he was going to make his fortune and how we were going Home to spend it."

"You were very homesick," I said, not needing to make a question of it.

She frowned and said, "At first it was much more than homesickness. It was a . . . a sickness of the spirit that went far deeper than just a longing for Home." She looked at me for a moment and then asked, "I wonder if you know what it's like to go on a long journey and then to arrive and find it's taken you nowhere?"

All my life I'd been going on a long journey that had got nowhere, but then it wasn't so bad for me, because I'd never expected to arrive anywhere.

I side-stepped the question, and asked, "How long did it take you to get to where you were going?"

"Much longer than it should have taken. Harper lost us several times, and once he didn't hobble the horses properly and they strayed and we wasted days looking for them. We never found two of the pack horses."

Another pot of tea had arrived, and she was busy pouring out. I felt as though my inside was drowning in tea, but I didn't want to cause a digression by refusing another cup.

"It was quite late in the spring," she said, "when we crossed another river and seemed to turn away from it as we travelled on for another day. Then, in the evening, we came back to it. We discovered afterwards that the river swept round practically at right angles. Our land was in the angle. Well, there we were. Jack's river that was loaded with gold. My little bit of land. Thick scrub, and that awful, awful silence. The bush grey-green all round us, hating us."

Late spring. The wattle would have been everywhere. Boronia, native roses, waratahs, wild violets, flannel flowers. They wouldn't have seen them. The bush would have been green-grey.

"And the eternal sunshine," she said. "Blue skies and sunshine. How we longed for a grey day." This reminded her that the afternoon sun was beginning to throw shadows, so she moved her chair a little so as not to be in the shade. "We hadn't seen a living soul since we'd left Bathurst. Jack had expected to find the valley teeming with prospectors, but it was three months before we saw anyone." She laughed. "Poor Jack and his gold. There wasn't time for him even to think about it. Not even time to build a place to live in. We lived in the tent while we made the clearing in the bush. The big trees had to be chopped down, sawed into movable sections, and then dragged away to be piled up to make fences. It was a job for bullocks, but we didn't have any, and we had to use the dray horse. It was slow work."

I'd marvelled that they'd been able to make the journey in the first place. I hadn't thought about what it must have been like when they got there.

"Then, although the bush seemed to be growing back on us as fast as we cleared it, we had to stop to build a hut to live in, because as it got hotter the tent became unendurable. That was the time, I think, when it was worst, because neither Jack nor I could think that we were achieving anything. It seemed, somehow, degrading to have come down to the level of working animals for no other reason than to keep ourselves alive. We worked and we ate and we slept. We dragged ourselves out of our blankets to face each day, and we went to bed at night with another day hanging over us."

I was trying to see it, to share it with them. My face must have looked rather odd, because suddenly my grandmother put her cup down and leaned over and patted my hand as though to tell me not to despair.

"Then Snowy came," she said.

I'd heard my mother and David talking about Snowy. I couldn't remember what it was they had said, but by the expression on my grandmother's face, I knew everything was going to be all right, because Snowy was here.

Cast in order of their appearance.

Snowy walking into the clearing.

Jack is fixing a slab of bark across the roof of the hut. Polly is carrying their belongings over from the tent, moving into her new home. Then a man leading a horse comes into the clearing. A big, fair man, heavily bearded. A bushman. The thing they first notice about him is the blue blueness of his eyes, and the wariness in them. Jack comes down from the roof, Polly puts down the mattress she's carrying. The stranger hitches his horse and comes a little farther into the clearing. They all stand looking at each other, suspicious. Then Polly tries to smile, but there isn't a smile left in her. The stranger seems to know that at least she's tried. His astonishing blue eyes become less wary. He says, "Good day," and Jack answers him with another, "Good day."

The stranger says, "It's a surprise finding a selector here. You weren't here when I was on my way up-country."

Jack explains that they've been here three months.

The stranger nods. "I was through here last autumn." He turns to Polly. "I won't bother you, ma'am. Just stopped for a minute to see if I could buy some flour and baccy from you."

Jack makes the mistake of asking, "Where are you from?" He's thinking of the goldfields, of course, but the stranger's eyes immediately become wary again. "All over the place," he says. Then adds, "I could do with some meat too, if you've got some to spare."

My grandmother, telling me this, made me laugh. It was the accent. She was trying to imitate Snowy, and making an awful hash of it. It wouldn't have been an Australian accent that he had, of course. As yet the dialects of Yorkshire, and Lancashire, and Scotland, and Ireland, and Devon, and Cornwall, and Wales, and London hadn't merged into a national speech form. His accent would probably have been closer to cockney than anything else, because he spoke the language of the old lags. But it was cockney with each syllable lengthened out into the drawl of a man with all the time in the world on his hands.

"He couldn't believe it," she said, "when we told him that the place was ours. He'd taken it for granted that we were the children of what he called the boss cocky. When we told him Jack was the boss cocky he didn't laugh, although I suppose he wanted to. He just said, 'Stiffen the crows!'"

The clearing has changed in the last few minutes. The evil has gone. The hate. This is the other side.

The stranger looks at the hut and says, "That's a nice humpy you've got there."

They've never heard the word "humpy". It was a hut to them. Now they accept his word for it. They've built a humpy.

The lethargy of the last few months is lifted. His eager,

inquiring, blue eyes give them something to hang on to, something by which they can drag themselves up out of the hell of despair. They show him the inside of the hut, the curtains Polly has made, the bed Jack has made to hold the mattress, the table, the pots scoured with river sand to make them shine, the floor of hardened clay, the half-dozen books. The fact that he obviously can't read makes these last things no less precious to him. He turns to them, his eyes shining. "I never thought I'd want to live in a humpy, because the only ones I've been in stank something awful. The men slept on sheepskins and the dogs too. Pooh!"

They both laugh, loving him, and the world is changed. They look with new eyes at this place which ten minutes ago was no more than a place to sleep and eat in. Suddenly it becomes something they've achieved. The journey they've made is not, after all, a descent into hopelessness. They've done something old hands would have feared to do. They're alive, and that, in itself, is surely triumph enough!

The stranger goes to the rough window, just a hole left in slabs, and fingers the curtains Polly has made out of an old dress. "Do you know what I heard?" he asks. "I heard there's humpies in towns with hard stuff in the windows that you can see through, yet it keeps out the cold and the rain."

Jack tries to tell him about glass, but he finds it difficult to understand. "But surely you've seen a house with proper windows!" Jack insists. The man shakes his head. "Never been in a town. I got within twenty mile of Bathurst once. Just to say I'd seen a town. Then I remembered the people. Too many people. I never got nearer than twenty mile. I can't abide people."

His name is Snowy. No other name. Just Snowy. He never knew who his father was. His mother was a convict assigned as a servant to a farm down on the Murrumbidgee. Nobody took much notice of him, least of all his mother, but they let him stay on the farm, just as long as he didn't get in the way. Occasionally someone would throw him scraps of food, but more often he scavenged, or shared the dogs' meals. He slept on sacks of potatoes among the rats. When

he was ten years old his mother was flogged for some mis-
demeanour, and a couple of days later she died. Snowy
pushed off then. He'd been on the go ever since, alone most
of the time, working for rations if he couldn't cadge any,
living as the abos did, mostly. He probably knew more than
any other white man about the country between the Murray
and the Darling Downs. He'd learned to live without people.

But he must have liked the look of Jack and Polly. He kept
shaking his head and saying over and over again, "Fancy a
couple of nippers like you coming all this way! I can't get
over it!"

They told him they'd had a guide, and when they mentioned Bill Harper by name, that wary look came back.
Then, seeming to sense their dislike of Harper, he relaxed
again, and asked if he could camp down by the river. "My
horse is lame," he said. "I've had to lead him all day. I'd
like to spell him for a few days."

Polly and Jack were delighted to have him there. He
could stay as long as he wanted. But Snowy, remembering
that he couldn't abide people, said he never stayed in any
place long. Just a couple of days for his horse to rest and then
he'd push on.

After Snowy had gone down to make his camp by the
river, Jack and Polly were alone in the humpy. They
watched him go, and then they just sat quietly for a long
time, not saying anything, liking being there together because the enchantment was back.

Snowy was still camped by the river a month later. He
earned his rations, helping Jack with the clearing and the
ploughing and the fencing, but he never went near Harper.
He was still there the day the squatter rode in.

Cast in order of appearance. Second character. The
squatter. Andy Cameron.

Polly is inside the humpy cooking a meal. Snowy is sitting
by the water-butt mending a piece of harness. Jack has just
come up from the sheep pens. Then, in rides the squatter,
stinking to high heaven, roaring like a bull. "Where's the
cove?" he roars.

Jack, astonished but standing his ground, explains that he's the cove. Out of the corner of his eye he can see Snowy sitting there grinning.

The squatter is a Scot. "You! Good God, I thought I was going to have to fight a man, and I find an unlicked cub!"

Jack is angry. "Who the hell are you?" he roars back. "What do you want of me?"

"I'll tell you what I want of you! I want you to get off my land!"

Polly has come out of the humpy to see what all the noise is about. Jack is shouting back: "Your land! This is my land!"

"You're a damned scoundrel! A landstealer!"

Then Polly takes a hand and says, "We've papers to prove it's our land!"

The Scotsman hasn't seen her come out of the humpy, and now his eyes nearly pop out of his head. The roar goes out of him. His horse has been plunging and rearing about, and he quiets it to a standstill. He drags the hat off his matted hair, and stares at Polly. He hasn't seen a white woman for years. He turns to Jack, "And you're a criminal lunatic, forbye, for bringing a woman here!" Then he jams his hat back on his head, wheels his horse round, and rides hell for leather out of the clearing.

Jack and Polly, gaping, turn instinctively to Snowy, who is still grinning from ear to ear. "Is he a prospector, then?" Jack asks. That kills Snowy. Andy Cameron a prospector! He laughs till his beard is wet with tears.

It was the silence that brought me out of the clearing with Snowy still laughing. My grandmother had stopped talking. She was looking at me with her head on one side. "You weren't listening," she said.

"Yes I was. I was there in the clearing with you."

"You looked as though you were wool gathering."

"Jan says I go broody every now and then."

"Who's Jan then?"

"My girl."

My girl?

"I'd like to meet her."

"Of course you'll meet her."

My girl?

Suddenly I wanted very much to talk to Jan. To get things clear. I'd take my grandmother back to the hotel now, and I'd go and find Jan and ask her what happened between her and David and I'd . . . Then I remembered that Jan would be at work. The whole of Sydney wasn't on holiday just because my road had come to a corner.

It was a glorious afternoon there in the Gardens.

"Are you tired?" I asked.

She shook her head, but I could see she was tired. That healthy glow had gone.

"Come on," I said. "We'll go."

But she didn't want to go. She wanted to stay while the sun lasted. She called for another pot of tea.

I wanted to leave. I didn't want to get back into that clearing again. What did it matter what had happened all those years ago? It had had a happy ending, hadn't it? All this wallowing in the past. It was the future that mattered.

What future?

The happy ending. My grandmother saying to my mother, "Sure you'd be surprised at the number of skeletons our family's stowed away in cupboards."

Lots of little happy endings. The curtain coming down over and over again, and then, each time, back to a beginning, back to a build-up to another little happy ending, and another curtain.

I was back in the clearing, of course. No escaping it.

It was when the squatter had gone, when Snowy had stopped laughing, that they learned they were dummies.

"We'd never heard the word before," my grandmother said. "We didn't know what it meant."

I am standing there in the clearing beside Polly, listening to Snowy, learning for the first time that you can't always trust kindness. Snowy is telling us about Andy Cameron, and how he's run his sheep on a million acres of this country for twenty years, how his lease has just expired. I am Jack Selway protesting that if this Andy Cameron hasn't had the sense to buy the land before his lease was up, that's his funeral.

Snowy shrugs and says, "Matter of money. He's had a run of bad seasons. First there was a three-year drought, then there was a bush-fire, then there was a flood. Andy couldn't get his wool down to Sydney because the bullock wagons couldn't make the trip in drought time. He had his three-years' wool clip in his sheds when the fire came through and wiped out the lot. He spent a couple of years building up again, then last year there was the flood." Then Snowy grins and adds, "You don't have to worry. There's always a run of good seasons after the bad ones. You're starting in at the beginning of the good ones."

But I'm not interested in talk about good or bad seasons. I want to know why I'm a dummy.

"Well, it's this way," Snowy says. "Andy's got no money. He goes to Sydney and asks the banks to lend him some. That's how Matt Cayley gets wind that Andy's broke. Cayley and Andy are old enemies."

Matt Cayley! What does Snowy know of Matt Cayley? Hasn't Snowy already said that he's never been in a town, let alone the city?

You don't have to go into a town to know about Matt Cayley. Biggest rogue unhung. Known through the length and breadth of the colony.

But how does Snowy know that I, Jack Selway, have any connection with Matt Cayley?

Snowy grins and gestures with his thumb over his shoulder at the sheep pens. "Bill Harper's one of Cayley's side-kicks. Cayley must have sent him with you."

It all becomes clear then. Cayley wants to get control of Andy's million acres. He knows that the whole enormous expanse of the run is no good to Andy without this river pasture, so all he has to do is get his hands on the river. Then he can starve Andy out. So he chooses me, green as grass, to be his dummy.

I'm not the only dummy, of course. Snowy tells us there are other selectors in the valley . . . other dummies put there by Cayley. Five miles up-river there's a family called Dooley. "Shanty Irish mob," Snowy says. "Father, mother, fourteen sons, and all of them as lazy as all get out." Beyond the Dooleys, another five miles up, there's an Englishman called Spencer.

Polly is astonished to find that we've neighbours only five miles away, but just now I want no truck with neighbours. I'm wanting to commit murder. I'm wanting to be back in that drawing-room in Sydney smacking my fist into that benevolently smiling face.

Then I stop being Jack Selway. I'm Harry Brandon again. Time waltzing round a bit because Polly Selway has grown up and grown old and become my grandmother, drinking tea.

"No gold?" I asked, being Brandon again.

She laughed and shook her head. "Not an ounce. Though Jack still swears there's some there in the river."

"The idea was that you and the other dummies were just to sit there on the river until Cayley was ready for it?"

"Until Andy Cameron faced the fact that he couldn't feed all his sheep on his own five-mile stretch of river. We dummies were stretched along fifteen miles. Cayley thought it would only take two or three years to starve Andy out. Then Cayley would clear us out of the river and offer to sell the land back to Andy at fifty times the Government price. He knew Andy wouldn't be able to pay, so then there would be a little business arrangement by which Andy would go on working the run, and Mr. Cayley would sit back for the rest of his life on the profit from it."

"Was that, in the the end, his proposition?"

"It was. But first he had to get the dummies out." My grandmother was beaming with delight now, because she'd got over all the agony and the despair. She was coming to the best bit. "He reckoned without Jack," she said, and stirred her tea as though she were ringing bells of triumph. "The idea, you understand, was that we dummies would just

G

about manage to exist. It was important that we should
exist."

"What if you hadn't?"

"Oh, he'd chosen us all very carefully. He knew we
would." She laughed and then had to blow her nose because of her cold. "But it was also important that we
shouldn't do well. That's what Bill Harper was there for.
He was there to see that we lost most of the lambs, that the
fences got broken down and the dingoes got in amongst the
ewes, that the rams would get sick so that we'd have to cut
their throats, and that, mysteriously, the crops we were trying
to grow would get trampled down. Then, when the time
came for us to be tired of just existing, along would come
generous Mr. Matthew Cayley offering to buy us out. Clearing his dummies out, you understand."

I said I understood.

She said again, "But he'd reckoned without Jack." And
then she added, on a smaller note of triumph, "And Snowy,
of course."

"Snowy stayed?"

She laughed. "He agreed to stay a couple of months till
we got straight. He was very angry."

"Angry?"

" I'm jumping a bit."

"Go back then."

She went back.

CHAPTER ELEVEN

As soon as Jack learned that he was a dummy, he rode up the river to see Andy Cameron, and told him how he'd been gypped. Andy was quite friendly when he heard the story, and even friendlier after Jack promised not to sell his land to Cayley without giving Andy first offer.

Then, the next day, to their amazement, Andy turned up in the clearing, all smiles, all apologies for his former uncouth behaviour. He'd had a bath, and his beard was trimmed, and his red hair stood straight up all over his head. Altogether he looked a much more alarming sight than he'd been on the first day.

Snowy said that he'd known Andy on and off for fifteen years and had never known him to have a bath or wash his hair before, and the missus was a good influence and no mistake.

After Andy had gone, Polly was feeling a bit smug because she knew that for the rest of time she had Andy Cameron eating out of her hand, and Jack was feeling happy because he'd made a friend out of an enemy, and Snowy was just sitting there laughing inside himself because people can be such damned fools.

"I must say," said Jack, sticking his chin out, looking a little pompous, "that the squatter isn't such a frightening ogre once you get under the dirt."

Snowy, thinking he ought to be taken down a peg or two, said, "Andy's all right. Why shouldn't he be friendly now he knows you're his dummy instead of Cayley's?"

"His dummy?"

"You promised not to sell to Cayley, so that means you're

dummying his best stretch of river till the time comes when he wants it himself."

"His best stretch of river?" Jack had never really bothered to look at the river. It was the symbol of his exile. All he wanted was to be shut of it.

Snowy said, "Sure thing. This is the part of the river that never runs dry even in the worst drought. The myalls call it Billabirra. Place of the deep water."

"Myalls?"

He was so innocent, this cocky little Johnny Newcome. Snowy couldn't imagine how he'd managed to survive as long as this. "Blacks," he said. "This used to be a meeting place of all the tribes hereabouts."

"Blacks!" Polly looked alarmed.

"It's all right" Snowy said. "They haven't been near here for years. They're scared stiff of Andy."

"Billabirra. It's a nice sound." Polly was looking dreamy, but Jack wasn't. He was thinking hard. Suddenly, he swung round to Polly and said, "Give me five years, lass. Give me five years and you'll be back Home living in the lap o' luxury. We're going to make our fortune and we're going Home to spend it."

Polly laughed, "Oh, you! A fortune out of three hundred and twenty acres."

"You heard what Snowy said. I've got the best of Andy's million acres, and I'm going to make it so valuable that when this land fight comes to a head, Cameron or Cayley, whichever of them buys me out, is going to pay through the nose!"

Snowy roared with laughter. "Now that's a pretty speech from a Johnny Newcome!"

"Don't you think I can do it?" Jack was all jaw.

Snowy had meant to take him down a peg or two, and somewhere things had gone wrong. There was still time, though. "Do it?" He laughed. "You've been here a few months. You haven't seen a drought yet! You haven't seen the mess the dingoes can make when they get into a mob of sheep."

Jack could stand being laughed at. He knew what he was about. "'I'll see the dingoes don't get among my sheep,'" he said.

That made Snowy even angrier. "And the lambing! You haven't gone through a bad lambing yet, with the bloody stupid ewes waiting for the wettest, coldest night in the year to drop their lambs! You haven't seen the crows perched on every tree and fence for miles around waiting to pick the eyes out of the lambs as they drop! You haven't seen anything yet, Johnny Newcome! You haven't seen a lambing in drought time when you've got to go round knocking the lambs on the head to save the ewes! You haven't seen a hot summer yet, with the sky hanging down in a haze till it's like a hot blanket over your head, so close that you want to put your arms up and push it back where it belongs! You've got the richest soil this side of the Great Divide, but you wait till the day comes when a shovel buckles when you try to dig into it! You! You're going to make your fortune and take it home!"

Snowy turned his back and walked away across the clearing, and there was Jack left without a dream to bless himself with. All he could do was fumble for his pipe.

It was Polly who went after Snowy. "Snowy," she said, "we know we can't do it on our own, but we could do it if you'd stay with us."

Snowy growled. "I stay nowhere."

Polly came closer to him. "We must send Bill Harper away."

"You will if you've got any sense."

"We can't manage alone."

Snowy turned round to face her. "I owe nothing to nobody and I give nothing to nobody. What a damned fool I'd be to stay here and get mixed up in your troubles. Do you think I want to run foul of Andy Cameron? Do you think I want my throat cut by Matt Cayley? You're going to make your fortune and take it home to spend! All right, you go ahead and make it, but you won't get any help from me!"

He'd break camp now. He could be thirty miles away from here by sundown.

Then Jack, with his hands trembling as he filled his pipe, said, "It's Cayley who'll pay, Snowy. And I'll tell you what he'll pay for. I don't give a hoot in hell about the land. It's what he's done to Polly that he's going to pay for. It's the trip up here, it's the sort of life she's had to live since we got here, and the hard work she's had to do and what it's done to her. Look at her hands, Snowy."

Polly looked at her hands. She hadn't realised how rough they were getting. She must do something about them.

Snowy looked at them too. Maybe he could even be forty miles away by sundown. Never mind the rations. They could keep them. He'd managed to live on the bush before now. He could saddle up and be away from here in ten minutes. Nothing to do except roll up his bluey and . . . He was surprised when he heard his own voice saying, "Well, get rid of Harper anyway. I'll stay around for a couple of months till you find someone else to help you."

Polly looked, for a moment, as though she were going to throw her arms round his neck, and he backed away from her, roaring at Jack: "I heard dingoes howling up in the foothills last night! If you don't want them to get at your sheep, you'd better do something about them!"

Jack, grinning with delight, said, "What do I have to do? You'll have to tell me."

Snowy said, "You can stop standing there flaming well grinning for a start."

So Jack stopped grinning.

Then Snowy said, "Here, if I'm going to work for you, what do I call you? I never yet called any man sir."

Jack said, "My name's Jack."

Snowy said, "All right, Jack. Come and see to your sheep if you don't want to lose the flaming lot!"

And that was how Snowy stayed at Billabirra, and was angry.

Harper went the next day, and after that the real work began, all three of them working from sunup till sundown, but getting somewhere. It turned out that Jack, hating sheep, seemed instinctively to know what was best for them. Rearing sheep out here was a very different proposition from what he'd known on his father's farm in Yorkshire, but even Snowy had to admit that he knew what he was about. Not that Snowy admitted it to Jack.

They got through the summer, and the beautiful autumn came. It hadn't the soft melancholy of an autumn at Home, but at least it was a cooling off, a softening of the sun's glare, a sighing of relief from the bush all round them.

Polly knew that she would have a child in the spring, and the only thing she prayed for was that it wouldn't arrive until they'd got the lambing over. Jack was terrified. She couldn't possibly have a baby here in the bush with no doctor within hundreds of miles. He'd have to take her to Bathurst. Polly pooh-poohed the suggestion. "Sure, a trip in that dray would do more harm than good."

She went on working, digging post-holes, splitting logs, setting slip rails, hoeing the garden.

The winter came. Clear, bright days, the mornings crackling with frost, and just enough rain to keep the paddocks green. Then the spring answered Polly's prayers, because the mild winter meant an early lambing. By the time the river paddock was full of new lambs all trying to hop about on all four feet at once, Polly was saying to the baby, "All right now, Jonathon. You can come now any time you want to, and I'm sure you'll be very welcome." But Jonathon didn't take the hint. The weeks passed and there was no sign of him.

Jack was frantic, and even Snowy couldn't concentrate on his work. They both found all sorts of odd jobs to do close to the humpy. Polly went about her work, trying to look serene, but it wasn't easy to hide her fears. Suppose something happened to the baby, just because she'd been so set on staying here with Jack? If only there were another woman somewhere near!

She thought she was seeing visions when the woman walked into the clearing.

Cast in order of appearance. Third character. Mrs. Dooley.

Polly has just come out of the humpy to get water at the butt. She hears a voice and there is Mrs. Dooley hurrying towards her. Mrs. Dooley, enormous and very hot because she's just walked five miles.

"Oh, a human face at last," she pants. "What kind of a country is this, that's full of things that stare out of the bush at you? Indeed I've been frightened out of my wits! There was a thing like a snake that stood up on legs! Whoever heard of a snake on legs! Oh, what a country it is, and no dear St. Patrick here to drive them crawling things away!"

Polly wants to hug her, but all she can do is stand, speechless with relief.

Mrs. Dooley doesn't draw breath. "You'll be young Mrs. Selway. I met Jem, the bullock driver, this morning, and he told me your time was near. So I said to my man, 'Sure we've not had the pleasure of meeting our neighbours, but how can I let that poor young one have her first all alone in a heathen land, while I, the mother of fourteen sons, sit minding my own business five miles away?' So here I am and a nice cup of tea wouldn't do any of us any harm."

Cast in order of appearance. Character number four. Jonathon Selway.

The clearing just isn't big enough to hold Jack, so Snowy thinks he ought to be taken down a peg or two. Snowy says that now the baby's born it's about time he moved on, because he's never stayed in any place, and this particular place is getting so full of people he can't hear himself think. That does the trick. Jack comes down so many pegs that Snowy can't help feeling sorry for him. Snowy says he doesn't mind staying on a couple more months.

Cast in order of appearance. Character number five. David Spencer.

The news of Jonathon's arrival has created a sensation. There's never been a white baby born in these parts before. Andy Cameron has already ridden over to pay homage, stopping on his way along the river to look with approval at the improvements Jack's made, and to reflect on the further improvements he'll make when it's back in his hands. All Andy's stockmen, most of whom have never laid eyes on the Selways, have had a high old time in the grog shop the blacksmith runs over in the foothills. The baby's head has been well soaked in rum.

Now David Spencer turns up. This is the Englishman reported to live fifteen miles up-river.

He's a young man, probably not yet thirty. Anybody looking less likely to make a go of life in the bush would be hard to imagine. He's frail, donnish, bespectacled, anxious. He'd run a mile if you said "Boo" to him.

Jack thinks, 'Good God, what was Cayley thinking of to put this one in as a dummy.'

Spencer doesn't know he's a dummy, of course. He thinks he owes a great debt to George Russell. Peering from behind his spectacles, he tells Jack all about the kindness of George Russell who befriended him when he first landed, found lodgings for him, introduced him to an influential wool exporter named . . .

Jack wants to laugh, but he remembers how he felt when the truth first came out, so he takes it gently.

Spencer flatly refuses to believe him.

"Did they send you after gold, too?" Jack asks.

Gold! Spencer is affronted. Of course he hasn't come for gold.

"What made you buy your selection then?" Jack asks.

"I bought it because I wanted land. When I arrived I found that all the land in the settled areas had been taken up. Then George Russell told me of the disgraceful state of affairs here in the outback where this Cameron, and others like him, control vast areas of country, making it impossible for the small man to settle."

A bit of a radical, this Spencer.

But Jack still takes it gently. "I'm sorry to have to tell you, Mr. Spencer," he says, "that George Russell and Matt Cayley are no more friends of the small man than Andy Cameron is. They're trying to get control of Cameron's land for themselves. When they've beaten him to his knees they'll have us out like a shot!"

Spencer isn't finally convinced until Jack takes him down to the lambing pens. Spencer is astonished. He himself has lost most of his lambs. The stockman Cayley sent with him has told him that this is only to be expected in the first season. Indeed, things have been going badly with him altogether.

Spencer isn't a fool. He faces facts in the end. He's a dummy.

"What are we going to do?" he asks Jack.

Jack says, "I'll tell you what I'm going to do. I'm going to work this bit of land into something worth while. Whoever buys it is going to pay through the nose for it, I can tell you."

Spencer is appalled. "But you won't sell!"

"'Course I'll sell. At a price!"

"I won't sell," Spencer says. "They won't get me out."

Jack finds himself liking Spencer, and pitying him too, because he knows perfectly well what will happen when Cayley turns up and says, "Boo."

Here they are then. Five characters, seven counting Jack and Polly, sitting in a valley miles from nowhere waiting for Matthew Cayley.

As you were. Eight characters.

Characters in order of appearance. Mick Dooley.

Mick Dooley, aged two, coming with his mother to drink tea with the Selways. Black-haired, smoky-eyed, the devil on one shoulder and £.s.d. sign on the other. Mick doesn't know that he's waiting for Cayley.

The cast is complete. But three years have to go by before the first happy ending and the first little curtain.

Snowy was right about the good seasons. Nothing could go wrong. Even Spencer prospered once he'd got rid of the man Cayley had sent with him. When Jack sent his first load of wool down to Sydney on Andy Cameron's bullock wagon, he made such a nice little profit that he was able to pay off the debt on the selection, and there was quite a tidy little nest egg left over. He decided to go to Sydney himself with the next clip. But first there was a little business to transact.

While things were going nicely with Andy, who was seeing the time when he'd be able to buy back the valley; with Spencer, who was looking forward to a prosperous middle age; with Jack, who was counting the days to the end of his exile, the Dooleys were rubbing along, just managing to keep alive.

There was a day when Spencer, his own shearing finished, had come over to help Jack and Snowy with theirs. He and Jack came up to the humpy for a mug of tea and found Mrs. Dooley and young Mick there. Polly had been making butter that morning. Mrs. Dooley was eyeing it admiringly and remarking in passing, "Sure, that old cow we've got is worse than a Dublin milkman for watering down the milk before she delivers it."

This was part of a ritual approach, and Polly made her ritual response. "Ah, now, why don't you take home a pound of this butter I made this morning?" Mrs. Dooley looked at the butter in surprise, for all the world as though she'd just, this very second, clapped eyes on it for the first time. "Well now, I'm sure that's very kind of you. A taste of butter is just what my poor boys would enjoy." This ritual varied accordingly to the commodity available. After Jack and Snowy had killed, Polly would wander out to where the carcass was hanging, and there, having appeared as though by magic, would be Mrs. Dooley inspecting it with a wistful eye. "I must say it's good to see a nice, fat bit of meat," she'd say. Then Polly: "Would you let me wrap up a leg and some chops, maybe, for you to take home?" Mrs. Dooley, astonished: "Are you sure you can spare it?" Polly: "Spare a bit of mutton? With a paddock full of old ewes fit for nothing but eating?" Mrs. Dooley, now convinced that she's doing the Selways a favour by relieving them of part of one of their old ewes: "Well now, I'm sure my boys wouldn't say 'no' to a bit of mutton, tough as it might be." If the Selways were digging potatoes, Mrs. Dooley could always be

persuaded to take home a few pounds for her poor boys.
The ritual also applied to beef, green vegetables, rabbits shot
by Snowy, and soap and candles made by Polly. Snowy re-
garded the whole thing with some disgust, and couldn't, for
the life of him, see why the Selways had to keep the Dooleys
in tucker; but Jack said he'd rather give them the stuff than
have them come pinching it, which he wouldn't put past
them.

On the day that Jack and Spencer came up from the shearing shed for their mug of tea, Mrs. Dooley had just accepted
the pound of butter for her poor boys as they walked in the
door. Spencer made polite conversation. "Is your shearing
finished, Mrs. Dooley?"

Mrs. Dooley snorted. "Oh, sure, the few mangy sheep
we've got take no shearing at all."

Jack grinned and said, "You shouldn't have eaten your
way through the whole flock, Mrs. Dooley."

"And why not? Were we to starve then? And sixteen of
us to be fed?" This with an air of outrage, just as though the
Dooleys had slaved their fingers to the bone to remain self-
supporting. Then the outrage changed to sadness, and Mrs.
Dooley shook her head in a bewildered way and said she had
reluctantly come to the conclusion that her man and her
boys were not cut out to be farmers. She hastened to add
that a finer lot of men were never born, mind, but facts had
to be faced. They weren't cut out to be farmers: indeed they
had a strong aversion to all matters relating to the soil and
its products.

When Spencer said he was surprised that they'd taken up
land then, Mrs. Dooley explained about this dear soul in
Sydney, may the saints preserve him. A soul called George
Russell, who had met them as they came off the ship, had
helped them to find lodgings, and . . .

And so on.

Jack was blessing David Spencer for giving him the opening he'd been waiting for for months.

"I suppose," he said, trying to sound casual, "you
wouldn't like to sell your land?"

Mrs. Dooley looked fierce. "And who's to buy it, pray? Who except that greedy, black-hearted squatter that takes the bread out of the mouths of little babes?" She hugged young Mick to her, as though expecting the squatter to come in.

Jack said, "Well, for instance, I might buy it."

He didn't dare to look at Polly.

"I've got the right to buy more land for young Jonathon," he went on. "I'd like to expand a bit."

He was praying that Polly would leave it to him to do the talking, but he needn't have worried, because she was too surprised to utter a word.

But Mrs. Dooley wasn't born yesterday. She took on a canny look and asked, "Now how much would you want to pay for it, Mr. Selway?"

Jack told her he'd pay the Government price. And all of it at once. Not just a deposit.

Then it came out about this dream Mrs. Dooley had had for a long time. The dream was to start a little inn. That grog humpy up in the foothills that Andy's blacksmith operated was a disgrace. All the stockmen and all her boys and her man got drunk there regularly. Now this offended Mrs. Dooley because the grog humpy was such a filthy place, and besides, think of the profit the blacksmith was making.

Mrs. Dooley had even chosen the place where she would build her little inn. It was on the river, at that place all the stockmen called Cameron's Crossing . . . the place where everyone who came into these parts had to cross the river. Now if Mrs. Dooley had her little inn there, and the cellar keys in her pocket so that her boys couldn't get at the stock . . . .

Jack told her she should have her little inn. He was going to Sydney himself with the next load of wool. He'd fix up the transfer of the land, and he'd bring her back a drayload of stock. Mrs. Dooley was so excited she couldn't get home quickly enough to tell her man and her boys that their long drudgery was over. They were going to become innkeepers.

Six months later, the trip to Sydney done, the Dooley land bought and paid for, Jack began to clear his new selection.

The Dooleys were already installed at Cameron's Crossing. This was the place where, many years earlier, Andy Cameron had tried to cross the river with a drayload of wool. He'd not realised how fast flowing the river was after unseasonal rains, and his whole year's clip had been swept away by the flood waters. He'd been furious when his stockmen had first dubbed it Cameron's Crossing, but after a while he'd become used it, and even called it Cameron's Crossing himself, just as though it had been some fictitious Cameron who had failed to cross it.

There was still no sign of Cayley.

They had a very festive Christmas. The scrub around them was ablaze with red trees which Snowy told them was Christmas bush, and in the gullies and creek beds they found red bells which turned out to be Christmas bells. It was funny, Polly thought, that no matter which hemisphere you were in, the colour of Christmas was red.

Andy Cameron turned up with a sucking pig. Snowy went out and shot some wild duck, and told them they'd like it better than goose. David Spencer brought the biggest pumpkin anyone had ever seen. He was prouder of that pumpkin than of anything else on his selection. The Dooleys, all sixteen of them, came with a bottle of rum.

They built a huge fire on the edge of the clearing, and set a side of beef to roast on a spit which was turned, in rotation, by the Dooleys, starting with Dad and going down to Mick. The potatoes were put to cook in the ashes. The pumpkin was cooked in the Dooleys' kettle.

Afterwards, when they were too full of food to talk, and everyone sat around drowsing in the shade of the three big gums that Jack hadn't wanted to cut down, Polly was thinking 'Whoever would have thought it would turn out to be as good as this?' Still it wasn't Home. It would be so much nicer to be Home.

Polly's and Jack's second son, Luke, was born the following July. No anxieties this time. He arrived exactly on schedule.

Mrs. Dooley was delighted with the efficiency of the proceedings, and Polly was up and about, working again, within three or four days. Luke could charm the birds off the trees from the very beginning.

Another Christmas had come and gone before Cayley turned up.

The rumour went round that he'd been sighted south of the river, driving with George Russell in one of those new-fangled buggies. The valley showed no sign of panic, but, as Cayley's buggy forded Cameron's Crossing, it did get stuck in a bog just in front of the Dooleys' place. All the Dooleys, who'd been toiling all night carting the water to make the bog in the first place, turned out to drag the buggy free, and that's how Cayley and Russell became Mrs. Dooley's first travelling guests.

Andy Cameron thought it was about time he made a move. He'd had three good seasons too. He had the money to buy Jack out now. He rode over to the Selways in fine spirits and said to Jack with no beating round the bush, "Well, Jack, I'll pay you two pounds an acre. Twice what you paid for it."

Jack frowned and scratched his chin the way Snowy did when he was thinking. "Cayley will pay me much more than that, Andy."

Cameron looked puzzled. "You said you'd give me first offer."

Jack said, quite reasonably, "Aye, I did that, and I'm still giving you first offer, but aren't you thinking I'm as green as I was when I first came here? What about my stock? What about the improvements I've made? Do you think three years' hard work is only worth a pound an acre?"

Andy thought carefully for a long time, and then said, "Maybe I could make it two pound ten."

But Jack was going to make his fortune and take it Home to spend. Two pounds ten wasn't enough.

In the end Andy stamped off in a great rage calling him a damned unprincipled scoundrel, and Polly, who'd been listening to it all at the humpy window. was worried.

"He'll make a dangerous enemy, Jack," she said.

But Jack only growled, "What do I care about that? In a month we'll be too far away to care about Andy Cameron."

"You'll sell to Cayley then?"

Jack grinned and kissed her and told her not to worry. "Andy'll pay my price in the end," he said. "He's got the money. He's had three good seasons the same as I have."

David Spencer arrived about an hour later looking very gloomy. He'd met Andy and heard the story of betrayal.

Jack snorted. "He takes me for a bloody fool! I've seen him for the last three years watching everything that was going on here, thinking I was improving his property for him. He's just greedy, that's all. Greedy!" He stopped then because David had a look on his face that made him feel uncomfortable. "I'm not greedy, David," he said.

David smiled. "I didn't say you were, Jack."

Jack wanted to justify himself. He liked David. "It's Polly and the boys I'm thinking about. I don't want my boys to grow up in a place that's three months' journey from anywhere!"

David said, "But, Jack, it won't always be like this! Can't you see the future? There'll be roads built, and railways, and towns, and . . . In twenty years . . .!"

Jack shrugged and said, "I'm not interested in what's going to happen in twenty years, David. I didn't come to this place to stay. I came to make money. I thought I was going to make it out of gold. Well, I'll make it out of land!" Because David didn't answer, he added, after a minute or two, "Don't forget you're in a position to name your own price, too."

Then it turned out that David Spencer's mild looks belied him. It seemed that he could be as pig-headed as the next man. "I don't want to name any price," he said. "I'm not selling."

Jack said impatiently, "You'll have to sell."

"But I won't! I want to stay in this valley. I want to marry and have children who'll grow up here."

Jack couldn't help feeling sorry for him. "Look, David,"

he said, "this future you talk about. It won't come true in our lifetime, nor in our children's lifetimes for that matter."

David looked eager then, ready to argue. "You see, you're wrong about that, Jack. While I was up at Cambridge I talked to a man who'd spent twenty years in the colony. It was he who persuaded me to emigrate. He said . . ."

Jack was scornful. "He persuaded you to come to a place he'd been only too glad to quit!"

David looked a bit sheepish and said, "Well, it wasn't that he was glad to quit . . ."

"Has he come back here then?"

"Well, no. But . . ."

"You'd better make up your mind to sell, David. Andy'll pay you a good price."

"I told you I'm not going to sell!"

They were back where they'd started. Jack began trying to reason with him. "Look, David, whichever of them buys me out, Cameron or Cayley, he's not going to let you stay."

"They can't make me sell!"

"If you don't sell they'll force you out!"

They argued for an hour until Jonathon became so bored he began to yell his head off.

Then Cayley and Russell arrived, and you wouldn't have known them from honest men, so glad were they to greet their old friends, Jack and Polly. They were delighted to find their other old friend, David Spencer, here too, since they'd called at his house and found he was away from home.

They inspected the humpy, and they chucked Jonathon under the chin and told him what a fine fellow he was, and they admired Luke, and they congratulated Jack on his prosperity, and they sympathised about the gold-strike false alarm, they inquired after everyone's health, the results of the lambing, the state of the soil.

It was Jack who interrupted a long speech by Russell to say, "Well, I reckon you've come to buy me out, Mr. Cayley."

Now that was what Cayley liked. Straight-from-the-shoulder talking. No beating about the bush. He said so.

H

So Jack, still not beating about the bush, said, "I must warn you that I've promised not to sell to you without giving Andy Cameron the chance to outbid you."

Cayley smiled his expansive, generous smile and said, "I'm glad to be dealing with a man that puts his cards on the table, Jack. Right. We'll pay you two pounds an acre."

Jack laughed in his face, but the bargaining went on. Fifty shillings. Three pounds. It got up to ten pounds.

Jack was thinking that six hundred and forty acres at ten pounds each made six thousand four hundred pounds. Not a fortune, but something to start them off when they got back to the old country. "I think," he said, "Andy'll pay me twenty pounds an acre. See, I know how important this little stretch of river is. As long as Andy owns my six hundred and forty acres, he controls a million."

Cayley looked at Russell and laughed. "And where do you think Andy's going to get thirteen thousand quid? The banks won't lend him a thousand, let alone thirteen thousand."

Spencer couldn't keep quiet any longer. "What are you going to do to Cameron? Are you going to break him completely?"

Russell raised his eyebrows. "Now, Spencer, you're not on the side of the greedy squatter, are you? Aren't you the one who talked so much in Sydney about breaking his monopoly?"

David said, "Andy's a muddler, but he's honest. I'd rather have his monopoly than yours."

Russell smiled then, and said, "You won't have to choose, my dear fellow. How much do you want for your elections? Will two pounds an acre satisfy you?"

Spencer said he wouldn't sell. If they offered him a thousand pounds an acre, he wouldn't sell! Cayley wasn't going to waste time with small fry. It was getting dark, and he badly needed some of Mrs. Dooley's rum. He went to the door, saying to Spencer, "If you don't sell now, you'll be begging us to give you five shillings an acre in six months' time." At the door he stopped and turned to Jack, "You think you're very clever, don't you?"

Jack didn't answer.

Cayley said, "I want this part of the valley."

Jack said, "I know you do."

"I'll have a look at your run tomorrow." Then Cayley
and Russell left, and Jack knew he'd won his battle. He
knew how badly they needed his six hundred and forty acres.
After they'd gone, David smiled at Jack and said, "Thirteen
thousand pounds, Jack. I can almost see your point of
view."

Jack tried again. "Sell to them for two pounds an acre,
David. They'll finish you if you don't." But David, blinking
behind his glasses, only shook his head and said he ought to
be going home.

Jack and Polly followed him into the clearing. Jack was
inwardly cursing. "Blast you, David! You've spoilt it all!
You've made a proper muck of it!"

Jack had waited so long for this moment, his moment of
triumph! He and Polly celebrating their revenge for three
years of humiliation! And now, here they were, glumly
following David out. Just as though the triumph had never
been.

Snowy came up from the river as they crossed the clearing.
Polly said, "Visitors, Snowy."

He nodded and said he'd seen 'em. Then he turned to
Jack: "I reckon I can be moving on, now, eh?"

Jack said, "We'll all be moving on, Snowy."

Snowy said, "That's what I thought," and turned back to
Polly. "I bagged a few rabbits. Do you want some or will
I give them to the dogs?"

Polly, without any enthusiasm, answered, "We'll have a
pair, Snowy."

Snowy said, "You can pick out the ones you want after
I've skinned 'em," and then he went off down to the river
again.

That was when they saw Andy Cameron. He was sitting
on the wood heap. When he got up to come to them he
looked about eighteen inches shorter than usual. Even his hair
drooped dejectedly. If Cayley had beaten him physically, he

couldn't more successfully have knocked the stuffing out of him.

Jack said, "They've offered me twenty pounds an acre, Andy. You can have it for that price."

Andy shook his head. "I can't pay it, Jack."

Thirteen thousand pounds piled up in sovereigns dwindled to less than seven thousand. Jack said, "You can have it for ten." He was thinking: 'Damn you, damn you! I'm daft to feel sorry for you! I'm proper bloody daft!'

Andy shook his head again. "I can't pay it, Jack. Matt's fixed it so that I can't get any more money from the bank."

Jack was furious. "But you've made money in the last three years!"

"I've used that to buy my own stretch of the river flat. Thought I'd better get in before Cayley put more dummies in. I reckoned on the bank giving me enough to buy you out."

"You actually own about a thousand acres, then?"

"That's about it. But I can't feed fifty thousand sheep on a thousand acres of river. It's all right now, while they're spread out to the west, but as soon as we get a dry season, I'll have to move them in to the river."

David broke in with, "What's Cayley's proposition, Andy?"

Andy grinned wryly. "That I buy back your three selections at fifty pounds an acre."

"They know you can't pay, of course."

"They've fixed it so I can't pay."

"What's the alternative?"

'That they lend me the money to buy a few acres here and there all over the run . . . the waterholes, and the creeks, and the good feeding places . . . the eyes of the run. That way I keep control of the whole run."

"And become their paid man! Their overseer! You work your guts out for the rest of your life as their paid man!"

Andy wasn't even angry. "What choice have I got? If I don't take their offer, they'll have me out of the valley as soon as they get their hands on your three selections."

"They won't get mine!" David said.

"Yours!" Andy laughed. "Yours doesn't matter, Spencer. Once they've got Jack's, you and I are both done for."

Jack was silently cursing them both so hard that it was a wonder the earth didn't open and the skies fall. Damn them! Damn them! It was thirteen thousand pounds! It was his dream come true! It was . . . He said aloud, "What if I don't sell, Andy? What if I stay?"

David and Polly couldn't believe their ears.

Andy put on eighteen inches and smiled broadly. "You've cheated me out of the best part of the river, but I could manage with you here instead of more of their dummies."

"You've only got a thousand acres of river flat. You'd have to cut down on your stock, be content with a smaller run."

Andy repeated, "I'd be all right with you here. I've got nothing against you as a neighbour. You'll make a good sheep man one day."

Jack stopped being angry. "Get away with you," he said. "I'm a good sheep man now, and you know it!"

That broke the tension and they all began to laugh.

David was jubilant. "Cayley will give us hell!" he said.

Andy roared, "There's not a thing he can do if we stick together!"

It was just then that Snowy strolled unconcernedly up from the river and went to the tin basin near the water-butt.

Jack called, "Snowy, we've got news for you."

Snowy filled the basin and began to wash his hands. "Dirty job, skinning rabbits," he said to Polly.

Polly went over to him. "Snowy, we're not going after all!"

"No?" was all Snowy said as he went on washing his hands.

Polly said, "We'll need to build another room on the humpy, and then there's . . ."

Snowy said they'd have to do it without him because he was pushing on. Then Polly said the trouble was that it was going to take time for them all to adjust themselves, now

that the decision had been made, and what with the shearing
starting soon . . .

So Snowy said he'd stay till after the shearing, but no
longer mind, and Polly thanked him, and . . .

A kookaburra started to laugh his head off not far away.

Not in the clearing at Billabirra, though. He was laughing
in a gum tree in the Sydney Botanical Gardens, and my
grandmother was looking round in wonder.

"A kookaburra! Here!"

"Why not?" I asked. "There was one quite near our
place a couple of weeks ago."

She couldn't believe it.

The kookaburra's being there meant that the sun was
going.

"Time we went home," I said. "There'll be no more sun
soon."

"I have enjoyed today, Harry," she said.

"There's just one thing I want to know," I said.

"Yes"

"You've told me that Jack didn't want to stay in the valley,
and that David Spencer did. You haven't said how you felt
about it. Were you glad when Jack turned down his thirteen
thousand pounds?"

She put her head on one side and looked at me for a while.
"Now can you see me sitting in London twiddling my
thumbs?" she asked. Then, before I had time to answer,
she added, "What a sight I'd have looked with my face
burned by the sun and my hands all covered with corns and
cuts."

"Your hands look all right now," I said

"I told you I'm a very vain old woman, Harry."

I said, "You liked being there at Billabirra. Come on,
admit it. You didn't want to leave."

She looked over my shoulder and went right away somewhere I couldn't follow her. Then she came back and said,
"Of course I liked it."

Then we returned to the hotel, and she said she thought
she'd go straight to bed because she'd had a very exciting

day. An early night would finish the cold off completely, and she'd feel fine tomorrow. David was waiting when we got back. He said he'd been anxious and why the blazes hadn't we left word that we were going out. She twisted the little finger round a bit, and he calmed down.

After she'd gone to bed, David and I went off to get a drink before the pubs shut. We didn't have much to say to each other, though. I was thinking that I wanted to get round to Jan's place as soon as I could, because I needed to be with her.

I suppose he was thinking about her too.

CHAPTER TWELVE

THE next day, Thursday, my grandmother said she felt a
lot better, because the cold had gone down to her chest
and she didn't have that awful sniffle any longer.

I was at work, of course, but my grandmother and my
mother went shopping. Her last-minute shopping, she said
it was, so that she'd be ready to go home on Friday night's
train, taking my mother with her.

I can imagine them trailing in and out of shops all day,
arguing as they went. "Now, Nell, the train goes at eight
o'clock." My mother: "I'm not coming." My grandmother:
"I've wired your father." My mother: "I'm not coming."

On Thursday night when I got home, there she was in the
kitchen. She'd bought us presents. A new winter coat for
my mother, some shirts and ties for me. She was too tactful
to overdo it.

The day in the sun hadn't done her so much good, after
all. She looked desperately tired, and she was coughing a
good deal. Later, she picked at her food and said she wasn't
hungry, but she was dying for a cup of tea.

My mother was worried about her. "You should have
gone straight to the hotel," she said. "That cold's much
worse than you admit."

My grandmother scoffed, "All this fuss about a little bit
of a cold. I'm not used to all this traipsing round shops,
that's all." She looked at me and smiled. "It's so much
easier at Cameron's Crossing. Everything's there in one
street."

My mother said, "Harry's going to take you back to the
hotel at once. I think you ought to go to bed."

To my surprise she didn't argue. I had expected her to say that she was going to sit there till Nell agreed to go home tomorrow night, but she meekly said yes, she did confess she was a bit tired.

Reserving herself for an all-out attack tomorrow, no doubt.

When we got to the hotel I kissed her good night and said I'd be at the station to see her off tomorrow night. She patted my hand and tried to smile, but she was so tired that there wasn't a smile left in her. I went to look for David, but they said at the desk that he'd gone out for the evening, so I left a message for him not to disturb Mrs. Selway when he got back because she'd gone to bed.

The Great Harry Brandon blundering about trying to do his best and succeeding in doing his worst.

I went home in the tram feeling miserable and lonely, and suddenly I wanted to talk to Jan again. It was only ten o'clock. Maybe she was still up. I started on my way round from the tram stop, and just as I got to the corner of the street, I saw Jan. She was with David. They'd just walked into the light of a street lamp. They were hand in hand, and I've never seen two people look so unutterably desolate. They were coming towards me, and it was the desolation I couldn't face. I turned and bolted round the corner.

It was a rough night. I wasn't sitting in the pavilion any more.

I kept going over and over in my mind what I should have done. I knew I shouldn't have bolted. I should have faced them. We should have had it out. I was cursing them, and pitying them. I was hating them for not telling me about it, and I was hating myself for being such a poor boob that they couldn't tell me about it. I got up in the morning feeling as though I'd already done a day's work, and swinging a pick was never as hard yakka as it was that day. In the evening all I wanted to do was get home, have a shower and fall into bed. Then I remembered that I had to go to the station to see my grandmother off. And David.

When I got home, Jan was sitting in the kitchen. She was just sitting there. I stood at the door and waited for her to

tell me that she was going back to Billabirra with David.
Come for an aunt, go back with a wife. Fair enough.

She didn't say anything for a bit, and I just stood there,
wanting to ask her not to go, wanting to tell her I loved her.

But when she did get up and move towards me, all I could
do was step aside a bit and say, "I'm dirty and sweaty."

"Harry," she said.

Now it was coming.

"You're to go to the hospital. Your grandmother's ill.
Your mother asked me to wait and tell you."

"How ill?"

"It seems serious. They took her to hospital. They've
sent for your grandfather."

The glands started pumping away at the reserve tanks,
and I came to life. I had my shower and got dressed and
went to the hospital. They'd taken her to St. Vincent's, so
it wasn't far to go. David was waiting for me. He looked
suicidal. "She has pneumonia," he said. "If I'd got a
doctor sooner, everything might have been all right."

It was my fault then. I'd left a message that he mustn't
disturb her. I'd done my worst all right. I said, "She said
she was tired. She wanted to go straight to sleep. I
thought . . ."

He shrugged and said, "I didn't get back till late last
night. I wouldn't have disturbed her anyhow."

How late?

He added, "I should have looked in on her early this
morning. I could have saved two or three hours."

He'd had other things on his mind early this morning.

"Aunt Nell came to the hotel about eleven o'clock. I was
still in bed. She called the doctor at once."

I would have been in bed too, if it hadn't been for the
appointment with a pick and shovel.

We sat in the waiting-room until my mother came down.
She said, "It's all my fault. I should have realised last night
how ill she was. I shouldn't have brought her to Sydney in
the first place."

I wanted to scream at them: 'For God's sake let's all stop

worrying about whose fault it is! Let's stop thinking about ourselves for a minute!'

But I didn't.

Mother took David and me up to the room, and there was an old lady lying in a white bed. There was nothing of Polly Selway there. Nothing more than an old lady trying to breathe. Her hands, brown, well cared for, not a corn or a cut to be seen, were lying quiet.

I'm a very vain old woman, Harry.

David and I went back to the waiting-room and . . . waited. About ten o'clock that night there was a bit of a commotion outside in the corridor, and then the door opened and two men came in. David introduced my Uncle Luke and my grandfather, Jack Selway. So this then, was Jason.

I knew then what my grandmother had meant. We didn't look in the least alike. He was short and stocky, and I towered over him. We had different features, different colouring. Yet, I felt like him. I felt as though I was standing face to face with myself. I think he felt the same way. In those few anguished moments of our first meeting, there was no barrier of time, or experience, or outward personality that stood between us.

The moment of recognition was shattered when the night sister came in, and Jason and I became separate entities again.

He went upstairs to Polly and the three of us sat down for more waiting. I could see in Luke Selway the gentleness of David, but there wasn't the strength there. He sat rolling cigarettes and dropping half the tobacco on the floor, and then smiling apologetically.

It was about two in the morning when they called us upstairs. The old lady on the bed was Polly Selway again, and Jason sat beside her stroking her hand. My mother was standing at the foot of the bed, and Luke and David went to her side.

I stood at the door, and looked at them. It was like picking up a book and starting to read the last chapter. There they all were, the present coming out of a past to which they all belonged.

I was only the onlooker.

I went out of the door, and down the corridor and into the lift and out of the hospital, and I walked along through Darlinghurst, and on through streets I'll never see again.

The streets are still there, but that night they were transformed by grief.

I wandered lonely as a cloud.

CHAPTER THIRTEEN

M^Y grandmother died that night.

The next day I knew that Uncle Luke and David were shocked by the way I'd flung myself out of the hospital room and disappeared. Even my mother was puzzled, and kept looking at me, trying to make me give some explanation. She wouldn't ask me outright.

What explanation could I give?

The only one who understood was Jason. The moment I saw him that Saturday morning I knew he understood, and that made it all right.

They decided to take Polly Selway back to Woollaby, the town that's about forty miles from Billabirra.

I didn't want to go. When my mother asked me to go, I refused. I was sick of being the outsider. Then an odd thing happened. Jason took me aside from the others, and he said, "I'd like you to come back with us, Harry. I'd like you to be there." And suddenly I knew that he needed me to be there.

So I went.

We caught the afternoon train, the slow train.

Polly Selway was going back home on Saturday afternoon instead of on Friday night. And my mother was going with her.

We had a carriage to ourselves, and everyone just sat there trying to make conversation. Ten hours worth of conversation that kept dwindling off into awful silences.

I went along the corridor to get away from the silences, and there was a party of commercial travellers playing poker in one of the carriages up near the Gents. I stood at the door and watched them for a while, and then one of them asked if I'd like to sit in on the game. I looked at the ten-bob and pound notes on the sample case they were using as a table and said I only had a few bob.

They laughed and said they wouldn't mind taking them from me. So I sat in on the game.

They let me win for quite a while, and by the time I started to lose it back to them again, I didn't mind at all. I'd had a good afternoon, and in the end it only cost me one and three.

I left them then, and thought I'd better go back to the silences.

Going back, I stood at the corridor windows for a while and watched the countryside going by. We were over the mountains and into the flat country. Every now and then we'd pass some tiny little house, miles from anywhere. How did they stand the loneliness? Then there'd be gangs working on the railway line with whole communities of tents that looked comfortable and permanent. There'd be tiny little townships. And all along the line, whether it was a single house, or a gangers' camp, or a township, the whole population turned out to wave to us. We were their one contact each day with the outside world. The express roared through at night, but here were we going somewhere, coming from somewhere, right there in broad daylight.

As we went along, the gangers would stop their work, or the kids would come running out of the lonely houses, and as they waved, they'd yell, "Papers! Papers!" And everyone on the train would throw out the midday papers, and bags of fruit, and chocolates, and we watched the kids scrambling for them.

While I was thinking what it must be like to live out here with one train a day to look forward to, a thought suddenly struck me. This was the way of Polly and Jack's nightmare journey. Out there, where the sheep were grazing right away to the horizon, had been the thick scrub they'd fought their way through that first time.

Now Polly was making another journey.

I went back to the silences.

We got to Woollaby at midnight. The typical bush town. A mixture of new stores with plate-glass windows, and old buildings with verandah posts and a first-floor verandah. We drove straight out to Billabirra. I couldn't see what it was like because there was no moon that night.

The next thing was the jumble of uncles and aunts and cousins. I didn't attempt to sort them out. I just hung around in the background and let the tears wash all round me. And Jason stayed by me. He never said anything much, but every time I moved a bit, there he was beside me.

The next day was Sunday, and I had a good look round. Everywhere I went, Jason came with me. I went down to the front gate, about half a mile from the homestead, and stood and looked up the hill at Billabirra.

"Not what you'd call a mansion," Jason said.

It was weatherboard with a corrugated-iron roof, and there was a wide verandah right round it. No gracious colonial-style house. An architect probably would have had a fit if he'd seen the original plans, that's if there'd ever been any plans. It was just built as a place to live, out of the timber of the country. On one side there was a clump of gums, and on the other side a citrus orchard.

There was no sign of a sheep.

They buried Polly the following morning in the churchyard at Woollaby. Near her grave there was a weathered stone that said: "In memory of Henry Peter Selway. Born September 3rd, 1888. Killed in action at the landing on Gallipoli April 25th, 1915."

The other Henry.

There were a lot of people there. There was a big, white-haired man surrounded by half a dozen black-haired men who looked very like him. Jason saw me looking at him. "That's Mick Dooley," he said.

There was a very old, very frail man who looked as though he should be ambling in a gown through some cloistered place. He stood between David and Uncle Luke, and he held his head up, staring straight in front of him all through the service, with the tears rolling down his face, making no attempt to wipe them away. David Spencer.

Jason never blinked an eyelid from start to finish.

We drove back to Billabirra, along the road by the river that had first been made by Andy Cameron's bullock wagons, and we passed through the one-street township that was Cameron's Crossing.

The house was full of people, and in the afternoon I escaped. I found a writing pad somewhere, then I went down to the outbuildings on the flat, and I searched round till I found the carpenter's shop, and on the bench I found a thick carpenter's pencil. I went back up the hill to the clump of gums, and I sat there and started to sketch the foot-hills.

Billabirra is in a bowl of hills. To the east, there are the foothills that gradually rise up to the mountains in the far distance. To the west, there are more gradually rolling hills that peter out into the plains.

I was letting the foothills watch me.

I must have been there an hour before I heard a match strike near by. I looked round. Jason was sitting there on a tree stump lighting his pipe. "You disappeared after we got back," I said.

"Aye," he said. "I wanted to be on my own for a bit."

I knew what he meant.

Then he came over and looked at the sketch. "I'd have thought The Bend's more like what an artist would want to draw," he said.

"What's The Bend?"

He pointed down the hill to the river, where it swung round at right angles on its way to Cameron's Crossing. There was a pretty little river scene, if you like. Willows shading a deep, fast-flowing river, a wide, clear stream with banks forty feet high. I said that wasn't my sort of drawing, and Jason nodded and went back to his tree stump while I went back to the foothills.

After a while I asked him where the original humpy had been, and he pointed down to the river flat where there was a clump of three gums.

"How did you know about it?" he asked.

"Grandma told me about it. We talked for a long time. Last Wednesday afternoon. We spent the afternoon together. She told me all about the beginning."

"Which beginning?"

Had there been so many beginnings?

I said, "She told me about how you came here. Up till the time you turned down Cayley's offer and decided to stay."

He left the tree stump and came over to stand beside me. He was looking across to the foothills. "I should have sold," he said. "I should have taken her Home. I had no right to sentence her to this sort of life." He looked round at me, and it was the first time he'd shown the slightest sign of his grief. "I didn't even ask her!" he said. "I'd promised her so much! I was going to take her Home, and then I didn't even ask her. I just made the decision to stay and she had to grin and bear it."

"She wanted to stay." He didn't hear me the first time I said it, so I said it again, "Grandfather, she wanted to stay."

He looked at me for a long time, and then asked, "How do you know?"

"She said so. Last Wednesday. After she'd finished telling me all about it, I asked her whether she'd wanted to stay at Billabirra, and she said, 'Of course I wanted to stay.'"

That was when he couldn't keep it all inside him any longer. He broke down and walked away from me, and sat on the tree stump. I went on sketching the foothills.

It was a long time later that I heard the match scraping on the side of the box again. I turned round and he was re-lighting his pipe. He was out of hell for the time being.

I thought I ought to make conversation, so I said, "I was surprised the other night when the train got in to Woollaby. Grandma'd given me to understand that the nearest big town was Bathurst."

"Oh," he said, "Woollaby wasn't here when we got here. It didn't come till much later. Let's see, it must have been about six months after Cayley went back to Sydney . . . no, not as long as that . . ." He grinned. "I'm not much good

I

at dates and details. Polly was the one for that sort of thing."

I said I knew that.

He thought for a while. "Cayley and Russell came just after Christmas. It must have been the following autumn that the settlers came and went north."

"Did you have any trouble with Matt Cayley when you told him you wouldn't sell?"

He laughed, thinking back. "He threatened to give us hell."

"And did he?"

"No. There was nothing he could do. We had the law on our side. He couldn't make us sell."

"What about Woollaby?"

"Well, we were all settling down after the bit of excitement with Cayley, when a big caravan of bullock drays and stock came up from the south and camped at Cameron's Crossing. Twenty families there were, travelling together. They'd all bought selections way up-river beyond Andy's northern boundary." He laughed again. "When they first appeared, you should have seen Andy! He had the wind up properly. He thought they'd come to take more of his land. When he found they were going north, he calmed down and was as nice as can be. You should have seen him being gallant with the ladies. Laugh! Polly and David and I were in fits."

"So they went north and started Woollaby?"

"They went north and started clearing land, and building humpies, and growing food, the same as we'd had to do."

I accepted the rebuke. As though a town could appear out of mid-air!

To show there was no offence meant, he grinned, and went on, "Just a little while after that, David Spencer went down to Sydney and came back with a wife."

"Nice for Polly," I said. I was thinking of her then as Polly, not as my grandmother.

Jack frowned and nodded.

"You don't seem too sure."

"Oh, Polly liked her all right, but she was an odd sort of

girl, Amy Spencer was. Not the sort of girl that could stand up to tough bush life at all. She didn't even try to, really. She gave poor David hell because the life here wasn't the sort of thing she'd been used to in Sydney. Now Rose Cameron, she was different. She . . ." He stopped. "I forgot to tell you that Andy got married, too. After David came back from Sydney with Amy, Andy said he'd better find himself a wife too, because he couldn't afford to have the whole valley overrun by other people's brats. So he disappeared for a week or so. We found out afterwards that he'd gone up north to where the new settlers were. He came back with Rose. She was the daughter of one of the settlers. Polly loved Rose." He laughed. "You never saw anything as timid as Rose. Bush bred, she was, because her father had been on the land down south before he came up here, yet she was frightened of everything. Like a tea cosy, Polly said she was. Little and plump. Exactly like a tea cosy."

"Was she frightened of Andy?"

"She doted on him too much to be frightened of him."

He knocked out his pipe and stowed it away in his pocket. "Funny, you know, about people."

I said it was very funny.

"There was David, quiet and sort of gentle, married to Amy who gave him hell, and there was Andy married to Rose, who never had a word to say for herself. It should have been the other way round. What Andy needed was someone to stand up to him and call his bluff. What David needed was someone like Rose to love him and look after him."

"Has it ever occurred to you," I asked, "that both Andy and David had settled for second best because you had already got the woman they really wanted?"

Jason looked at me in astonishment. "By God," he said after a bit. "By God, you could be right about that."

I wanted to kick myself for having reminded him of Polly. A moment ago he'd been laughing about Andy Cameron, talking about Polly as though she were still there. Now he was remembering.

I started off another tack. "You must have been feeling very much the patriarch of the valley. All these newly-weds and you with two sons, already."

He looked at me, knowing my thoughts. "Don't worry," he said. "I've got to talk about her. A lot better to talk about her." He was silent for a while, then he said, "I'd like to go on talking if that's all right with you."

I said it was all right with me.

"I was just thinking," he said, "about the way I was always telling her how I was going to take her Home, and how she was going to drive down Piccadilly in her own carriage." He smiled. "I was always telling her that."

"You were just staying until Andy Cameron could afford to buy you out."

"Aye, I was that."

"You went on expanding, though?"

"It was the only sensible thing to do. After we'd stopped worrying about whether Cayley was going to pull some dirty trick or other on us, I bought another three hundred and twenty acres on the other side of the river. That was for Luke. We made the humpy bigger, too, and put a verandah round it. Oh, you never saw such building as was going on. Andy had to build a bigger place for Rose, and David put two more rooms on his place just to keep Amy quiet. That was because Amy had to have things just a bit bigger and better than anyone else's, see? If we had three rooms, she had to have four. David planted a lot of saplings round his place and called it New Park. That gave us all a good laugh. All except Amy, that is. She didn't see the joke. She said that where she came from every house had to have a name. It might have been because of that that we started calling our place Billabirra. That was the old name the aborigines had given to this part of the river."

I told him that Polly had talked about that.

"It was just in fun at first, of course. But somehow, the name stuck. Andy thought we were getting a bit above ourselves, and said that his place was Cameron's, and that the bullock drivers would only get confused if he tried to call it anything else. The homestead's still called Cameron's. All the time we were building, there were more people coming through Cameron's Crossing, going north. Ma Dooley was coining money in her pub. In a couple of years there was quite a sizable community up there. A little township had sprung up, and that was the beginning of Woollaby. A couple of years later, they started a post office there, so we could have sent a telegram if we'd had anyone to send it to; and, round about the same time, Cobb and Co. started a monthly coach service between Woollaby and Bathurst to carry the mails. The coach service made a difference. A lot of people started settling all along the coach route. It must have been just about then, too, that Ma Dooley opened the general store in Cameron's Crossing."

"Progress," I said.

"I didn't notice it," he said. "Just took it for granted. There was a lot of work to be done, and I don't suppose I'd much time for looking round me. After a while Snowy and I couldn't handle all the work by ourselves, so I took on three stockmen, chaps Andy didn't need any longer. Oh, I forgot to tell you! Before that David and Amy had a daughter." He smiled. "Vicky. She was a beauty, Vicky was. Oh, and there was Rose Cameron expecting too. Andy had the whole valley in a proper shemozzle about that. See, he was bored to tears with poor little Rose. He always liked people best if they stood up to him. Anyway, he was going to have a son, and that was going to put everything right! When I think of it now! The plans Andy had for his son!"

He seemed to want to think of it now, and so he didn't speak for quite a while. Then suddenly he started off again "One morning, right bang in the middle of the shearing, Patrick Dooley rode hell for leather over here to ask Polly to come quick to Camerons, so Polly dumped Jonathon and Luke down in the shearing shed with Snowy and me, and saddled up and went over there. She found Mrs. Dooley there and in an awful state. She said she'd had to send for Polly because she couldn't take the responsibility all to herself. See, things weren't going well with Rose, and Andy, stinking of the shearing sheds, was ranting and roaring round the house that he'd kill Mrs. Dooley if anything happened to his son." He stopped for a few moments, and then he finished it off. "Polly and Mrs. Dooley fought all that day and the next night to save Rose Cameron, and in the end she was saved all right, and her daughter was born. It was Polly who told Andy that he had a daughter. And Polly told me afterwards that she'd never forget the look on his face when she said the word 'daughter'. He never spoke. Never asked about Rose. He just walked out of the house, and back down to the shearing sheds. After that he went into the house to get his meals, and that was all. For years nobody ever saw him even speak to Alison. Alison was the daughter, of course."

I started on another sketch of the foothills, and he came over from the stump and watched me for a while. It was obvious he didn't think much of my talent. He didn't say anything, of course, but he kept shaking his head and talking about how The Bend was so much prettier. Then he went back to the stump and lit another pipe.

"It was that year," he said, "that Ted was born." He chuckled. "The great Edward Selway."

It suddenly occurred to me that Uncle Edward hadn't been at the funeral.

"Doesn't he know about Grandma?" I asked.

"Oh, yes, I sent him a cable. He's over in Europe, see. The Government sent him over. This League of Nations lark."

"My mother came next, didn't she?"

"That's right. Nell was next. After Ted came, Polly said to me, 'I've given you enough sons, Jack Selway. The next one's going to be a girl.' She was right, too. The next one was Nell. I don't mind telling you that much as we wanted a daughter, we had our doubts about producing one. The boys never gave us any trouble, see. Good as gold, all of them. But from what we could see of other people's daughters, they were inclined to be a bit contrary. There was Vicky Spencer, now. If ever a man loved a child as much as

David loved young Vicky, I'd like to be told about it. It was
as though he was giving her all the love Amy didn't seem to
want. But Vicky treated David like dirt, ordered him round,
stamped her foot at him. Proper little madam." He smiled
again. "You couldn't help liking her though. There were so
many times when I'd have liked to smack her backside for
her, but still I couldn't help liking her. Then there was
Alison Cameron. Her father never spoke to her or went
within feet of her, but she worshipped him, followed him
round, yearning after him." He shook his head. "Contrary."

"Was my mother contrary, too?"

He laughed. "Funnily enough, no. Not at first, that is.
She was no more trouble than the boys had been. She didn't
want all your attention as Vicky did, and she didn't want
your pity as Alison did. No. Polly and I were both very
happy about Nell."

I was trying to picture my mother here, as a child growing
up in the bush. I couldn't see it. The picture I had was of a
woman sitting frowning over a typewriter.

Jason was talking again.

"It was just after Nell was born that Amy Spencer was
killed."

"Killed?"

"Aye. By that time, the monthly coach was bringing
great parcels of books and papers and periodicals to David.
You could hardly move in the house for books, and Amy
hated them. Then, one morning, the coach brought a
specially large parcel, and Amy was in an awful state about
it and said you couldn't get into the house for books, and
then she tried to burn some of them, and it all ended up in an
unholy row. The upshot was that Amy flounced out of the
house, and saddled up the black mare and went riding away
from New Park. That mare was a vicious brute, and Amy
must have been in a vicious temper. God knows what sort
of battle of wills there was between them that morning, but
the mare won. She limped back to New Park in the afternoon, by herself. Later on we found Amy down at the
bottom of Boulder Gully. Her neck was broken."

One of the little curtains.

Then afterwards, back to a new beginning.

"After Amy died," Jason said, "David decided it was time Jonathon had some schooling. I must confess I'd been starting to worry about that myself. I didn't want him growing up illiterate, yet I knew it'd break his heart if we sent him away to school somewhere. So David solved the problem for us by taking on the teaching of him. As the others got old enough they went to David, too, and in the end New Park was turned into a very good little school. David knew how to teach kids, and he loved doing it. He'd never had much interest in being a sheep man. It was just living in the valley that he liked. So he put an overseer to look after things for him, and took on two or three hands, and set his mind to being a schoolteacher. We all owe a lot to David. He . . . Oh, there's one thing I forgot to tell you!" He began to laugh at the joke that was coming up. He sobered for a minute, and asked, "I'm not jumping round too much, am I?"

I said, "No. Go on."

He started to laugh again. "Mick Dooley," he said. "Mick was a couple of years older than Jonathon, and he was always round here with the boys when they were little. After they started to go to school, he still came over here, and I thought he must be lonely without them, so I said to him one day, 'Why don't you go to school with them, Mick?' and he looked at me with that butter-wouldn't-melt-in-my-mouth look of his, and said, 'Ah sure, what could their old school teach me?' Well, as it happened I was doing some sums myself at the time. The shearing shed wall was covered with tally marks, and I was trying to add up, so I said, 'Well, it could teach you to do arithmetic for one thing.' And he said, 'Sure, I can do it already.' And blow me down if he didn't! He could do sums in his head quick as a flash. I told David about it, and David set him all sorts of really hard problems, and he just polished them off in no time. David reckoned we had a mathematical genius on our hands, so he talked to Mrs. Dooley about Mick coming to school, and

Mrs. Dooley said school was the very thing for him to keep him out of mischief. He never went to school, though. Every time anybody tried to get him there, he saddled up his horse, filled his saddle-bags with food, and disappeared into the hills. In the end we gave up." Jason looked at me, and added, "Funny thing is, he must have got some schooling somewhere. He's not an illiterate man by any means."

There was a silence for a long time, while I went on sketching and Jason sat looking into the distance. Then he said, "Henry was the last one. Unexpected, he was. Nell was seven. Funny little nipper. We all loved Henry."

"You were expanding the property all this time?"

"I was that. Every time a new one arrived, I added a bit more land. I had to, see. With all that brood I was going to need a tidy fortune to keep them in the lap o' luxury once I got 'em back Home."

He was jeering at himself as he said this.

"You were still wanting to go Home?"

He looked at me in amazement. "Of course."

"But why didn't you go? You must have been a wealthy man by . . ."

"Well, it was always one thing or another. First there was the flood. That was when Nell was about three. Funny thing, I'd been thinking to myself that day that it was time I sold out. We'd had a winter of heavy rain, see, and this day, in a short spell of sunshine, I came along to the house, and there were all the kids playing Bobbies and Bushies, and they were mud to the eyebrows. I thought to myself, 'It's time we left here. They're growing up like savages. I'll sell next season.' Well, just after that, Snowy came up to tell me that he didn't like the look of the way the river was rising. He said it was still raining up in the mountains and there'd be a lot more water coming down. I never argued with Snowy about things like that, so we went and called all the hands and set to work to get as much of the stock off the river flat as we could. By nightfall, wreckage was starting to come down . . . fences, trees, dead sheep and cattle, the roof of a house. There was nothing we could do except pray the river banks'd hold. We put the kids to bed, and then Snowy came up to the house, and he and Polly and I just sat there and waited. It was round about midnight that the water started to trickle under the door. So Snowy and I grabbed Nell and Ted out of bed, and we told Jonathon and Luke to take what clothes and blankets they could carry, and by that time Polly'd collected all the food she could, and we left the house with the candles still burning and the fire crackling away in the stove. We thought we'd be coming back, see? We thought it would be just a matter of washing the mud out next day."

I was looking down the hill to the place where the three gums were. I was trying to see the humpy there, with its candles burning.

"Well, when we got outside, it was worse than we'd thought. There was a log fence just by the house, and the water was all dammed up behind it. In front of the house it was up to my knees, but behind the fence it was feet deep. We knew if the fence gave way we were all done for. We started up towards the hill here, but the water was swirling round us so strong, I was worried about Jonathon and little Luke. Luke was such a little chap. I was trying to carry Nell, and a bundle of clothes, and hang on to Luke at the same time. Snowy had Ted and a great load of blankets and stuff, and Polly was struggling with a box full of food. With our arms full, there wasn't one of us that could give a hand to Jonathon. There he was, with Luke's clothes as well as his own under one arm, and hanging on to the fence with the other arm to stop himself from being swept away. God, he was game. I've never forgotten how game Jonathon was that night. Fighting it out all by himself. All the rest of us could do was pray to God that the fence would hold."

He was praying again. He was living through it again. I kept quiet and let him live it. After a while, he went on, "We got up on to the hill in the end, and just as we got here, there was a noise like . . . a sort of ripping, roaring noise, and the fence gave way, and we looked down on the house, and we could see the candlelight in the windows for a while.

Then, suddenly, there wasn't any more light, so we knew it must be under water." He was quiet again, for a long time. Then he said, "In the morning, there was nothing but water as far as you could see."

"You were marooned here on the hill?"

"For four days. Then some of the Dooleys managed to get across with some supplies for us. When the flood waters went down, there was nothing left of the humpy. After that we built a new house here on the hill."

Just like that. There was nothing left, so they built another house here on the hill. He sounded so matter-of-fact about it that I was able to raise a smile myself as I asked, "And that was the end of selling out and going Home?"

"Just for the time being. Just till I could get things going again." He was jeering at himself again. "It took quite a long time to get on my feet. Then just as I was getting things straight, there was the fluke epidemic; then there was the bank crash of the nineties; then just as we were getting over that, there was Luke to be sent Home to Cambridge." He grinned. "One thing after another."

I laughed, "You men on the land! You've always got something to grouse about!"

He laughed too. "Happen we have. Any road, there we were, still talking about making our fortune and going Home to spend it."

"When did you finally make up your mind not to go Home?"

He looked at me, and the laughter went out of him. "Last Friday night when Polly died," he said. "I wouldn't want to go Home without Polly."

CHAPTER FOURTEEN

I STARTED to get a bit restive after a couple of days at Billabirra. I'd made a lot of sketches of the foothills and I was anxious to get back to Sydney to have a shot at putting them on canvas.

My mother was going through her own private hell, so there was nothing I could do for her by staying. Jason was beginning to potter about, finding work to do, and that was a good sign. In the old days, they all said, he was always in and out of the house, popping up to the kitchen at all hours demanding cups of tea and a chat with Polly, but now he only came up to the homestead for meals. My mother had rigged up a cow-bell on the back verandah and she rang it when he was to come in.

I could feel the whole family looking at my back. Face to face with them it was all right. They were charming, and friendly, and anxious to make me feel at home. But my back told me that they were looking at it and wondering how the hell this oaf of Nell's was managing to keep the old man so cheerful.

My Uncle Jonathon I could have liked, but the word "artist" had frightened the living daylights out of him. He wouldn't come within cooee of me. If you wanted to paint a portrait of a typical outback Australian, you only had to ask Uncle Jonathon to pose for you. It was a wonderful face.

The young ones, my cousins, were no less suspicious.

David avoided me. I thought he was hating my guts because of Jan.

One day, however, I was in one of the rooms, and a group of cousins were lounging around on the verandah. It was

impossible, at Billabirra, to be in a room that didn't open on
to the verandah, and it was impossible to find a bit of verandah that didn't have someone lounging round on it.

I heard one of the cousins, Frank, I think, say, "I always
thought artists wore long hair and corduroy pants."

David growled, "Break it down. Harry's been working as
a navvy."

"Do you like him, Dave?" It was another voice.

David said, "Yes. But I don't think he thinks I'm much
chop. I made a bit of a fool of myself the first time we met
in Sydney. As a matter of fact, I don't think he's too keen on
any of us Selways."

"Well, surely he doesn't blame us because Auntie Nell
buried herself for years!"

David's voice said, "I don't think it's that exactly. I
could be wrong of course. It's pretty hard to know what
Harry thinks. He's a casual sort of bloke."

Another voice: "I thought artists were supposed to be
sensitive. He looks about as sensitive as a bullock."

Well, there's that one about what eavesdroppers hear
about themselves. Still, at least I knew that David didn't
hate my guts. That was something.

Why the hell should I feel guilty?

Well . . .

Anyway, I wanted to go back to Sydney. Apart from anything else I had to get back to my road. The foreman had
given me a week off to go to my grandmother's funeral. I
knew damned well he was convinced I'd never even had a
grandmother.

Everyone spent hours arguing round and round. Why
should I go back to Sydney and work on a road? Why
couldn't I stay here? I said I didn't know the front end of a
sheep from the back, so what the hell could I do here? And
they said there were plenty of things I could do here. Anyone that could work on a road could work at Billabirra. And
I said I'd got very attached to my road. I'd started with it
when it was no more than a mess of potholes, and I'd proudly
watched it turn respectable. I told them about how we'd

come to the corner, and not known where it went from there, and how we'd ferreted out its secret, and . . .

The whole family was sitting there staring at me in astonishment, and my mother, with her eyes smiling for the first time in days, said, "Harry, stop it!"

So I stopped, and the argument started again and went on until Jason suddenly banged his cup down on its saucer and said, "Be quiet, all of you! The boy wants to go back to his road!"

So it was settled that I'd go back.

I went on sketching for a couple of days, because I had to get it firmly in my mind so it would still be there when I got back to Sydney. Sometimes Jason would come and sit on the tree stump. Sometimes it would be old David Spencer. He was a dear old boy. The first time he came, he asked me for my candid opinion of Picasso. I didn't have any opinion, candid or otherwise, for the simple reason that I'd never even heard of Picasso. David Spencer was appalled and insisted right there and then that I should go back to New Park with him.

I spent a wonderful morning at New Park. Books everywhere. Books about painters, books of criticism, books of essays. David Spencer talked all the time, telling me about this man's work and that man's work, showing me reproductions and getting furious because I couldn't see the originals It would have been very easy to spend the rest of my life at New Park being educated in art by David Spencer, but I knew that if I stayed there I'd be so busy listening I'd never pick up a brush again.

The next occupant of the stump was Uncle Luke. He must have been there quite a long time before I heard a little cough, and there he was, smiling apologetically, rolling a cigarette and spilling the tobacco.

"Have a tailor-made?" I asked, reaching for a packet of cigarettes I had in my pocket.

He said no thanks, he preferred to roll his own. There was a long silence, and then he said suddenly, "Harry, I'd like to make you an allowance!"

That made me see red! I knew why there'd been all this fuss about my going back to Sydney. The Selways were ashamed that one of the family was a navvy on the roads. They were all seeing the time when one of them would be driving along a road, and there, at a stop at an intersection, would be Harry Brandon stripped to the waist, or maybe in a singlet, swinging a pick. Imagine Mr. and Mrs. Luke Selway during one of their periodic visits to whoop it up in Sydney, coming face to face with a nephew who was a labourer. Since I was seeing red, I said all this to Uncle Luke.

I got my come-uppance all right.

I've never seen a man change so much in a matter of seconds. My quiet, apologetic Uncle Luke got up from the tree stump and he let out a string of language that would have made a bullocky blush. He certainly didn't learn those words at Cambridge. He called me for everything. Putting the adjectives aside, I managed to learn that the Selway were not snobs and never would be. That if anyone was a snob I was. Inverted snobbery! Adjectival inverted snobbery it was, the way I kept stuffing my adjectival road down their adjectival throats.

I was lost in admiration. I decided that I liked my Uncle Luke very much.

I said to him, "You're all right, Uncle Luke. You'd do well on the road. The boys'd like you."

He gave up then and sat on the tree stump and said, "I'll have one of your cigarettes, after all." So I gave him a cigarette, and then we both laughed like a couple of idiots, and then he came over to look at my sketches.

"You ought to have some painting things here," he said. "We could order some up from Sydney. If we phone today, they can come up on tomorrow's train."

I told him I'd rather wait till I got home and use my own stuff, because it was battered about and familiar.

"About the allowance, Harry," he said.

I said it was very kind of him, but I didn't much like the idea of being a remittance man.

"Your mother tells me you've had no training. I'd like to make it possible for you to go to an art school."

I said I could always go to the Tech if I wanted to.

"I was thinking," he said, "of a couple of years in Paris perhaps."

That almost did for me. A couple of years in Paris! I didn't give myself time to think about it. I just said, "I'm not ready yet, Uncle Luke. I want to blunder around a bit first."

The extraordinary thing was that he seemed to understand. He didn't argue any more. He just stood looking at me for a while, and then he said, "Why the hell should I expect you to be the means of my salving my guilty conscience?"

And then he went off.

Guilty conscience?

The memory of my grandmother's voice: "Sure, you'd be amazed at the number of skeletons this family's stowed away in cupboards in the last thirty years."

CHAPTER FIFTEEN

YOU just don't go round asking people why your uncle has a guilty conscience. You keep your ears open, that's all; and every now and then, this one drops a remark here, or that one says something else there. Perhaps you don't even connect the two things, until a third person, years later, happens to say, "Do you remember the day we . . .?" and then things click into place. Sometimes Jason would say something, sometimes it would be David Spencer, or Uncle Jonathon, or Uncle Luke, or . . . Over the years, that is. The last bits of the pattern have fitted into place only quite recently.

First of all, you've got to see them as they were back in the eighties and nineties. A closed little community. Exiles, not only from the place thirteen thousand miles away that they still called Home, but from the rest of the colony of New South Wales too. The railway to Woollaby wasn't completed until 1894, and the trip to Sydney by coach was only undertaken for the settling of matters of world-shaking importance. But nothing of world-shattering importance happened in the valley, so nobody went to Sydney.

Woollaby, forty miles away, seemed to them to be a thriving metropolis. In its one street it had a post office, a bank, a grocery store, an ironmongery, a produce store, an establishment grandly known as a Drapery Emporium, and two pubs. Going to Woollaby was a big event. Jack would harness up the buggy, and he and Polly and the youngest of their offspring would sit up in the driver's seat, while the others, rigged out in their best clothes, would sit in the back. On arrival, Jack would line up the boys and march them off to have their hair cut at, surprisingly enough, the ironmongery.

K

In the meantime, Polly, with Nell, and then later on with
the new baby, Henry, would make for the Drapery Emporium. During the morning, the two parties, transacting their
various business deals, and moving from one store to another,
would meet in the street with the harassed formality of those
engaged in great commerce. At lunch-time they'd become
less formal as they met at one or other of the pubs to eat an
enormous meal. After lunch Polly would bustle off to do
more shopping, while Jack found a couple of cronies on the
pub verandah to whom he could yarn about lucerne, and
fluke, and blow flies. When they'd arrive back at Billabirra
in the evening, they'd always feel as though they'd been
away for weeks.

Once a year there'd be the Picnic Races, and buggies and
sulkies would come from all over the district to the big
paddock outside Woollaby. There the young ones would
show off themselves and their horses, and everyone would
stuff themselves with food, and the men would have an
eighteen-gallon keg to keep them cheerful.

Once a year, too, someone or other in the district would
clear out his wool shed, and the sulkies and buggies would
come from miles around, the women would bring food, the
men another eighteen-gallon keg, and young Tim Dooley
would play the fiddle and they'd have a high old time dancing till way into the morning. All the kids would be there.
Once they got too tired to keep their eyes open any longer,
someone would doss them down on heaps of blankets, and
by midnight, all round the wall of the wool shed, there'd be
kids sleeping so hard that all the noise in the world couldn't
have wakened them.

But, for the most part, the Selways and the Camerons, and
the Spencers, and the Dooleys just stayed in their valley, and
if there was shopping to be done it was done at Ma Dooley's
store at Cameron's Crossing, and if there was any drinking
to be done it was done at Ma Dooley's pub, and if there was
any eating to be done it was done in Polly Selway's kitchen.

There they were then. Polly absorbed in bringing up her
family; Jack absorbed in his sheep; Ma Dooley absorbed in

counting her profits; David Spencer absorbed in his daughter and his books; Andy Cameron absorbed in despising his wife because she wasn't Polly Selway, and his daughter because she wasn't Jonathon Selway.

And all the time the young ones were growing up towards adulthood, towards middle age, towards old age.

All except young Henry, Polly's beloved little Henry. He was growing up towards a beach at Gallipoli.

There was Jonathon, the sheep man already, wanting nothing more than to get this school business over and done with so that he could get out in the paddocks with his father and Snowy. There was Alison Cameron, Jonathon's slave. There was Vicky Spencer, the golden girl, beautiful, lazy, arrogant, yet loved for all that. There was Luke Selway, the golden boy, the handsome one, the brainy one, the one who could charm birds off trees.

Jonathon and Alison were always together talking sheep. Luke and Vicky were always together talking God knows what glorious dreams into becoming realities. Ted Selway was always talking. Just talking. Moving from pair to pair, laying down the law. Unsnubbable. Then there was Nell Selway talking to nobody.

Watching them all was Mick Dooley, talking most likely, to the devil on his shoulder.

Jack was just starting to recoup his losses after the bank crash and slump of the early nineties when David Spencer suggested that Luke should go to Cambridge, adding, as though it were something that had just come into his mind, "Of course I shall foot the bill."

Jack grinned at that. "Come now, David, don't take away my one little conceit. Think of it. The son of a Bradford warehouse hand going to Cambridge."

Spencer protested, "That's all very well, but I know how things are with you, and . . ."

Jack patted him on the shoulder, and said, "Happen we'll manage. Be a good chap and let me talk it over with Polly."

When he talked it over with Polly, she declared that of

course they'd manage. Jack said he was wondering whether it was fair to the other children. Polly was scornful. "Now how would they suffer? They've all the food they want, and there's no children better clothed."

"What about the future, lass?"

"Oh, you and your future, Jack Selway! Where's there a man more fitted than yourself to cope with the future? And what about me? Aren't I here, too?"

Jack kissed her and said she'd better be, because there'd be no coping by him without her, and she told him to get away with him. So it was decided that Luke would go to Cambridge . . . if Cambridge would have him.

It transpired that Cambridge would have him, and the following year, washed by the tears of all except Vicky Spencer, a very frightened Luke was driven in the buggy to Woollaby and put on the train which was to be the first leg of his journey Home. Jack, watching him go, made up his mind that by the time Luke was through Cambridge, the whole family would be there in England with him.

Everyone, except Nell, was very surprised that Luke and Vicky had parted in such an offhand way. After they'd been such friends too! You could never tell with children.

By now, of course, Jonathon had left school and was jackerooing, and the girls found New Park very dull. Alison was the first of them to go. She took a chance on her father's scorn and asked him if she could work on the property with him. He didn't even bother to answer her. So the following day she went down to where Andy and the hands were branding cattle, and without even turning a hair at the smell and the noise, she set about making herself useful. Andy pretended not to see her, but he didn't send her away, and after that she became the general rouseabout at Camerons.

The time came when they had to begin thinking about whether Ted should follow his brother to Cambridge. Ted irritated the life out of David as a pupil, but there was no getting away from the fact that the boy had brains. He didn't take learning for the pure joy of it as Luke did. He worried at it, probing, measuring, arguing, questioning.

What irritated David was that all this was not curiosity so much as a predilection on Ted's part for the sound of his own voice. David tried to be extra-patient with Ted because he was ashamed of his irritation.

So here was the problem of whether or not they could afford to send Ted overseas, and Polly and Jack did a lot of arithmetic. It turned out that they could have saved themselves the trouble, because Ted had made up his mind that he was going to Sydney University. Heated arguments followed, but they might as well have saved themselves that trouble too, because you couldn't win an argument with Ted. So Ted went away to Sydney University, and Jack admitted to Polly that he was glad Ted's education wasn't going to be as costly as Luke's.

By the time Nell had learned everything David could teach her, it never occurred to any of them to work out ways and means of sending her either to Cambridge or to Sydney.

Nell was the one who puzzled David most. She was the one who had, after all, turned out to be contrary. The others fitted into their pigeon-holes, but there was no pigeon-hole that was the right shape for Nell.

Alison, for instance, had grown up from a silent, pathetic little girl, into an inarticulate and still pathetic adolescent. She had transferred her worship from her father to Jonathon, and that was the only change.

Spencer had no illusions about Vicky. He knew her faults and didn't love her any the less for them. Indeed, everyone loved Vicky, and that's why David knew that she'd get away with murder if she wanted to. This didn't worry him, however, because murder was unthinkable in the valley.

Nell, now. There was no knowing what she'd get away with, because of this difficulty about pigeon-holes. Nell was at once gregarious and solitary. She'd join in the larking with the others and appear to be having the time of her life, and then suddenly, right in the middle of some game perhaps, she'd go off by herself somewhere. She was at once affectionate and withdrawn. She'd give out love and she'd take love, till a kind of saturation point was reached, and then off she'd go again to be alone. She had brains, too. She was just as brainy as the boys, but it was a cluttered-up braininess. She read everything she could lay her hands on, all David's books, periodicals, and newspapers, and her brain was a seething mass of all she'd read. Sometimes David tried to unclutter it a little so that he could push in a Latin tag, or a bit of trigonometry, or a speech of Shakespeare's but he always had to wait until Nell's brain was good and ready to make room for him.

Polly was always saying, "I don't know what to make of you, Nell, with your nose always stuck in a book."

Polly was a great believer in what is now known as inner cleanliness. She believed that if your bowels were open, so was your soul. She'd line them all up every Saturday morning, inquiring into the state of their bowels, and then she'd dish out senna tea or sulphur and treacle, and she expected that in reporting on the state of your bowels, so, too, you would report on the state of your mind.

It was never possible to get a full report on the state of Nell's mind, and that made Polly cross, because she liked to know what people were thinking. Jack left all the probing, both physical and mental, to Polly. He took Nell just as she was, and he loved her very much.

By the time Luke had been gone a year, Alison Cameron was working their property with Andy. He still hated her guts, but she saved him the expense of another hand. Jonathon had nobody of his own age to talk sheep to now, so it seemed only natural that he and Vicky should team up. Nell often watched them together, frowning a little.

Then there came the night just before Christmas, their second Christmas without Luke. It was hot, and they were all sitting on the verandah. Jack was talking about a letter they'd just had from Luke. He was doing well at Cambridge. Suddenly young Henry broke in to ask when Luke would be coming home.

Jack puffed away at his pipe and said he reckoned Luke wouldn't be coming home at all. "There's nothing for him here," he said. "He'll stay over there in England till we all get there. I reckon I'll be selling out within the next couple of years. Then we'll all go Home." Nobody commented, because all their lives Dad had been talking about selling out and going Home.

It was the next evening when Jonathon announced, sounding as though he scarcely believed it himself, that Vicky had promised to marry him. Everyone was overjoyed. Polly cried, and Jack said nothing could have pleased him more, and David Spencer said this was what he'd been dreaming about ever since Vicky was born. Nell just stood in the background, looking puzzled.

Jonathon and Vicky were married at Easter, and they cleared out the wool shed at Billabirra, and invited everyone from far and wide. The whole district turned up, including all the Dooleys and their wives. Most of Mrs. Dooley's boys were married by now, and their wives had been put to work in the pub and the general store. All the Dooleys, that is, except Mick. Jonathon said he wouldn't be surprised if Mick was in gaol.

It took a couple of weeks for everyone to settle down again after the wedding, but eventually they were back into the old routine, and the only difference was that Vicky now lived at Billabirra.

Snowy was very unsettled by all this wedding lark. He hadn't talked for a couple of years of moving on, but now he said that since Jack had Jonathon shaping up so well, there was no need for him to stay around any longer. Jack said, "You might as well stay another season, Snowy. I reckon to sell out next year. No harm in you staying till we go." Snowy thought about it for a while, and then agreed that there was no harm in seeing another season out.

It would be nice and dramatic at this point to say: 'And then came the seven stark and dreadful years of the Great Drought!' But you can't talk about droughts as though they arrive with the morning post. Droughts don't begin. They only end; if you're lucky.

There had been no rain to speak of in 1896, but that wasn't

much to worry about, because they often got a dry season. There was no rain at all in the next year, and everyone began peering at the sky each morning, saying: "Never mind. Tomorrow maybe." When the third rainless season had come and gone, Jack was thanking God for the river at Billabirra that never ran dry.

There was precious little grass in the paddocks now, and Jack, knowing the danger of being over-stocked, began to sell off quite a lot of his sheep. Alison tried to persuade her father to follow suit, but Andy told her to mind her own business. "Look at Selway selling for a few shillings a head," he said. "He'll be sorry when we get rain in the spring."

But they didn't get rain in the spring, and by then, even less was being offered per head. However, Jack sold half his new lambs, and let Andy scoff his head off.

In the autumn of 1898, Vicky and Jonathon's son was born. He was called John, and he caused so much excitement that for a long time they all stopped talking about rain.

The following year they had something else to take their minds off the drought, because Luke wrote and told them he wasn't doing so well in his last year, and that he might fail his Finals. While they were still recovering from their bewilderment at this news, another letter arrived from Luke. He hadn't failed, but he'd taken only a very mediocre degree. By the time they received this letter, Luke was already on his way back to Billabirra.

At first, Jack was very cross about that. He thought Luke had had no right to take matters into his own hands and just get on a ship like that. He should have waited in England for the rest of them. But after he'd simmered down and looked out at the dry, yellow paddocks, he came to the conclusion that, since it might be some time before they'd all be going Home, it wouldn't do Luke any harm to come back for a last look at Australia.

I've left out a few other things that had happened while all this was going on.

For instance, I mentioned the train Luke caught from Woollaby, so it's obvious that, by that time, the railway had been built. Also, there was young Henry. David Spencer had felt that since Henry was so much younger than the others, he ought to go away to school to be with boys of his own age. So he'd just finished his first year at boarding-school in Armidale when Luke got back from England.

I mention this here because it makes a nice little picture. Brothers meeting on Woollaby railway station. Henry was coming home for the Christmas holidays, and his train got in from Armidale at eight-thirty in the morning. At nine o'clock the other train got in from Sydney, and Luke was on it, with Ted, also coming home for the Christmas holidays.

Jonathon met them all in the buggy.

The only record of their conversation I can find is that Luke said, "I say, the country looks dry!" And Jonathon said, "We'll be all right when we get some rain." And Henry said, "I'm hungry." And Ted started to talk about politics.

The only one who didn't seem overjoyed by Luke's home-coming was Nell. Polly couldn't understand her at all. Nell had always loved Luke, and yet here she was going round like a cat on hot bricks, dropping things, looking dreamy. And so much work to be done, too!

There was to be a dinner-party for Luke, with all the Camerons and David Spencer coming. On the big day, Polly had Nell up and in the kitchen while the cows were still being milked. There was scarcely room to work on the enormous kitchen table, because of the food there waiting to be cooked.

Polly was flour to the elbows. "I'd like my mother to see me now," she said. "The secret of good pastry is to keep everything cool, she used to say. Cold hands, cold water. And look at me making as good a bit of pastry as anyone ever tasted in a temperature of ninety-two degrees."

Nell was beating egg whites. She didn't answer.

"Well," Polly said, "you could say something nice. You could say it is indeed better pastry than anyone ever tasted."

Nell came out of her dream, or nightmare, and smiled and said, "Oh you! You're always looking for compliments."

"Well," said Polly, "it seems to me that if I don't blow my own trumpet, nobody else is going to blow it for me."

Vicky came in just then looking very cool, and very languid, and very beautiful. "I thought you said you were going to have it all done before the day got too hot," she remarked.

Nell went on beating and said, "If you'd come and given us a hand we'd have been finished hours ago."

Vicky smiled good-humouredly and said, "I had the baby to see to."

Nell snapped at her. "Every time there's work to be done, you have the baby to see to. When there's no work, he damned well sees to himself!"

Polly was astonished, she told Jack afterwards. Nell and Vicky usually got on so well together! And now Nell picking on Vicky like that! But Vicky didn't seem to mind. She only smiled good-humouredly and said, "Well, he's seeing to himself now. What can I do to help?"

Polly put the cream jug in her hand and said, "I want you to run down to the dairy and fetch this morning's cream."

Vicky, still smiling, said, "I won't run, but I'll fetch it," and then she went out.

Polly turned to Nell and said, "What in the world made you speak to Vicky like that?"

Nell finished beating the eggs and said, "I'm sick of fetching and carrying for her. She's bone lazy!"

Polly knew very well that Vicky was lazy. Everybody knew it. But it had never occurred to anyone to remark on it before. The whole Selway family took it for granted that it was their job to wait on Vicky.

"Now Nell . . ." Polly began.

But Nell didn't let her get any further. "Oh, for goodness' sake, Mother, leave me alone!"

Polly, telling Jack about it later, said she couldn't believe her ears. "Don't you dare to speak to me like that, my girl!" she said. "What's the matter with you, at all? You've been like a bear with a sore head ever since we heard Luke was coming home. What's the matter with you?"

And then Nell slammed down the knife she was just going
to peel apples with, and said, "There's nothing the matter
with me except that I want to be left alone! I'm sick of
everyone prodding and prying and talking and talking! I
just want a little privacy, that's all!"

And after that she stamped out of the kitchen.

Jack came in soon afterwards, and Polly was still seething,
so he sat down at the kitchen table and talked to her for a
while, and that calmed her down. He talked about the tank.
He'd just been tapping it. The water was down to the last
rung. That meant they'd have to drink well water from then
on, so Polly had to concentrate on plans for conserving water.

By the time the boys arrived, Polly's and Nell's little tiff
was forgotten. Henry made straight for the kitchen. Ted
tried to buttonhole everyone to tell them what he thought
about things. Luke just stood there in all his glory.

He looked so elegant in his London suit. He was so good-
looking, so sophisticated, so much a man of the world. You
wouldn't have known him for their little bush boy, until,
after all the greetings were over, he sniffed and said, "The
smells of home. Burning gum, axle grease, wool, Mother's
pies!" They loved him for not having changed. David
Spencer, watching him, knew he had changed, of course.
David also knew he was unhappy about something.

None of them, except Nell, noticed that Vicky was the only
one of the family who didn't attempt to welcome Luke home.

They all ended up in the kitchen, and Polly, pretending to
want to be rid of them, shooed them all away while she put
the sucking pigs in the oven, but they were all back in no
time at all talking about the drought, and about Cambridge,
and about politics, and about how hungry Henry was. It
was pandemonium. Polly kept saying that if they didn't all
get out of the kitchen there'd be no dinner, but she loved it
just the same.

When Luke asked who was coming to dinner, she said that,
since Uncle David was already here, there were only the
Camerons to come. And Jack said to Ted, "Now for
heaven's sake don't start talking politics to Andy," and he

said to Jonathon, "And don't you mention the river to Andy."

And Polly said to Luke, "Now, Luke, I want you to be nice to Alison."

Luke protested that he'd always been nice to Alison, but Polly was insistent. "I want you to be specially nice to Alison today. Promise me!"

So Luke promised that he would be specially nice to Alison, and that was how all the trouble started.

CHAPTER SIXTEEN

LUKE sat next to Alison at dinner, and he was amazed to find that it was very easy to be specially nice to her. At first she just sat there, tongue-tied and embarrassed, and then, responding to him, she began to relax. It gave him a great sense of power gradually to draw her out of her shell, to make her laugh, to make her talk.

He saw his mother watching him with approval.

Ted was talking about the federation of the Australian states. Jack was scornful. "What rot!" he said, stuffing sucking pig into his mouth. "They've been talking about Federation ever since I arrived in the colony thirty years ago."

"Longer!" said Andy Cameron with his hair standing straight up, looking surprised at having had another wash.

"Well," said Ted, "they're not just talking about it any longer. It's really going to happen. Barton's leading a delegation to England. The bill ought to be brought before the House of Commons early next year."

Jack snorted. "It won't go through. Do you think the House of Commons is going to allow a tuppenny ha'penny colonial government to be in a position to overrule the Imperial Government?"

Ted said there was no question of overruling, but Jack insisted that he'd read somewhere about them wanting to take over the powers of the Privy Council. Ted pointed out that they didn't want to take over any powers. They only wanted to have the right to interpret the constitution, that's

all. Jonathon wanted to know what good Federation would
do, anyhow. Ted told them to look at the States.

So they looked at the States.

"Here we have," said Ted, laying down the law, "six
different colonies scattered over a continent larger than
Europe. Six different Governments! Look at the mess we
have now! Each State building its own railways on different
gauges, so that if you want to go from Sydney to Melbourne,
you have to change trains at the border. All the stupid old
State jealousies dating back to the first settlements. Each
State trying to stab the others in the back, jostling for position. The States ought to be working together instead of
against each other!"

Andy Cameron scoffed and said they could have their
States, federated or otherwise. As far as he was concerned,
Scotland was the only country on the map, anyhow, and
since none of these States could ever be Scotland, it was up to
them to mind their p's and q's, and stop trying to pretend
they were something they weren't.

Ted got a bit heated then, and Polly had to take a hand
and tell them to stop talking their old politics, for goodness'
sake, and eat their dinner. But Ted had to have the last
word.

"The Commonwealth of Australia, the Federation'll be
called. If all goes to schedule, the Queen will make a procla-
mation next year, and on the First of January 1901, the
Commonwealth of Australia will come into existence. A new
century, and a new country!"

Ted was already training for the time when he'd address
Electors, and he couldn't resist the last bit. He added for
good measure: "So, from next year, Dad, we won't be New
South Welshmen, or Queenslanders, or Victorians. We'll be
Australians."

Jack grunted, "Don't be daft. There's no such thing as an
Australian. There are only Englishmen, and Scotsmen, and
Irishmen and Welshmen who live in Australia."

Henry stopped stuffing himself with food long enough to
say, "I'm an Australian."

They all looked at him.

"I don't have to wait till next year to call myself an Australian," Henry said. "I'm one now."

Jack slammed his knife and fork down and roared, "I won't have any son of mine calling himself an Australian!"

David Spencer smiled and asked, "What is he, Jack? A Yorkshireman? An Irishman?"

Henry looked at David indignantly, and said, "I'm not a Pommy."

Jack had been about to pick up his knife and fork again. He sat with his hands poised. "You're not a *what*?"

Henry said, "A Pommy. We've got one at school. He talks funny. La-di-da. Like Luke."

Jack was appalled. He turned to David. "Am I or am I not sending him to the most expensive school in the State?" he demanded to know.

David smiled and said, "I'm afraid you've got to face facts, Jack. When you throw your Englishman and your Scotsman and your Irishman and your Welshman into the pot, the concoction turns out to be an Australian, with an Australian accent."

An Australian accent indeed!

David added, "A mixture of you, and Polly, and Andy here, and Ma Dooley, and me."

This was too much for Jack. A son of his turning out to be an Australian! Imagine it! He began to say that drought or no drought he was going to sell out and take the whole boiling of them back to the old country, but Polly knew it was time to put her foot down.

She put it down and they all began to eat again. The men talked about the drought, and Luke talked to Alison about Cambridge, and Polly talked to Rose Cameron about quince jelly, and Vicky didn't talk to anyone, but looked as though she didn't have a care in the world. Nell didn't talk to anyone either, but she looked as though she had all the cares in the world.

The dinner was a great success, and afterwards the men retired to the cool side of the verandah to recover.

The women washed-up.

Alison was still glowing with pleasure. She had never realised before how nice Luke was. How very nice. Nobody, not another soul, had ever asked her questions about herself before. He hadn't laughed at all when she'd told him how much she preferred working out on the property to being cooped up in the homestead. He'd asked her all about her work, not just out of politeness. Really sounding interested.

Alison was wiping a plate and dreaming away as they all chattered round her, when she suddenly became aware of Vicky. Vicky, too, was wiping a plate, and she looked so lovely, her dress was so becoming, her hair was so well groomed, and her hands were so white. 'How on earth does she manage it?' Alison thought. 'You'd think she lived in the city with a dozen servants to look after her.' Alison looked down at her own home-made dress, at her own brown, neglected hands, and came out of her dream.

Vicky wiped two more plates and then said she was sure she'd heard the baby crying, and went out.

Nell said, "Of all the lazy . . .!"

Polly said, "Now, Nell!" and handed her a vegetable dish.

Alison was horrified to hear her own voice say, "I was looking at her hands, at how nice they are."

Nell said sourly, "No wonder. She never does any work." And Polly said, "You've nice hands yourself, Alison. A nice shape."

Alison had gone too far now to back out. She held out her hands. "Look at them. Just look. Corns, scratches, cuts! I can't get the dirt out of them!"

Alison's mother began to say that if she would work out-side with the men . . . But Nell took the words out of her mouth. "What can you expect?" she asked bluntly. "You work as hard as Jonathon does."

An echo out of the past for Polly? A voice out of the past? Jack saying, "Look at her hands, Snowy!"

Polly said, "I used to work harder than Jonathon does.

Look at my hands." Without a blush she held them out.

Alison inspected them and asked, "How do you keep them like that?"

Polly looked smug. "Bran. I soak them in bran. I have for years."

Rose Cameron looked terrified and fluttered the tea towel and said, "Bran. Oh dear!"

Nell banged a plate very hard on the table and said, for no good reason at all, "When will it ever end!"

Nobody had the slightest idea what she was talking about, but Polly looked severe and said, "That plate came out from Ireland with my mother, and if you break it, my girl, you'll end soon enough with a clip over the ear."

The rest of the washing-up passed without incident.

David didn't have an opportunity to talk to Luke all day. If Andy wasn't haranguing them about the state of the country, Ted was haranguing them about the future of the country.

"Future, future! Don't talk to me about the future," Andy said. "There'll be no future for any of us if it doesn't rain soon."

David said, "You ought to talk to Mick Dooley, Ted. He's the one who's always talking about the future. Expansion and progress and so forth."

Jonathon asked, "Is Mick Dooley back?"

And Luke asked, "Why? Has he been away?"

Jonathon explained that he'd been away for about three years, and Ted said, "He must have got out just in time."

"Out of what?"

"He's been blackbirding. The police were after him."

Jonathon echoed, "Blackbirding!" and Luke wanted to know what blackbirding was, so Ted explained about the slave traders who'd been kidnapping Kanakas from the Islands and selling them to work on the Queensland sugar plantations.

David said, "But I thought there was a law passed to stop blackbirding years ago."

L

Ted was pleased to be the centre of interest. "The law was passed all right. That's why there's so much money in it now."

David turned to Jonathon and said, "No wonder Mick looks so prosperous. He's been driving round in a new sulky, a very splendid turnout. He didn't get his horse at the sale-yards, either."

Jonathon said, "There's a rumour going round that Ma Dooley's buying up all the land she can around Cameron's Crossing."

Andy Cameron laughed. "Aye, I sold it to her myself." He turned to Jack. "What the deuce do you suppose she wants it for? Even the rabbits can't live on it."

Jack replied that he couldn't imagine. Jack was still smarting from the sting of discovering that he was the father of an Australian. He didn't join in the talk very much.

Eventually the Camerons went home, Andy stalking out followed by his womenfolk. Luke went to see them off. Then Ted and Jonathon disappeared somewhere, and Polly and Nell went to do the last-minute chores. After Vicky had kissed her father and gone off to bed, Jack and Spencer sat on to smoke a last pipe.

After a while Luke came back and sat on the verandah step. "I've not had a real opportunity to talk to you all day," he said to Jack. "Is it true you've had no rain for nearly four years?"

"No rain to speak of," Jack said.

"Why didn't you tell me in your letters?" Luke demanded.

"What could you have done? Held a rain-making ceremony?"

"But, Father, you've let me go on spending all that money . . ."

"We're not broke yet," Jack said. Then he got up and added, "We've a good crop of lucerne. The river's holding. We'll be all right." Then, saying he wanted to go and have a word with Snowy, he left Luke and David together.

Luke didn't waste time beating about the bush. "Are you very disappointed in me, Uncle David?" he asked.

David knew it was no use lying. He said, "I had hoped you'd do better. What happened, Luke? You were going along so splendidly. Why was your last year such a failure?"

Luke didn't answer that. He went off on another tack. "Ted should have been the one to go to Cambridge," he said.

"Oh, I wouldn't say that. He seems to be doing very well where he is."

"Why did he go to Sydney? Because there wasn't enough money for him to come abroad?"

"Money had nothing to do with it. He wanted to go to Sydney University. Insisted on it."

Luke said, "I've wasted four years that he could have used to advantage."

David said, "I think you'll find, in the end, Luke, that the four years weren't wasted."

Luke got up from the step where he'd been sitting, and walked impatiently along the verandah. Then he turned back to David. "I'm sorry, Uncle David. Perhaps we'll be able to discuss it all a bit more profitably later on. I'm a bit confused at the moment."

David paused before he asked, "Could it be that you didn't want to come back to Australia?"

Luke protested, "Oh, no! I was dying to get back! I was terribly homesick!"

"Well, you're back. Why the confusion?"

Luke came back along the verandah, and stood for a moment, looking uncertain. At last he said, "Because now that I'm back, I'm going to be terribly homesick for England."

David gave a sigh of relief. So that was all that was worrying him. He laughed. "Oh, Luke, that's the usual problem of the ex-patriate, even the temporary one."

Luke burst out, "But of which country am I an ex-patriate? That's my problem. Am I an Australian? Or am

I an Englishman who just happens to have been born in
Australia? Where are my roots? I don't know. Here, at
home, everyone looks on me as something of a freak . . . the
elegant sophisticate who has no place in the bush. At
Cambridge I was the brash colonial who had to have allow-
ances made for him. Where do I really belong, Uncle
David?"

David knew that was a question he couldn't answer, so
he simply said, "You've only been back a day, Luke. Give
yourself time." Then David thought he ought to be getting
back to New Park, so he went off to say good-bye to the
others, and Luke was left there on the verandah with his
problems.

Being an ex-patriate wasn't Luke's only problem. There
was Vicky and the fact that he was still in love with her.
Homesick or not, Luke knew damned well that he shouldn't
have come home.

While Luke was sitting on the verandah at Billabirra
thinking about Vicky, Alison Cameron was thinking about
Luke.

At least, she was thinking about Luke in between moments
of horror in case she should walk on a snake or a rat. She
was in the feed shed at Camerons. She'd only just come in,
and she didn't dare to light the hurricane lamp until the door
was closed. As well as the snakes and the rats, there was the
added horror that her father might see the light. Once she'd
closed the door and could risk the light, she couldn't remember what she'd done with the matches. There were all
sorts of nasty rustlings and scamperings in the dark all round
her, and she gritted her teeth and hoped they were mice. At
last she found the matches, and lit the hurricane, and held
it up over the sacks and the bins. There didn't seem to be
any snakes or rats, so, clutching the bowl she'd brought with
her, she went to the bran bin and began to scoop some of it
out.

The next moment she dropped both bowl and lamp, because with a noise loud enough to wake everyone between
here and Woollaby, the tin door of the shed swung open and

she saw her father standing there silhouetted in the moon-light. Even terrified as she was, her first thought was for the lamp. If she were to start a fire there'd be no stopping it with everything so dry.

She picked up the lamp and waited for Andy to come into the shed. "What the devil are you doing here?" he yelled.

"I was . . . I was getting some bran."

"What for? The fowls don't get fed in the middle of the night."

"It . . . it isn't for the fowls. I was just taking a handful."

"What for?"

"Nothing really, Papa."

He hated the way she cringed away from him.

"What do you mean, nothing really! What are you going to do with it?"

Alison swallowed hard and knew there was no way out. She'd have to tell him. "It's for my hands," she said.

"Your hands!"

"To clean them. They're such a mess. I . . ."

Andy grabbed the lamp out of her hand and held it up to her face. "Have you gone mad, girl?"

She turned away from the light, but he grabbed her arm and held her. "What's made you start worrying about your hands all of a sudden?"

Alison tried to get away from him but he held her firmly. "Luke Selway," he said.

She was praying that he wouldn't see how she was blushing as she tried to sound surprised when she said, "Luke Sel-way?"

Andy let go her arm and pushed her away. "I saw you ogling him today. Making a fool of yourself. Everyone laughing at you!"

"Everyone laugh . . ." She was so appalled that she forgot her embarrassment at being caught out in this ridiculous situation.

"All through dinner," Andy said. "All of them laughing their heads off."

'Oh, no,' she was thinikng. 'Oh, no!'

Andy went on: "You don't think he'd be likely to look twice at you, do you? My God, to go and pick on that namby pamby! If it had been Jonathon now . . . But no! You had to let that slut of Spencer's get in first with Jonathon!"

Alison heard her own voice shouting at him, "Papa, please be quiet!"

Nobody had ever raised a voice to Andy. Nobody had ever tried to outshout him. It took him ten seconds to get over the surprise of it, and then he roared, "Don't you tell me to be quiet, my lady!"

Alison picked up the bowl and began to move to the door, but Andy wasn't finished with her yet. "Bran on your hands, indeed! And feed costing me a fortune!"

Those few seconds of defiance had given her courage. She'd actually told him to be quiet! Now she even had the courage to laugh. Feed costing him a fortune, and she'd wanted a handful. Andy couldn't see her laughing because he was talking to her back. "As though Luke Selway would want a gawk like you! He'll be away looking for some city woman! A woman as soft as himself!"

At that Alison swung round and said, "Luke isn't soft!"

For the second time Andy was surprised. He dropped his voice and sounded almost bewildered as he said, "They're all soft. All except Jonathon. Great God, a man has the good fortune to have four sons, and he sends three of them away to be educated! The man's mad! But let me tell you this. Jack Selway's riding his good fortune too hard. He's had all the luck so far . . . the best land in the valley, land that should have been mine, four sons while all I've got is a daughter, a wife to help him while all I've got is . . ."

And then Andy got the shock of his life because Alison lost her temper. "I used to think you were the most wonderful person in the world!" she shouted. "But now I hate you! You're a bully and you're mean! Mean!" She threw the bowl at the bran bin. "If I'm going to do a man's work for you, you pay me for it! From now on I get paid the same as the other hands! Do you hear? Union wages paid monthly! Then if I want twopennorth of bran, I'll buy it from you!"

And Alison marched out of the feed shed, leaving Andy standing there with every red hair on his head and beard bristling.

"By God," he said aloud. "By God, she's got spunk! I thought she was as spineless as her mother. By God!"

And then he laughed and felt better than he'd done for years.

This all happened on Luke's first day back at Billabirra.

CHAPTER SEVENTEEN

IT's very difficult to get middle-aged people to talk seriously about their youthful indiscretions. Looking back in tranquillity, in the light of experience, they like to think they've developed a sense of humour. "How could I have taken myself so seriously?" or "Good lord, I must have been mad!"

All those skeletons waiting to be stowed away.

Jack thinking about the drought, and Polly making pies, and quince jelly, and pickles, and sponge cakes, and thinking how lovely it was that Luke was back home and were they feeding little Henry properly at that school.

And all the time a tiny little hell getting bigger and bigger and waiting to be big enough to break loose.

Nell was the one who knew about the hell. She'd known it from the time it was so small you could scarcely see it, back in the days before Luke went away and he and Vicky were in love with each other.

When Vicky and Jonathon were married, Nell had hoped for a while that the little hell had withered away and died, but the day Luke came back she knew it had only been hibernating. Watching Vicky watching Luke that first day made Nell feel a bit sick inside. Then watching Vicky watching Luke and Alison made her even sicker.

Vicky and Luke hadn't spoken to each other all day, except for a rather formal greeting when he first arrived, but Nell watched them being aware of each other, even the backs of their heads being aware of each other.

And Nell prayed that they'd be sensible.

But the little hell was getting ready to break loose, so it got very busy.

First of all it sent Jonathon out to Ten Mile Creek. The kangaroos, coming in close to the river to look for grass were making an awful mess of the fences out at Ten Mile. So Jonathon went out there with Danny and Bob to do something about both fences and kangaroos.

The little hell also made Polly forget to put kerosene on the grocery order, so Nell had to harness up the sulky and drive into Cameron's Crossing for it.

Then the little hell prompted Luke to go for a ride. A kind of tour of inspection. After an hour or so, it also prompted him to work up a prodigious thirst which could only be slaked by a glass of cold beer at Ma Dooley's pub.

As Luke rode into Cameron's Crossing, there was Nell getting into the sulky in front of the store, and there was Mick Dooley stowing a tin of kerosene under the seat.

And what a difference there was in Mick Dooley! Whether he'd been blackbirding or in gaol, he'd obviously done well for himself. Good clothes. An air of knowing just what he was about. Good looking, too. Butter still wouldn't melt in his mouth.

All the Dooleys came out to welcome Luke. Nell got out of the sulky again, and they all sat on the pub verandah; Luke had several nice cold beers and Nell had some lemonade, and Luke told the Dooleys all about the old country. All the time he was telling them how wonderful it was to be home, Luke was thinking, 'I've come out of beautiful Cambridge to this. To one dusty little street, and a flyblown pub and a general store.' Then he remembered how, sitting on the banks of the Cam, with the Colleges all round him, he'd longed for this same dusty street. Where in hell did he belong, anyhow?

Just in hell, the little hell was saying.

After a while Nell said she'd better get back with the kerosene or there'd be no lamps lit that night, so Mick Dooley said he'd ride a bit of the way with them, and he went and brought round the most expensive looking horse that had ever been seen in these parts.

And then, as though they were going off on a long journey

into the interior, the sulky drove off with Luke and Mick riding on each side, and all the Dooleys waving good-bye. About a mile out of the township, Mick said he'd leave them here, so he rode off, but he didn't ride back in the direction of Cameron's Crossing.

The sulky and Luke's horse went on at a walking pace, and after a while, Luke said, "Mick's done very nicely for himself."

Nell nodded and said, "It's the first time I've seen him since he got back. I never realised before how attractive he is."

Luke laughed easily. "Well, I suppose if you like that sort of Irish charm."

And Nell laughed too. "You know, I think I do!"

Luke stopped laughing, but Nell didn't. She asked, "Have you ever thought about the disadvantages of being a Selway woman in a closed community like this, Luke? At least Vicky and Alison have the pick of my brothers. What men are left for me?"

Luke looked so shocked that she thought she'd better stop laughing.

"If I catch you with Mick Dooley," he said, "I'll break both your necks!"

"Oh, come now, Luke, don't tell me you've turned into a snob!"

"It's nothing to do with snobbery! Do you know where he got his money? He's been blackbirding!"

Nell looked so interested when he said that, that he thought he'd better say something else. All he could think of was, "You see that Mick Dooley keeps his distance."

Nell said, "Oh, you don't have to worry about me. Mick's already involved."

"Involved? With whom?"

Would it help to tell him? No. Mind your own business, Nell Selway. Let things work themselves out.

"With whom, Nell?"

"Oh, nobody you know. Luke, I must hurry. Mother's waiting for the kerosene. Are you coming home?"

Luke said he was hot and he thought he'd go down to the river for a swim, so Nell whipped up her horse and bowled away at a fast trot.

Luke turned his horse towards The Bend, where they always swam. He was thinking about Nell, about what she'd just said. What was it? The disadvantages of being a Selway woman in a closed community? There she was, month after month, year after year, in the kitchen at Billabirra. She never got away anywhere, never met anyone. That was his fault, of course. There was no money for her to go anywhere, because he'd spent it all. It had never occurred to him, while he was spending his very generous allowance, to think about Jonathon slaving away and Nell slaving away. Jonathon, he knew, was perfectly content to slave, but what about Nell? It was so damned hard to know about Nell. You could never tell what she was thinking.

He came down towards The Bend through a patch of heavy scrub, and just as he was about to ride into the clearing, he saw Mick Dooley's horse tethered there under the willows. There was another horse, a big bay, tethered near it. Luke reined in and backed his horse into the scrub. He saw a flash of colour. A woman's dress.

'Oh lord,' he thought, 'that was a close thing. Jolly embarrassing if I'd ridden straight into that.'

He walked his horse, hoping they wouldn't have heard him, and then when he was far enough away he broke into a gallop, and went up-river towards the homestead. At a place where the willows were thick again, he stopped and had his swim. Normally the river was very deep here, but now there weren't more than five feet of water. It was cold, though, and he felt refreshed.

Riding back towards home, he was thinking with amusement that it was just like Mick Dooley's nerve to conduct his amorous affairs on somebody else's property, and he made up his mind to warn Mick to be more careful in future. Suppose one of the girls had blundered into the scene?

Then he began to wonder who the woman was. That bay horse. He hadn't been home long enough to know all the horses in the district. What women were there? Alison Cameron? Good lord, that was hard to imagine. Not Nell. Thank goodness he knew for certain it wasn't Nell. None of the Woollaby girls would be likely to come all this way, forty miles, for an assignation. It could be that Mick was playing fast and loose with one of his sisters-in-law. That was probably it.

He didn't let himself think that it might have been Vicky.

As he rode on, he was thinking that of course he couldn't stay here. A Cambridge degree and he wasn't even worth his keep at Billabirra. Nothing he could do here. He couldn't see himself settling down like Uncle David to a life of books and educating other people's children. Much better to get away quickly. Find himself a job in Sydney. Enlist and go and fight the Boers. Work his passage back to England. He should never have left England in the first place.

He'd forgotten all about Mick Dooley and the woman by the time he got back to the homestead. He unsaddled and turned his horse into the paddock and then came up to the harness shed to put his saddle away. As he came out of the shed he heard hoofbeats, and presently a big bay appeared from behind the shearing sheds. It was the bay he'd seen tethered at The Bend. Riding him was Vicky. He'd known it all the time, of course. She smiled as she rode up to him and dismounted. "I don't seem to have been out of the house for days," she said. "The baby was asleep so I thought a ride might blow the cobwebs away."

It was the first time she had spoken to him since the formal greeting. She began to unsaddle. Luke said, "I'll do that."

"Thank you."

And then as she began to walk away, he asked, "What the devil were you doing with Mick Dooley this afternoon?"

Vicky stood stock still for a moment, and then she turned to him, perfectly relaxed, perfectly tranquil. "Yes. I did meet Mick. He was out for a ride too." Then she turned again to go, but he grabbed her arm.

"What's going on between you and Mick Dooley?"

"Nothing," she said. "Nothing at all. I went out for a

ride and I met him. I told you. I was miserable. I had to get out of the house. I couldn't stand wondering every time I walked into a room whether I was going to find you there. I didn't know how long I could go on pretending."

No emotion. All perfectly flat, calm, matter of fact. Anyone watching her from a distance would have thought she was talking about the weather.

Luke said, "Vicky, why didn't you wait for me to come back?"

He was still holding her arm. She made no attempt to pull away from him. "They said you weren't coming back," she said.

That last year at Cambridge wasted. Completely wasted.

"You should have known I'd come back no matter what they said!" Then he let her arm go, and saw the dead white mark of his hand on it. She held it up, and rubbed it so that the white mark turned red. "I shall have a bruise there," she said, and then added in exactly the same tone, "Oh, Luke, it's been so dreadful without you. So dreadful."

Nell, coming out of the kitchen on her way to the dairy, saw them locked in each other's arms. Her first thought was, 'The fools! Anyone might see them!' She turned quickly back into the kitchen.

Then she just stood there feeling sick because she knew that the hell had finally broken loose.

Once loose, of course, there was no stopping it. It behaved very goatishly and sired more little hells all over the place. Each one was sent to lie in wait for someone in the valley.

Nell didn't see hers, because you only foresee disaster when it's brewing for someone else. It arranged for her to go for a ride one afternoon a few days later.

Jonathon was still out at Ten Mile. Luke and Vicky were going about the house being elaborately unconcerned with each other. Polly was making green tomato chutney, because the tomatoes weren't going to ripen without water. Nell had been thinking all the morning about something she wanted to write down in her notebook. Nobody at

Billabirra knew about this notebook, and she was determined that for the time being it should go on being a secret. It would be nice and cool at The Bend. She'd ride over there and swim first, and then she'd write in the notebook.

Nell's black mare was old and too close to giving up the ghost to bother much about trying to stand up to the drought. Her ribs stuck out, and her head drooped, and she looked so tired and dejected that Nell hadn't the heart to put a saddle on her, so she went to ask Vicky whether she could borrow the bay.

Vicky was in expansive mood. She was ready to give the moon to anyone who asked for it.

She said, "Of course, Nell. Take him whenever you want him."

So Nell saddled up the bay and rode off towards the river. As she got to The Bend, she was so impatient to make the best of her hour by herself that she urged the bay into a gallop, and had burst out of the clump of scrub into the clearing before she saw Mick Dooley's horse tethered there. She reined quickly, horrified. Perhaps he'd come to swim! If he was here alone he was probably swimming naked! If she . . . But he was neither naked nor swimming. He was lying on his back with his hands behind his head looking up into the trees. He was waiting for someone. Of course! He was waiting for Vicky! They'd been meeting here a couple of times a week ever since he'd come back to Cameron's Crossing.

He turned over on his side and smiled at her. "Good afternoon, Eleanor Selway," he said.

He was certainly good-looking. Those smoky eyes. What she'd give to have lashes like that.

"Good afternoon, Mick Dooley," she said. This was a formal game they'd played ever since they were children. "You look as though you're waiting for someone," she added.

He got to his feet and took an expensive looking watch out of his pocket. "The . . . the fellow I was waiting for is an hour late. He won't be coming now." Then he looked up at her and said, "I'm glad he's not coming. I'd much rather it was you here."

She knew perfectly well she should have said good-bye and ridden off then, but she didn't. The next thing she knew he was helping her to dismount just as though she weren't capable of hopping off a horse by herself. While Mick tethered the horse she went down to the river and looked over.

"It's fallen two feet," she said. "Even The Bend's going to dry up eventually."

He smiled and said, "Ah, now, it'll rain before long. You'll see."

The smile did peculiar things to her stomach, so to take her mind off it, she said, "My brother said you've been black-birding. Is that true?"

Mick went on smiling. "And which of your nosy brothers would it be that said a thing like that, Eleanor Selway?"

"There's a law against blackbirding. They probably would have hanged you if they'd caught you."

Mick agreed that it was likely they would have.

"Where did you go?"

"All round the Islands."

"Kidnapping poor natives. You should be ashamed."

Mick, grinning, said he was mighty ashamed.

Nell thought about the notebook in the saddle-bag. If he told her all about blackbirding, she could write it down, but just at the moment she wasn't in the mood for writing anything down.

"What are you going to do with all the land you've been buying?" she asked.

Mick said, "Come to think of it, you're the nosy one of the family."

"I like to know about things," she said.

Mick stretched himself out on the grass beside her. "You do? Well, now, that's very interesting because I'm just the boy that likes to tell about things."

Nell moved away a bit. "Why did you stop blackbird-ing?"

"Because I'd got all the money I wanted."

"You did it for money then? It wasn't just the adventure of it you liked?"

Mick looked at her for a long time and then said, "I did it for money."

"You like money so much?'

Mick paused again before he answered, "I like what money can buy."

She'd forgotten about the peculiar feeling in her stomach, She was interested. "What sort of things can money buy for you, Mick?"

The pause again. "Just one thing, Eleanor. Land."

"Land!"

He nodded.

"What are you going to do with it, Mick? The land?"

At that Mick roared with laughter. "I never knew a girl so nosy!"

Nell leaned closer to him. "Mick, I asked you what you're going to do with the land."

He sat up and said, "Own it, Eleanor. Just own it."

Nell was trying to imagine Mick as a sheep man. The picture wouldn't come right.

Then he put a hand on her hair and said, "Your hair shines."

Nell's stomach started feeling peculiar again. What on earth did one reply when a man said a thing like that to you? Did you dismiss it and say, 'Oh rot, it's as dull as ditchwater, really,' or did you say, 'As a matter of fact I know very well it shines, and so it ought to after all that brushing!'

She didn't say either of those things because Mick didn't give her the chance. "I remember when you were a little girl," he said. "I used to watch you riding that black pony you had. The way you both shone so bright it was a wonder to see."

She was so surprised at this that all she could think to say was, "It was?"

"When you were teaching him to jump, you used to go down by Boulder Gully . . ."

"I never knew you were watching, Mick," she said. "I never saw you."

Mick said, "I was about. Wherever you were I was always about somewhere." His hand that had been on her hair pulled her face down closer to his, and he kissed her very gently. Nell's stomach stopped feeling merely peculiar. It turned over altogether. Then Mick put his arm round her, and kissed her again, not gently this time. Nell thought, 'Now I understand about Luke and Vicky.'

CHAPTER EIGHTEEN

THE day before I left Billabirra to go back to Sydney, I was standing on the back verandah looking out over the paddocks that stretched away to the horizon.

They were green and had their most benevolent smile on. It was as though nature was making up for the fact that the world wasn't in much of a position to buy wool just then.

Not, of course, that the Selways were, by any means, down to their last yacht.

While I was standing there, Jason came bustling up from the river paddock where he'd been watching the boys breaking horses. He looked cocky, important, but preoccupied. I didn't say anything to him as he came up the verandah steps and went into the kitchen. He was only in there for about ten seconds. He'd come up, of course, for a chat with Polly. He'd forgotten.

I heard the kitchen fly-proof door close, but I didn't look round. He came and stood beside me, leaning on the verandah rail. When I thought he'd had enough time to get over it, I said, "I was just thinking how different it must all have looked during the great drought."

He looked round at me with blank, disinterested eyes.

"Uncle Jonathon and Uncle Luke were talking about it last night," I said.

He nodded and said, "The drought. Aye, that nearly did for us, that did."

I couldn't stand the blankness.

"Did the river hold out?" I asked.

That did the trick. He warmed up a bit. "The river at

Billabirra never runs dry," he said, and laughed. Then he added, "String of waterholes it was, by the summer of 1901. Above and below us it was bone dry. Poor old Andy Cameron. Not a drop of water to bless himself with. He and David Spencer and the Dooleys used to come over with drays of empty drums to carry away what water they could. I just hoped the waterholes'd hold to keep the lot of us going. Look," he said, pointing to the homestead garden and the citrus orchard beyond, "see that? Dead. All of it dead. Had to be replanted afterwards. All the water we used in the house for washing and so forth went on to the vegetables after we'd done with it. Didn't keep them alive, though. It was all too dry, deep down."

"It was as bad as that in 1901!" I said. "But you had another two years of it after that!"

"Funny the things that keep you going," he said.

He was quiet for a while after that, and I waited.

"Something Snowy said," he said.

I waited.

"We were burning dead sheep. Oh, I've just remembered. That was the day we heard that the old Queen was dead. It'd been a sort of personal blow, if you know what I mean. See, she was on the throne when I was born. I'd reckoned on her being there when I died. Well, any road, we'd heard that she was dead, and it somehow seemed the end of things in a sort of way. What was I saying? Oh, yes. Snowy and I were burning dead sheep. Have you ever seen a sheep just lie down and die? Damn' silly things. Those silly little legs. They get sort of top heavy. Well, poor devils, I suppose, when their legs get weak . . . See, once they get on their backs they can't get up again. You see 'em lying there with their legs stiff and stark just pointing straight up. There's another thing, too. The way the stupid idiots play follow my leader. There's a mob of them coming down the hill to the river for water, see. A whole bloody paddock for them to move round in, but they've got to form a line and come down one by one. The big ram in front is so weak that he falls. Do the others go round him? Not on your life! They try to climb over him. Climb over him, mind you! Before you've got time to do anything about it, there's a small mountain of sheep all trying to trample each other to death. And still the back ones are trying to climb over. Fifty merinos fit for nothing but burning in a matter of seconds!"

He mourned silently for his dead sheep for a while, and then turned to me and asked, "Where was I?"

"You and Snowy were burning sheep," I said.

"Oh, yes. Well, as I told you, I was feeling beaten because of the news about Queen Victoria. I was ready to throw in the sponge. There was the Agricultural and Grazing Company, see. They were ready to buy me out. For a song, mind. No more than a song. It would have just given us a little bit of capital to start again when we got Home. And I was thinking I ought to sell. I said to Snowy, 'Well, Snowy, you always said the bush would beat me in the end.' And Snowy chucked another sheep on the bonfire and he said, 'I was wrong, Jack. It won't beat you. It couldn't beat you when you were a Johnny Newcome, it's got damn all of a chance of beating you now.'"

Jason looked at me, with his eyes shining now. "I'd been waiting thirty years to hear Snowy say I was a good sheep man." Then he looked embarrassed, suddenly realising that this all sounded like sentimental tosh. "Funny," he said, "the things that keep you going."

I agreed it was very funny, and then I asked, "How did you get through the last two years?"

"God only knows," he said. "We had to start hand-feeding, of course. There was no lucerne. We bought chaff from South Australia. Cost us fifteen pounds a ton. We had to cart water out to the paddocks, too, because the sheep were getting too weak to come to the river. We watered the horses and the cattle at the well. We put the chaff for the sheep in hessian troughs. Polly and the girls had red raw hands from making the troughs."

I think he was back in the kitchen watching Polly and the girls sewing hessian, because he was silent for several minutes. Then suddenly he turned round and said, "People

never realise that their children are growing up and having
lives of their own."

The young Selways living and a country dying all round
them.

"I suppose," he said, "Polly and I should have known.
Trouble was, there were all those silly little things on our
minds. We didn't have time to notice the big things. There
was me, for instance, working out how long I could go on
paying fifteen pounds a ton for chaff, and there was Polly
wondering how the blazes she was going to feed the lot of us.
We couldn't eat the meat, see. It just made us sick to look at
it. We could grow precious few vegetables. Poor Polly, she
was at her wits' end to know what to do with us. You take
breakfast, just breakfast alone. After a couple of hours work
in the morning, I could put away a big steak or a couple of
chops and some eggs, and as for Jonathon . . . Well, anyway,
there was Polly wondering how she was going to feed us.

"Funny part about it was," he went on, "that we thought
everything was going along like nine o'clock with all the
young ones. There was Ted, for instance. Passed all his
exams in great style. Was called to the Bar. Then he decided
he was going to stand for Parliament. Federal Parliament,
of course. By that time we were the Commonwealth of
Australia." He grinned about that. "Fat lot of good it did
us being the Commonwealth of Australia. Rain would have
been better."

"Oh, and then there was Nell. You could have knocked
us down with a feather the day Nell came in with a copy of
the Sydney *Bulletin* under her arm. And there was a story
she'd written, with her name on it and everything. Well, you
should have heard Polly!" He laughed quite a lot. "See,
Polly didn't know whether to be very pleased or mad as a
hornet."

"Why mad as a hornet?" I asked.

"Because of the secrecy. Nell never telling any of us that
she was writing little stories. Just going away by herself, and
doing it. One minute Polly was saying, bursting with pride,
'There now, that's my father she gets that from, writing

little stories,' and the next minute she was saying, 'The deceit of it! I can't get over the deceit of it!'" He laughed again, and added, "I must say I was very pleased. Gave me something to boast about when I went into Woollaby." Then he stopped laughing. "That first story was about blackbirding. We all wondered at the time where Nell got her information about blackbirding. We decided, in the end, she must have got it from Ted. Ted was the one who always knew everything."

He was frowning when he turned to me again and said, "I wouldn't have had it happen for the world, Harry. I loved Nell. I was a daft, blundering fool."

I didn't know what he was talking about then. I've found out since, of course.

Then he was off again, talking about the young ones. "There was little John, Jonathon's son. He was growing into a fine boy. There were Jonathon and Vicky. You'd have sworn they were happy. Until Jonathon started to get a bit odd and grumpy and irritable, but that happened later on. There was Luke. I must say I wasn't very happy about Luke staying on at Billabirra. It didn't seem right that, after the education he'd had, he should be hanging round doing the work of a stockman who didn't need to know how to write his own name. Of course, when we started hand-feeding, I was glad he was still there, because we needed as many hands as we could get."

At the time I knew none of the story behind all this, so I wasn't particularly interested. I was still thinking about the drought. So I asked, "What about Cameron's and New Park? How were they getting on?"

"Well," he said, "by 1901 David didn't have any sheep left. But he didn't seem to mind. He just shut himself up with his books and waited for the drought to break. Andy, of course, was hand-feeding the same as we were." He laughed. "And was he complaining about the price of feed!"

"Oh, there was another odd thing that happened," he said. "Remember I told you about how Andy never even spoke to Alison, or faced the fact that she existed, for that matter?"

I said yes, I remembered.

"Well," he said, "he started to change. It was just after Luke got back from England. I said something or other to him one day, I don't know what it was. Some suggestion I had. And Andy said, 'I'll talk to Alison about it. See what she thinks.' Well, I couldn't believe my ears. Then, all the next year, when we had to make a lot of decisions about how we were going to carry on, Andy'd never make up his mind about anything without Alison was there to advise him. And do you know what? This is the odd part. Where Alison had always been the one that took a back seat, just sitting there imploring Andy to take notice of her, suddenly she'd changed too. She was the one that ignored Andy, treated him like dirt, said what she thought when he asked her, and went on treating him like dirt."

Jason shook his head, still wondering about it. Then he added, "We didn't see much of Alison that year. Up till then she'd always been in and out of Billabirra like one of the family. Then the day Luke got home we were all so glad to see the way he and Alison got on so famously. But after that day, she never came near us, except for some business conference with her father."

Andy Cameron, in the feed shed that night Luke came home: "Making a fool of yourself. All of them laughing their heads off." And Alison seeing them, in her nightmares, laughing their heads off.

The story of what was going on with the young ones comes of much later knowledge. Snippets picked up here and there over the years and finally fitted together. I've got to tell it here, though, just to keep things in proper sequence.

There was Alison avoiding Billabirra because she loved Luke and they all knew it and were laughing.

There was Luke torn between loving Vicky and hating himself, thinking that he must go away next week, tomorrow.

There was Vicky going on placidly, calmly, being a good

mother to little John, and a good wife to Jonathon. Having her cake and eating it too.

As for Nell. Well, for Nell there was Mick Dooley. He wasn't like anything she'd read about in books, but she loved him just the same. The trouble was that she didn't trust him. She didn't trust him an inch. That was the thing she couldn't understand, the thing that didn't match up with the books. How in the world could you be in love with someone you didn't trust an inch? When she was with him she forgot about not trusting him, because he was so tender and gay. But when she wasn't with him, the distrust would start again. All the family laughed about Mick, and said what a devil he was with the women. That made her doubt very much that Mick really meant it when he talked about marriage. Then, too, she could never get that first day out of her mind. The day when she'd asked him what he was going to do with the land, and he'd said, "Own it, Eleanor. Just own it." Suppose Mick wanted to own Billabirra? Suppose it was Billabirra Mick wanted and not Nell Selway? He had money. Her father had almost none now. Suppose . . . But for the time being, anyway, Nell just got on with the business of loving Mick, and tried to forget about not trusting him.

For a long time Jonathon had nothing on his mind except dying sheep.

Then he overheard two of the stockmen talking. After they began to hand-feed, Jonathon and Danny and Bob spent most of their time out at Ten Mile looking after things there, and one night after Jonathon had turned in, Danny and Bob were sitting yarning. Jonathon heard them laughing about Mick Dooley and some woman. He wondered who the woman was, but he was too tired to think much about it.

About a month later, in the late summer, when he was back at the homestead, he decided one evening to ride over to Boulder Gully because someone had reported some strays out there. As he was going by The Bend, he saw Mick Dooley's horse tethered. Jonathon wanted to get out to the Gully and back by nightfall, so he didn't stop to say hullo to Mick. He thought Mick must have come over to The Bend

for a swim. When he'd ridden on a bit farther, Jonathon
heard another horse a long way off, and he turned to look.
Someone was riding down to The Bend to join Mick. Jonathon was up on the ridge that was the start of Boulder Gully,
and he could look down on The Bend. The horse that was
going down to The Bend was a bay, and there was a woman
riding him, because Jonathon could see the long riding
habit.

A bay? The only woman round here who rode a bay was
Vicky. Uncle David had given him to her before she was
married.

Jonathon watched, and then both horse and rider disappeared among the willows. Vicky? How on earth could it be
Vicky? He'd left her playing with little John on the homestead verandah. Anyway, what if it was Vicky? No reason
why she shouldn't go down to swim at The Bend, was there?
No reason why she should know that Mick Dooley was
there.

Mick Dooley and some woman.

It was crazy to go thinking it was Vicky. Why, the rider
might not even have been a woman. From this distance you
couldn't be sure. From this distance you couldn't be sure
that it was Vicky's bay.

But all the way out to Boulder Gully, he went on thinking
about it, remembering how Bob and Danny had laughed
that night. In the Gully he found that all his strays were
dead, so he decided to come back and burn them tomorrow.
When he got home, Vicky was putting John to bed.

By the time winter came, they were all having to go round
every morning with sledge hammers to break the ice on the
water-troughs. The crows were everywhere, waiting to pick
the eyes out of the sheep as they fell over, too weak to
walk.

One afternoon Jonathon left the homestead to spend
another couple of weeks out at Ten Mile. When he got out
there, he found Danny shivering and burning with a fever.
At first he thought he ought to try to get Danny back to the
homestead, but then he realised he was too sick to be moved,

so he told Bob to keep an eye on him, and Jonathon rode as fast as he could back to his mother to get medicines.

It was getting late, going on for nine o'clock, as he saw the lights of the homestead in the distance, but it was bright moonlight. About a mile from the homestead there was a big clump of gums, and Jonathon was only fifty yards from it when he saw Dooley's horse, and tethered close to it was the bay. There was no mistaking it this time. He was close enough, and the moonlight was bright enough for him to have a really good look. It was Vicky's bay all right.

He wanted to stop then, but he didn't dare to because of Danny. In a blind fury, he urged his horse into a gallop, then he remembered that the poor beast was in no condition for galloping, so he slowed down again, and rode the rest of the way telling himself that there was some explanation, and that of course it had not been Vicky with Mick Dooley.

When he got home he told his mother about Danny. She began to bustle about getting medicines out, and then Snowy, who was there in the kitchen with Jack having a warm and talking about whether the hand-feeding was doing any good, said he'd take the stuff out to Danny because his horse wasn't in bad condition and was fresh. So Snowy went out to Ten Mile, and Jonathon went to see if Vicky was in the bedroom.

She wasn't there. She wasn't with young John either. He was sound asleep. She wasn't in the front room, she wasn't anywhere on the verandah. Jonathon went to bed, but though he was dead tired, he couldn't go to sleep. Vicky came in about an hour later. Jonathon pretended to be asleep, and Vicky got undressed and got into bed, and snuggled up close to him to get warm. But he went on pretending to be asleep.

While Jonathon was pretending to be asleep, Luke was getting into his own bed. He'd just had an awful scene with Vicky. He'd made up his mind that this time it was finished. He was sick of feeling guilty. Sick of everything. He was going away. Good God, he hadn't so much as opened a book in the past year! Here he was, wasting his time, wasting his whole life!

He'd tried to make Vicky understand, but there was no getting through to her. You just couldn't get past that cool, calm complacency. She knew she had him. Well, not any longer. She didn't have him any longer. He was going away.

Luke didn't sleep very much, and was out of bed at dawn. He dressed and went out to his usual job of watering the cattle and horses at the well. He was thinking that somebody else would have to do this next week. After he'd attended to the watering, he went to get the bundle of green branches they'd chopped off the river gums yesterday. The cattle liked the green. The air seemed to be full of the cawing of crows. Everywhere he looked, fences and branches were black with them.

He went back to the house for his gun, and then went down to the lucerne paddock that was now no more than a brown vacancy. He clambered through the slip rails, eyeing the crows on the fence. They weren't even afraid of him. Waiting for him to fall down so they could get at him, probably. Well, he wasn't going to have any trouble with his aim. Even shooting at random, he'd not be able to help hitting one. Then he saw something moving in the paddock. An enormous, fat hare. And there was another one, and another. The paddock was full of them! How the hell did they stay so fat? They must have come down from the foothills after the lucerne roots. He got one with the first shot, and the crows rose from the fence and the trees in a black, screaming cloud. He shot six hares before the rest managed to escape, and he felt very proud of himself as he gathered them up. Mother had been wondering what they were going to eat. She'd be delighted about the hares.

Before he was out of the paddock, the crows were settling again.

Up in the homestead, Polly and Nell were getting breakfast, and Polly was wondering how much longer the last side of bacon was going to last.

Vicky came in with little John, and Nell put him up in his high chair. Polly cooked him the one egg that the six remaining scruffy-looking hens had managed to lay between them, and he tucked into it without any unhappy thoughts about food shortages.

Then Jonathon and Jack came in, rubbing their hands to get the circulation back.

Vicky was very bright and very cheerful and wanted to know why Jonathon hadn't stayed out at Ten Mile. She'd gone out for a walk, she said, and she was very surprised to find him there in bed when she got back. He'd been so sound asleep, she hadn't wanted to waken him.

Jonathon only grunted and left Polly to explain about Danny. None of them took much notice of Jonathon's grumpiness, because he was often irritable lately. They all had other things to think about. Even Nell was off guard, because she was feeling pleased with herself. Another one of her "little stories" had just been accepted by the *Bulletin*, and she was waiting for a moment to break the news.

So it was then, when everyone was thinking of something else, that all the little hells decided to get together and make one glorious eruption.

Vicky started it. She said chattily to Polly: "While I was in Cameron's Crossing yesterday, I was talking to Mick Dooley, and he said he was driving into Woollaby today and would bring back anything we wanted. So I thought . . ."

Polly was just on the point of saying how very nice that was of Mick, when Jonathon exploded.

"When you were in Cameron's Crossing yesterday! My God! That's the flaming limit!"

Everyone stopped eating and drinking and stared at him in astonishment.

Then Jonathon got up and went over to young John, picked him up out of his high chair, thrust a piece of bread into his hand and took him out to the verandah. "See if you can count the crows, will you, son? I want to know how many there are this morning." Stoning the flaming crows was one of John's favourite games. "We'll have to know how many stones we'll need," Jonathon said.

John nodded and sat on the verandah steps and began to count the crows on the nearest fence. He could only count up to ten, so each time he reached ten, he started from the beginning again.

Back in the kitchen they were all trying to behave as though nothing had happened, but Jonathon hadn't finished yet. "So you're having the nerve to rub my nose in it, are you?" he said to Vicky.

It was the first time any of them had ever seen Vicky frightened. "I . . . I don't know what you mean," she said.

"Mick Dooley's what I mean," he said. "Mick Dooley and you!"

Nell thought she was going to be sick, so she hung on to the table and dug her nails into the wood, hoping that would keep her stomach in the right place. Jack sat paralysed with surprise. Polly put her hand on Jonathon's arm, and said, "Jonathon, I'm sure . . ."

Jonathon said, "I'm sorry, Mother. I didn't mean to come out with it like this in front of everyone!"

Vicky had got over the first shock, but she was still frightened. Even Jack could see that. "Jonathon," she said, trying to laugh, sounding shaky, "what are you talking about?"

Nell was still praying that she wouldn't be sick.

So Jonathon told them about hearing the boys laughing about Mick Dooley and some woman, about seeing Vicky's horse at The Bend, but not being sure enough that it was hers, about seeing it again last night.

Vicky said, "I wasn't there, Jonathon! It wasn't me!"

Jonathon said, "Where were you last night then? I was awake when you came in. Where were you till nearly midnight?"

That was when Vicky looked more frightened than ever.

Jack hadn't been able to say a word. All he could do was sit there, staring at Vicky and Jonathon. Then Nell's voice made him turn to her. Nell, swallowing hard, said, "You're on the wrong track, Jonathon."

And then they were amazed to see calm, complacent Vicky turn to Nell and snarl, "Keep out of this, Nell!"

Jonathon ignored Nell. "Where were you last night?" he asked Vicky again.

"I . . . I told you. I went out for a walk. It was such a lovely evening. I went down to the river and . . ."

"You went for a walk! You went to meet Mick Dooley! I saw your horse, and . . ."

"I didn't, Jonathon! I swear I didn't!"

Nell could see through the kitchen window. Luke was coming up from the river with a gun and something that looked like a rug slung over his shoulder.

Jonathon said, "If you weren't with Dooley, I demand to know where you were!"

Nell knew she had to do something before Luke came in. Luke would ruin everything. She had to do something. She said, "It wasn't Vicky who was with Mick Dooley last night, Jonathon. It was I."

There was a dead silence.

They could hear little John out on the verandah. "Seven, eight, nine, ten, one, two, three . . ."

Vicky relaxed back in her chair and closed her eyes. Jonathon and Polly turned to Nell, and Jack got up very slowly from his chair. "You, Nell?" he asked.

Nell said to Jonathon, "It was me you saw last summer. I'd borrowed Vicky's horse. I've often borrowed him lately because mine's in such bad condition."

Jack said, "You and Mick Dooley?"

Luke was coming closer. She had to get it over and done with. "Yes. Mick Dooley and me. I've been sneaking out every chance I could get during the past year to meet Mick Dooley."

Jack was surprised to hear how loud his voice sounded when he yelled, "Get out!" He hadn't meant it to come out like that. He'd expected it to sound more bewildered than angry. Nell said, in a tired sort of voice, "Are you ordering me out of the house, Father?"

"Go to your room," he said. "I'll give you Mick Dooley! I'll take a stockwhip to you both! Get out!"

And very slowly Nell went out of the kitchen. Polly made a move to follow her, but Jack said, "Let her alone, Polly." So Polly stayed in the kitchen.

Jonathon was still standing beside Vicky. "I'm sorry," he said. "God, I'm sorry." Vicky got up from her chair and, without looking at him, went out.

It was at that moment that Luke burst in the back door looking as pleased as punch. "Look, Mother, "he said, "I bagged half a dozen hares!" He turned to Jonathon and Jack. "The lucerne paddock was full of them this morning. After the roots. Look, they're as fat as butter! How do you think they've managed it?" He held the hares up, waiting for Polly's cries of joy, but she only said, "They'll do nicely for dinner," and turned away to the stove.

It was only then that Luke realised something was wrong. He looked from one to the other, Jonathon miserable, his father both bewildered and angry, his mother uncertain. He knew then that he had to watch his step. "Anything wrong?" he asked warily. Nobody answered him. He felt ridiculous standing there with his hands full of rifle and hares. "Did I interrupt something?"

Jonathon mumbled, "I've just made a complete bloody fool of myself, that's all."

Luke waited for the rest.

"I accused Vicky of messing about with Mick Dooley."

The hares were heavy, but Luke didn't dare to put them on Polly's scrubbed-white table.

Jonathon added, "And it turns out that it was Nell."

Luke almost dropped the hares. "Nell!" He turned to Jack and Polly. "You don't believe that, do you?"

Jack said, not angrily, just hopelessly. "She admitted it. She's been carrying on with him for the past year."

Luke put his rifle on the table and then stamped out of the back door to get rid of the hares. On the step young John was still counting, but Luke didn't notice him.

Nell was alone in her room. Vicky had come and knocked, but Nell had ignored her. Then Luke came. She let him in.

"Is this true?" he asked. "You and Dooley?"

Nell nodded.

Luke took her hand, and his eyes were troubled. "Why didn't you tell me, Nell? Why didn't you let me smooth

things over? Why did you have to go and blurt it out in front
of the whole family?"

Nell said, "It seemed the only thing to do. Jonathon was
demanding to know where Vicky was last night. I saw you
coming up from the river, and . . ." She stopped and then
said again, "It seemed the only thing to do."

Luke let her hand go. "So that's what happened."

"That's what happened."

After a while he said, "Nell, it's over between Vicky and
me."

Nell nodded, trying to believe him, but knowing it wasn't
true, knowing it would never be over between Vicky and
Luke.

"You've known about us all along, haven't you?" he asked.

She nodded again.

"At first," he said, "I wanted to make a clean breast of it
to Jonathon so that we could go away somewhere together,
but she was always saying, 'Not yet. There's my father, and
your mother and father, there's little John. Let's wait a
while.' Always it was 'Let's wait a little while.' Well, I
never did have any guts, anyhow." Luke walked away to
the window and stood there. Then suddenly he turned back
to her. "It's you we have to talk about, not me."

Nell shrugged because it didn't seem to her that there was
any sense in talking, anyhow.

Luke asked, "Nell, are you in love with Mick Dooley?"

She didn't know how to explain about Mick, so she didn't
attempt to.

Luke said, "If you're in love with him, I'll damned well
take a whip to him and beat him into agreeing to marry you.
I can't say I relish having that crook for a brother-in-law,
but . . ."

She broke in with—"He isn't a crook, Luke. He just can't
help making money, that's all. He isn't a crook!"

Luke asked again, "Do you want to marry him, Nell? If
you do, I'll see that it's all right. I'll fix the family, too."

Nell only said, "Go away and leave me alone, Luke dear.
I want to think."

So Luke went away and left her thinking.

Afterwards they remembered that day with horror. They tried to work, but none of them had any heart in it. Nell stayed in her room, and although first Polly, then later Jonathon and Jack went to her, she wouldn't open the door. Vicky made one brief appearance for the evening meal, but she didn't speak to anyone.

The roast hare was the best food they'd had for weeks, but nobody enjoyed it.

The next morning Nell was gone. Polly went to her room expecting to have to plead to be let in, but the door was unlocked, and Nell's bed hadn't been slept in, and her clothes were gone. When Polly came into the kitchen and told them, Jack said to Luke, "Go and bring the horses up." He turned to Jonathon. "She's with Dooley. We're going after them."

Luke went out and Jack said, "I'll make that blackguard wish he'd gone to gaol for life!"

He wasn't bewildered now. He was angry and he didn't mind who knew it. He was ready to tear Mick Dooley apart. Then Luke appeared again at the kitchen door, and said, "Mick Dooley's here," and before any of them could move or say anything, Mick Dooley himself was standing in the doorway. Not the flash boyo of Cameron's Crossing, not the butter-wouldn't-melt-in-my-mouth charmer of all the Woollaby girls, not even the good-looking Mick who'd made Nell's stomach turn over. There'd been a little hell waiting for Mick too. He was right down there with it.

Jack had started off being angry and he couldn't stop himself. "Get out of my house!" he said.

Mick said, very quietly, "I will, after I've delivered my message." He turned to Polly, wearing misery like a chasuble. "She wanted you to know she's safe. She didn't want you to worry."

Polly asked, "Where is she, Mick?"

Mick said, "I drove her into Woollaby last night. She caught the train to Sydney."

Jack was still angry. "Where is she in Sydney?"

Mick said, "That I don't know, sir."

N

"You don't know! What's the use of lying, Mick?"

Mick answered, "Before God, I don't know. I wish I did."
He looked round at them one by one. "She's walked out
on me too, you see." He paused for a moment, and then
added: "I wanted to marry her. Did she tell you that?
Aren't I the stupid one, thinking I was good enough to marry
a Selway!"

They were all silent, staring at him.

Luke was thinking how he'd been going to horsewhip him
into agreeing to marry her; Polly was thinking, 'Poor Mick.
Oh, poor Mick,' and Jack was thinking, 'Good God, what
kind of a mess have I made of things!' Mick, taking the
silence for hate, turned to go, but Luke put a hand on his
arm, and said, "I'm sorry, Mick."

Mick didn't know what Luke was apologising for, but he
turned back to Jack and Polly. "She was a queer nosy one,"
he said. "Always asking questions about what it was like in
the rest of the world. And yet, the funny thing is, this is the
only bit of the world she ever really wanted." Then Mick
walked past Luke and he and his hell went out.

Jack turned to Polly. "Did she think I meant it when I
said 'get out'? She couldn't have thought I meant her to get
out of the house. I wouldn't have sent her away."

Polly said, "No, love. Of course you wouldn't."

Jack went to the back door and stood looking after Mick.
"It was all . . . it was all talk, what I said about horsewhip-
ping. He's not so bad. Mick isn't so bad. I've always known
he was the best of the bunch." Then he turned back to
Polly. "The little fool! The daft little fool! Why couldn't
she have talked to me about it!"

And that was why Nell Selway left home and, I suppose,
how she became, ten years later, Nell Brandon, and then
three years later the mother of an oaf.

CHAPTER NINETEEN

O N the day of my grandmother's funeral, I saw a middle-aged Nell Brandon meet a middle-aged Mick Dooley. You could see that he must once have been a hell of a fellow. He still had the smoky eyes, but he also had a paunch with a watch chain on it. It seems that he'd always had money written all over him, but it wasn't so subtly written by the time he was in his fifties.

Seeing them meet, you'd have taken them for old acquaintances glad to see each other again after thirty years. No more. No fireworks. But I didn't know the story then. I wasn't sniffing round minding other people's business. So I didn't register much. But just recently I asked my mother about it. She started to do the old act of shying away, but I'm up to her tricks now, and I didn't let her get away with it.

First of all I asked her, "Were you really in love with Mick Dooley?"

She considered for a moment, and then said, "As much in love as any girl of eighteen is in love." After another moment she added, "Of course, that's an awful lot of being in love."

Then I asked her, "Were you in love with him when you met again?"

She laughed and said, "Harry, that watch chain."

"It was all gone, then?"

"Harry," she said, "it was thirty years later."

Thirty years, twenty years, ten years. The number of years didn't seem important. But I'll come to that later.

"Did you really think your father was ordering you out of the house?" I asked.

She said, "Everything is so exaggerated when you're eighteen."

"Why did you leave home?" I asked. "You knew, really, that Grandfather didn't want you to go."

She thought about it for a long time, and then she said, "It's so difficult, you know, to say why one has done things. I was pretty mixed up."

Well, why not? No reason why they shouldn't have been crazy mixed up in the nineties, too.

"I wanted to know what the world was like outside Billabirra," she said, "and at the same time I never wanted to leave it. I was in love with Mick, but at the same time I was ashamed of being in love with him." She smiled. "You see, even in those days, he was very flash, over-dressed, too good-looking. Yes, I think that was it. I was ashamed of being in love with Mick."

"Did you really think he wanted to get his hands on Billabirra?"

She nodded. "I was pretty sure of it." Then she laughed. "As it turned out, I needn't have worried about that. Father would never have got through the last year of the drought if it hadn't been for Mick. If he'd wanted to, Mick could have taken over Billabirra lock, stock and barrel, but . . ." She stopped, and then went on, "There was another reason for my running away. A cowardly reason. I knew that sooner or later there was going to be an awful bust-up about Luke and Vicky. I wanted not to be there. That, I think, is the thing I'll never forgive myself for. I ran out, and left Father and Mother to bear it. I could have helped if I'd been there."

A skeleton looking for a cupboard.

They tried to find Nell after she disappeared. Luke went to Sydney, and Ted came up from Melbourne to join in the search. They spent weeks inquiring at all the hotels where they thought she might have hidden herself, but Sydney had grown a good deal since the days when Jack and Polly had known it. Nell had managed completely to lose herself.

When Luke got back to Billabirra he said their only course

was to report the disappearance to the police, but both Jack and Polly vetoed that because they knew Nell would hate it so. Luke had made up his mind to go back to Sydney. He'd even organised a teaching job in between his inquiries about Nell. But when he got to Billabirra, he only had to see Polly and Jack bewildered, defeated, to know that he couldn't leave them. So, poor Luke, without being able to help himself, set about deepening the bewilderment, dragging them farther down into despair.

They all thought that winter would never end.

The river at Billabirra, the river that never ran dry, was no more than a string of ever-shallowing waterholes and the paddocks were brown and parched. The cold wind would come razoring down from the mountains; its sharp edge would raise the surface of the soil that was no longer bound by grass, and the dust would rise in little eddies and blow into the house, on to their food, and into their clothes, into their eyes and their mouths.

For a while it had seemed that their hand-feeding was going to save them, but then they had to face the fact that each day there were more and more sheep to burn. The chaff had plenty of grain in it too, but it couldn't save Billabirra from dying.

They were in the seventh year of the drought.

They had longed for the summer, but when it came they regretted their longing, because the hot wind was harder to bear than the cold one had been, and the blistering sun opened great cracks in the parched paddocks. By midsummer, their staple diet was hare, and damper and treacle.

Mick Dooley came often to the house, a subdued Mick Dooley, not as flash as he had been. There was something he kept trying to say, but he never seemed to be able to get it out.

Luke had promised Nell that he was through with Vicky, and he meant to keep his promise. It was easy for a couple of months, because Vicky had had a bad fright that morning of the showdown with Nell. She kept out of Luke's way as much as possible.

Then, one day, Alison Cameron rode over to Billabirra
with some message for Jack from her father. Luke saw her
ride up and went to help her dismount. Alison was just as
unused as Nell to being handed down from a horse. She was
bright red with the embarrassment of it.

Luke had scarcely seen Alison in the past year. When she
did come to Billabirra she always scuttled away if Luke
appeared on the scene. In the days when he'd still been able
to laugh, before Nell's going, Jack had teased Luke about it.
"You frighten the life out of the poor girl!" he said. "What
have you done to her that she's so terrified of you?" Luke
hadn't the slightest idea what he'd done to Alison.

On this day, though, he was determined that she wasn't
going to scuttle away, so he went with her while she delivered
her message to Jack, and then he saddled up his own horse
and said he was going to ride part of the way back to Cameron's with her.

Vicky stood on the verandah and watched them go.

Luke was lonely. He was feeling that he'd go mad if he had
to stay here any longer, but he knew that he had to stay and
see it through. It couldn't be much longer, anyhow. You
could hear the death rattle quite clearly now. Luke wanted
someone to talk to. At first, as they rode slowly to save the
horses, Alison was monosyllabic. She wasn't going to be
caught a second time. All of them at Billabirra laughing at
her. But then the old Luke charm started to do its work.
Not that Luke was the golden boy any longer, the elegant
man of the world, nor for that matter the brash young
colonial undergraduate. He was a bag of bones riding another bag of bones, but he could still talk, and he could make
Alison talk. They were talking nineteen to the dozen by the
time they got to Cameron's.

Alison was horrified when she realised how close they were
to the homestead. Suppose they should meet her father!
She began telling Luke that it was nice of him to have come
this far with her, and she hoped she'd see him again soon, and
shouldn't he be getting back now because it was a long ride,
and . . .

But Luke didn't take any of the hints, he just went on riding beside her, and then the worst happened, because they rode up off the dry river bed, and there was Andy shaking his head over a dead bullock.

"Damned fool animal," he said as they rode up. "Must have wandered off by himself to die."

Alison began again to tell Luke that it was nice of him to have come this far, and good-bye for the present, and . . .

But Andy stopped shaking his head over the bullock and slapped Luke's horse on the rump and said, "By the look of him, he'll be next." Luke said he wouldn't be surprised, and started to turn his horse round heading for home, but Andy looked very affable and said, "You can't go home without coming into the house for a bit. Better stay to tea now you're here. Come on." Alison was suspicious. What was her father up to? Luke said he'd like to stay to tea.

It wasn't a very comfortable meal, because Alison had gone monosyllabic again, and all his efforts couldn't bring more than a 'yes' or 'no' out of her. Rose fussed and apologised for the meal, and kept telling him not to eat the food because she was sure it was dreadful, and then piling more of it on to his plate. Andy was more affable than Luke had ever known him, and he, too, kept trying to draw Alison into the conversation, but Alison wouldn't be drawn. Luke was puzzled. They'd all watched, during the last few months, how Andy seemed more and more to defer to Alison, and how she had seemed more and more to despise him for it, and they'd laughed about it. But Luke didn't want to laugh now, because for some unknown reason he was feeling terribly sorry for Andy. If Luke hadn't known Andy over all these years, he'd have sworn there was a sort of . . . tenderness about the way he kept trying to draw Alison into the conversation. Tenderness! What a word to couple with Andy Cameron! Luke thought about it all the way home.

It was because he was interested, curious about this extraordinary new Andy Cameron, that he started going quite a lot over to Cameron's. Inside the house, while her father was around, it was always the same. Alison tongue-tied, while Andy talked his head off. But when Alison and Luke were alone together, it was different. They got to know each other very well during the next months. Not that Alison imagined Luke loved her. She knew it was Vicky he loved. You only had to see Luke and Vicky at Billabirra, avoiding each other, but so much aware of each other, to know how things stood between them. But Alison was grateful not to have to scuttle away from Luke any longer. It was nice being friends with him.

At Billabirra they were beginning to be able to laugh again. Jack even said to Polly one day when she was preparing the hare for dinner, "There's one thing about it. Our Nell won't be living on a diet of hare," and they both laughed and felt that they were getting used to Nell's not being there.

Vicky was the one who didn't seem to be able to laugh. They were all worried about Vicky. Jonathon had a long talk with Polly about it. She was so thin. She looked ill. She'd no interest in anything any more. Look at the way she and Luke had always teased, and quarrelled, and laughed about things. Now she scarcely ever spoke to Luke.

Polly could only say what they were all saying a dozen times a day lately, "She'll be all right when the rain comes."

One morning Luke came up to the kitchen with a couple of hares he'd shot earlier. He looked quite cheerful as he handed them into the kitchen to Polly. "How are we going to have them today?" Polly thought she might curry them, and added that she'd just made a pot of tea.

Luke said he'd have his out on the verandah because he was too filthy to go into the kitchen. He had been helping to burn sheep, then he'd skinned and cleaned the hares. It was a long way down to the river to wash.

He went along the verandah, and Vicky was sitting there. 'How thin she's got,' he thought. 'Poor Vicky. She's stopped being beautiful. This is what I've done to her.' She looked round as he came along the verandah and said petulantly, "I wish you wouldn't burn sheep when the wind's blowing in this direction, Luke. The stench is awful."

"Better than the stench of fly-blown carcasses," he snapped back, to stop himself from taking her in his arms.

He wished his mother would hurry with the tea because he wanted to get away. He couldn't stand seeing Vicky sitting there, not beautiful any more, needing him to love her.

She got up and began to move away. Then she turned round, and Luke could see that there were tears in her eyes. Luke had never seen Vicky cry. He had to get away. He wouldn't wait for tea. He had to get away. Now. Now!

Suddenly Vicky grabbed his hand and said, "Luke!"

He pulled his hand away and said, "Leave me alone. I'm filthy. I've been gutting hares!" And because he knew he'd be lost if he stayed another moment, he rushed off down the steps. When Polly came out a few moments later with the tea, Vicky was standing there, looking blankly out at what had once been the vegetable garden.

Luke couldn't get Vicky out of his mind all that day. He'd been telling himself that it would work. That it was just a matter of keeping away from her. That soon, when Billabirra's fate was determined one way or another, he'd be able to go. That once he'd gone she'd settle down with Jonathon and be the old, selfish, complacent and likable Vicky again. He hadn't really looked at her for months until this morning's encounter on the verandah.

That evening he went over to Cameron's, hoping that Alison's good sense would help him to forget about Vicky. It was late when he got back to Billabirra, and everything was in darkness, and he was glad because that meant that everyone was in bed, and that there'd be no chance of his running into Vicky.

When he walked into the harness shed with his trappings, she was sitting there, on the step of the buggy, and she'd been crying.

He knew this was it.

The moonlight was shining straight in on her. It was as though she was sitting in a spotlight. The moon highlighted all the bones of her face, and left deep shadows in between. She looked hideous. The first thing she said to him was, "Luke, take me away." He didn't dare to touch her.

"It's too late now," he said. "If you'd come away when I asked you to, if you'd let me have it all out with Jonathon then . . ."

"We could go, Luke! There's nothing to stop us from going!"

He went and very carefully hung up his saddle and bridle.

"I can't stand it, Luke," she said. "I can't stand it any longer." She moved out of the moonlight and he was glad he couldn't see her face any longer. "After . . . after Nell went I told myself that I'd get over loving you, that I'd make it up to Jonathon for what I'd done to him, that . . . But it hasn't worked. I can't go on with Jonathon. I'm going to tell him everything!"

Luke said, "Tell him, Vicky. We long ago lost our chance of coming out of this with any decency." Although she was standing in the darkness, he could still see her face in his mind. Then Vicky came up to him and put her hand very gently on the side of his face, and said, "I love you, Luke."

He had to clench his hands to make them stay down by his sides, heavy.

Then she said, "You love me too, don't you?"

And Luke said, "Love and hate. I love and hate you."

She took her hand away from his face and said, "I shall die with Billabirra."

And because he could still see her face in his mind, thin and haggard, once-white skin turned yellow, once beautiful eyes dull and black ringed, because he knew that all this was his fault, Luke put his arms round her and tried to comfort her.

So it was that for the second time in four months, Polly went to call one of her children in the morning, and she found the bedroom empty. Luke had left a note. He and Vicky had gone.

It was Snowy who went over to New Park to fetch David Spencer.

David said afterwards that he was glad it was Snowy, because he wouldn't have wanted to hear the news from anyone else.

So David and Polly and Jack sat in the kitchen, just the way they used to sit together in the old humpy kitchen years ago, and David said, "All those dreams I had. Do you remember? When Jack wanted to leave here during the first years, I talked so glibly about the future. This was the place of the future, I said. This was the place in which our children were going to grow up and take advantage of all the things we were fighting for. And now my child has grown up and destroyed all our futures!"

And Polly said, "No. It's us, David. We were the ones who went wrong somewhere." She turned to Jack, and asked, "Where did we go wrong?"

Jack only shook his head, and wondered vaguely through his misery how it was that Polly managed to stay beautiful when the rest of them were as cracked and parched as the paddocks outside. He was telling himself that he'd think about Luke and Vicky later. Later. His brain was too dead to accept it just yet. He'd think about them later. He heard David asking Polly where Jonathon was, and Polly replying that Jonathon had gone off by himself somewhere. Then he heard David say, "While he's not here, we ought to talk about little John." Then Polly's reply, "What is there to talk about? I'd bring him in to see you, only Jonathon's taken him with him." Then he heard the relief in David's voice as he said, "Oh, I see."

That got through to Jack's numbed brain. "Good God," he said, "you don't suppose what's happened would make Jonathon turn against the boy, do you?"

And it was while David was smiling apologetically and saying that Jonathon would only be human if . . . that Alison knocked on the door.

Polly called, "Come in," and then Alison appeared, and just stood there.

It was a long time before she could speak. Then she said, "I had to come."

So the news had got round already? None of them knew what to say to her.

"I was at Cameron's Crossing," she said, "getting some stores. Mick sent me ahead."

Mick sent her ahead? What was the girl talking about?

Alison came away from the door and went to Polly. "They'll be here in half an hour. I've got to tell you."

Both David and Jack got to their feet. "They?" Jack asked. "You mean Luke and Vicky are coming back?"

"Luke's coming back," Alison said.

They were all staring at her. "Oh, why is it that I can never find the right words! Why do I have to tell it to you like this!"

Jack and Polly looked at each other, not daring to speak. It was David who had the courage to say gently, "What is it you have to tell us, Alison? Don't bother about the right words."

It all came pouring out then. Luke and Vicky had taken the sulky, and it had overturned about ten miles from Cameron's Crossing. One of the bullock drivers had found them about two hours ago, and had ridden back to fetch one of the Dooleys. Mick had taken charge. He'd sent one brother to Woollaby for a doctor, he'd sent another couple of brothers to put a mattress in a dray and bring it out to where Luke was. They didn't know yet how badly hurt Luke was, but . . .

"So Vicky's dead?" David asked.

And Alison nodded.

Polly put a hand on David's arm, and he smiled at her and said, "If they're bringing Luke back, you've a lot to do, Polly."

So Polly went off to prepare things for Luke's second homecoming, while David and Jack rode off to Vicky.

Mick and his brothers brought Luke home, and then Mick waited for Jack to come back. He sat on the verandah step, and as Jack walked up, he got up and waited.

Jack was in his middle forties, but he looked seventy that day. He was thin, as they were all thin. He was burned dark brown by the sun, and his hair was bleached white. The stuffing was knocked out of him.

Mick said, "The doctor's in there now, Mr. Selway."

Jack said, "I'll never be able to repay you, Mick."

"Ah, sure, it's only what any neighbour would have done. My mother's always talking about how good you were to us all way back in the beginning."

Jack said, "We all had to look after each other in those days, Mick. She helped us too."

So Mick said, "Well, I'll say good day then."

And Jack answered, "Good day, Mick, and thanks again."

Mick went to the top of the steps, and then turned and came back. "Look, Mr. Selway," he said, "there's been something I've had on my mind to say for quite a long time. It's expensive all this hand-feeding. It's expensive trying to keep going."

Jack thought Mick was advising him to throw in the sponge, so he nodded, and said, "I'm finished, Mick."

Then Mick said, "But you can't be finished! Look, there's this thing I've had in my mind to say, I've got money in the bank, you understand. A lot of money. You've only got to say, Mr. Selway, and it's yours."

Jack was so startled that all he could do was stand and stare at Mick.

"And that's not just being neighbourly," Mick said. "It's an investment. I'm quite a boy for investments. Look, I'll tell you what, Mr. Selway. I'm going to make a town out of Cameron's Crossing. A big town. If it's the kind of town I want it to be, it'll need you and Mr. Spencer and Mr. Cameron here the way you were at the beginning." And before Jack had time to say a word, Mick had turned and was running down the steps.

Luke had a broken leg and several broken ribs, and for a week they thought he was going to die. Alison stayed at Billabirra all that first day, because Polly never left Luke's side. Then Alison faced the fact that she had to go home. Home to hearing her father chortling about how Jack Selway had ridden his luck too far.

As she rode towards Cameron's, she saw her father standing by the home paddock slip rails. She gritted her teeth and waited for it to begin.

Andy made no attempt to lower the slip rails for her to go through, and she was just about to dismount to do it herself, when he came over to her. "I didn't expect you back," he said. He was neither gleeful nor gloating.

She didn't know what to say because this was so unexpected.

Andy asked, "Has the doctor seen Luke?"

She nodded and said, "He may not live."

Then Andy surprised her even more. "Polly'll need your help," he said. "She can't nurse Luke and look after them all. You'd better go back and lend a hand." Then he turned her horse round and said, "Go on. Get going. And tell Jack and Polly I'm here if they need me."

So Alison went back to Billabirra.

Jack and Andy and David Spencer took Vicky to the new cemetery in Woollaby the following day, and just as the service was beginning, Jonathon came in. Afterwards he went back to New Park with David, telling his father he'd like to stay there for a while. He didn't inquire after Luke.

Luke didn't die, but it was four months before he could manage to get round on the crutches Snowy had made for him. After the first month, when Polly no longer had to sit at his bedside night and day forcing him to live, Alison took over the nursing, and that was when Luke really began to see her for the first time. Up till then he'd been using her as someone to talk to, someone to take his mind off Vicky, someone to help him forget his self-loathing. Now he found himself waiting for her to come into the room, missing her when she wasn't there.

Glad as he was to get back on to his feet at last, he was sorry that it meant Alison could now return to Cameron's. He told her how much he'd miss her on the morning she left, and Alison thought about it all the way home.

All her life Andy had avoided the homestead as much as possible, coming into the kitchen for meals, and then disappearing God knew where, but on the evening of Alison's return, to the astonishment of both Rose and Alison, he pulled up a chair to the kitchen fire and lit his pipe.

Rose was immediately thrown into a flap and began to fuss about inquiring if there was anything he wanted, anything she could do for him.

Alison waited for him to get first irritated, and then enraged, but he didn't. He simply let Rose circle round him while he drew contentedly on his pipe and told Alison what had been going on at Cameron's while she'd been away. He wanted her advice, too. Mick Dooley had lent him some money. Did Alison think he dared to ask for more?

Mick had lent Jack Selway some money, too, but Jack knew it was no use asking for more, although Mick had said there was plenty more where that came from. Jack had made up his mind it was no use sending more good money after bad. There was no saving them now. No reason to save anything, anyhow. Nobody to save it for, except young Henry away at school. The paddocks were dead, most of the sheep were dead, and the cattle. And the worst thing was that both his sons were behaving as though they, too, were dead.

Luke kept to his room when Jonathon was in the homestead. They had never spoken since Luke had been brought back.

At the beginning of the winter there were thunder and lightning storms over the mountains, and the first few times it happened, Jack and Polly would rush out on to the verandah saying, "Perhaps it'll rain." But it didn't rain.

Jonathon never came near the house during the day, so one day Luke ventured out on to the verandah to try his new crutches. He was standing on the verandah watching the vicious flashing of the lightning in the north east, and he didn't hear Jonathon come up the steps. When he did see him, it was too late, because he wasn't sufficiently used to the crutches to get away quickly. Jonathon stopped at the verandah rail a foot or two away from him and nodded towards the distant mountains. "That happens every night round about this time."

Luke didn't say anything, and they both stood and watched the lightning for a minute or two. Then Jonathon said, "As soon as you're fit enough, you'd better have a look at the accounts. I've made a hell of a mess of them."

Luke said, "Jonathon, I don't think I want you to be friendly and forgiving."

Jonathon shrugged and answered, "It seems to me we've got more to worry about than personal feuds. We've got to stand by the old man. He can't carry this by himself."

Luke said, "Look, we've got to get things off our chests. You see, Vicky and I . . ."

Jonathon said, "Don't kid yourself, Luke. It was never Vicky and you, any more than it was Vicky and me, or Vicky and Mick Dooley for that matter. It was Vicky and whoever was most useful to her at the moment."

Luke had always known that. He'd never had any illusions about Vicky. He said, "Jonathon, I had been wanting to tell you about it. I . . ."

Jonathon shrugged again and said, "That wouldn't have suited Vicky at all. She wanted to be certain which one of us would come out on top. There was always the chance that I might end up owning Billabirra. She wouldn't take a chance on throwing that away to go off with someone who'd probably end up as a badly paid school teacher or a civil servant or something."

Luke winced at that.

Jonathon said, "In the end, of course, two things helped to swing the balance. Billabirra wasn't worth anything, anyhow, and you were in danger of falling for Alison Cameron. Vicky thought that even a half-baked schoolmaster was better than a bankrupt property owner."

Jonathon had been saying all this perfectly calmly and unemotionally. Now he added, "I'm being deliberately brutal, Luke. I've got to get the hate out of me if we're going to get back on to the old footing."

All Luke could say was, "I'm sorry, Jonathon." Jonathon said, "you don't have to be sorry for me, Luke. I came out of it best. I've got young John. Anyway, I don't deserve anyone's sympathy. I knew what Vicky was when I married her. From the very first I was a man striking matches into a keg of dynamite knowing damned well something was going to have to blow up some time. Don't think I didn't hate your guts at first. I've had four months to think about it, that's all. Now, what are we going to do to help the old man?"

It turned out that they didn't have to do anything to help the old man, because the bush had decided it had given Jack Selway enough of a beating.

A couple of days later, Jack was standing on the verandah watching the lightning and thanking God that Jonathon and Luke seemed to have made it up, when there was a hell of a hallooing and a yelling, and the noise of a horse being ridden to death. Jack was just thinking that he'd tear the lights out of whoever was trying to kill the poor beast, when Mick Dooley and his foaming horse appeared in a cloud of dust round the side of the house.

Mick flung himself out of the saddle, and came hurtling up the path.

"Mr. Selway! Mr. Selway!"

Jack said, "Mick, what the devil's the matter?"

And Mick, the Irish Greek messenger, yelled, "It's raining in the mountains! Mr. Selway, it's raining in the mountains!"

Mick was dancing about with excitement.

Jack yelled, "Mick, you're drunk!"

But Mick yelled back: "As God's my judge, I haven't had a drink. My brother's just got back from Woollaby. He heard the news there. It's raining in the mountains. He came home yelling fit to wake the dead. They said it'll be raining in Woollaby by nightfall."

People started appearing from all directions to see what all the noise was about. Polly from the kitchen, Luke from the front room where he'd been wrestling with accounts, Jonathon from the harness shed, Snowy from the smithy. As each one of them appeared, Mick went on yelling, "It's raining in the mountains! It's raining in the mountains!"

Jack yelled above him, trying to bring some sanity to the

o

whole business, trying to stop them all from having to face another disappointment.

"Mick," he yelled, "that thunder and lightning's been happening every night for weeks!"

Mick stopped yelling. He was pleading to be believed. "It's God's truth," he said. "It's raining in the mountains."

Then Snowy said, "He could be right, Jack. I've got a feeling he's right."

Jack grabbed Mick by the lapels. "It's not just a rumour, Mick?" He was almost crying. "Your brother was sober?" By then Mick was almost crying too. "I swear. I swear he was sober!"

Jonathon said, "The wind's coming from the north-east. It'll blow it here."

Snowy said, "Round about midnight, I reckon."

Luke, swaying on his crutches, was praying aloud, "Oh God, don't let the wind change!"

Snowy said, "Jack, we'd better get to work. The earth's as hard as a rock, and it'll be days before any water can soak into it. The rain'll all just run off into the river. The river'll be running a banker by morning."

The river running a banker!

Jonathon ran to tell somebody to ride over and warn Andy Cameron, sombody else to warn David Spencer. Snowy turned to Mick and said, "You'd better get that no-good family of yours to work, Mick. Cameron's Crossing's going to be under water tomorrow."

And you'd have thought, to see Mick riding off, hallooing and yelling again, that he couldn't wait to see Cameron's Crossing under water.

Snowy said to Jack, "We've got plenty of time, but I reckon we ought to start moving everything on to high ground."

Luke said, "Oh this damned leg!" and Jack grinned at him, and said, "There's plenty of ways you can make yourself useful," then he threw his arms round Polly and said, "It's going to rain, love! It's going to rain!" They all began to laugh and Jack threw his arms up to the sky and yelled, "Come on, you beautiful rain! You bloody beautiful rain! Put us under six feet of water and see if we care!"

They all went on laughing, and were still laughing when Jack and Snowy went off to put all hands to work.

At midnight they were all in the kitchen, the family and Snowy. They'd driven what was left of the stock up into the foothills, and everything that was movable had been cleared out of the sheds and storerooms. The verandah was piled high with saddles, and harness, and drums, and sacks, and packing-cases.

They sat in the kitchen and waited. Even young John was there, for it had been no use trying to get him to bed.

And then, at midnight, the first drop fell on the iron roof. They rushed out on to the verandah, and stood there and watched it as it came down in enormous isolated drops at first, and then there was a great crash of thunder, and a flash of lightning that seemed to split the sky open and let out all the rain that had been waiting there for seven years.

In a few minutes they couldn't hear their own voices because the rain was drumming on the roof with a noise that could have been made by a mob of wild horses.

And while they hugged each other and laughed and cried and wondered how long the flood was going to keep them marooned, young John stood at the verandah rail and stared out in astonishment.

He was nearly six years old, and he'd never seen rain before.

CHAPTER TWENTY

I REMEMBER, when I was a kid, how my mother used to tell me about when she first came to Sydney in the time of the Great Drought. She lived in a boarding-house in Strathfield. She told me how food was short, and there were no fresh vegetables, and how fruit was too expensive to buy, and how the water-carts would come round selling water, and how there never was enough water for washing.

She also told me how the children had to begin each morning at school with a prayer for rain, and how the same prayer was said before they went home from school in the afternoon.

It may have been this powerful offering up of prayer that did the trick, because my mother said that one night when she was in bed, sound asleep, she was wakened by a great commotion in the street. She got up and went to the window and the whole neighbourhood seemed to be gathered there, and they were all yelling at the tops of their voices. She put her head farther out of the window to see what it was that they were yelling about, and an enormous drop of water fell on her cheek. She said she looked up to see where the water was coming from, and then two more drops landed on her face. Then she heard what it was they were yelling in the street.

"It's raining! It's raining!"

She got dressed very quickly, and by the time she, too, was in the street, it was raining hard, and the gutters were beginning to run, and everyone had joined hands and they were dancing round and round, singing: "It's raining! It's raining!" There were children in their night clothes, and people half-dressed, and people fully dressed, even some people in full evening rig.

And there they were, all soaked to the skin in no time, dancing round and singing.

My mother told me that story over and over again.

On the night before I left Billabirra to go back to Sydney, most of the family came over to the homestead for dinner.

Uncle Luke and Aunt Alison came over from Cameron's, and Frank, their son, David's older brother, came with them.

My cousin John came over from New Park. He managed New Park for his grandfather. When I say managed, I really mean that he was looking after it for himself, because when Mr. Spencer died, New Park would belong to John.

Uncle Jonathon ran Billabirra, with Jason, of course. And Aunt Alison and Frank ran Cameron's. Uncle Luke was the business manager of all three properties. David called himself the general rouseabout. He worked on whichever property needed him.

I was starting to get them all sorted out.

Uncle Luke and Aunt Alison had another son and two daughters. The son, Andrew, their eldest boy, was a doctor in Woollaby, the two girls were married. One of them to that Parker of Woollaby, and another one to a grazier in Queensland. They weren't there on my last night. They'd all come to Billabirra for the funeral, of course, but had only stayed a couple of days.

The family were beginning to get over the shock of Polly's death. My mother had even reached the stage where she could say half a dozen words to someone without bursting into tears.

While we were having dinner they all started talking about old times, catching my mother up on everything that had happened while she'd been away, and everyone was being gay and cheerful. At one time David turned round to Aunt Alison and said, "Do you remember the Christmas Night Grandfather got drunk and fell in the river?"

Jason looked scandalised and banged his fork on the table

and said he'd never in his life been drunk enough to fall in the river.

They all laughed and David said, "Not you, Grandfather. I'm talking about Grandfather Cameron."

Then Jason said, "Good lord, yes!" and he turned to my mother. "I never can get used to the idea of sharing grandchildren with Andy Cameron." Then he turned back to David. "It wasn't the river he fell into. It was the sheep dip." Then he roared with laughter.

Uncle Jonathon grinned, "It was the river, Dad."

Jason looked very knowing. "I heard a rumour it was the sheep dip."

Uncle Jonathon said, "You started the rumour yourself. Don't you remember?" Then Jason roared with laughter again, and nodded. "So I did."

Aunt Alison, smiling, put in, "I happen to know it was the river, because I had to go in and fish him out. My best dress was ruined."

David got his gentleness and his charm from Uncle Luke, but it was from Aunt Alison that he got his strength. Not that she was one of your tough hombres, even though she did run a sheep station. She was tall, thin, had the most beautiful red hair I've ever seen. Not ginger, or copper, just red. My mother said she'd never been attractive as a girl, but she was certainly attractive in middle age. She and Uncle Luke made a most impressive couple.

While they were still laughing about Andy Cameron falling in the river, my mother said to David, "I used to be terrified of Andy."

David laughed, and answered, "He was a wonderful old boy. He and I got on like a house afire."

Jason laughed delightedly and said to my mother, "You wouldn't have known him in the last years, Nell." Then to Aunt Alison, "Turned into a regular Father Christmas, didn't he?"

I kept watching Aunt Alison to see whether she minded all this, but she didn't seem to. She was as much amused as the others.

When she turned to my mother, she was smiling.

"I'll never forget the evening I had to break the news to him that I was going to marry Luke."

My mother, laughing too, said to Uncle Luke, "Don't tell me you left the poor girl to do it all by herself."

Uncle Luke said, "What could I do about it? I was still on crutches. No chance of my riding fifteen miles to Cameron's to ask formally for her hand."

"What happened?" my mother asked Aunt Alison.

Aunt Alison said, "It was just after the flood waters had gone down, and we were in a sea of mud. I got back to Cameron's covered in mud from head to foot. All the way over I'd been rehearsing what I was going to say, how I was going to break it gently. I never was much of a one for long speeches"—she looked at Uncle Luke, smiling—"but I knew this one would have to be long. I think I thought if I could befuddle my father with words, I'd have it all confessed before he had time to fly into a rage. Well, I walked into the kitchen and there were Papa and Mamma sitting on either side of the kitchen range like a couple of strangers in a railway carriage, and then I . . . I completely forgot the speech I'd rehearsed, and I said, "Luke and I are going to be married."

The rest of the family had obviously heard this story many times before, but that didn't stop them from laughing. Then they all began to butt in with their own particular stories about Andy. Knowing the end themselves, they'd completely forgotten that Mother didn't.

She had to yell to make herself heard. "Wait a minute, Alison hasn't finished." Then to Aunt Alison, "What happened?"

Aunt Alison said, "For about ten seconds I thought he was going to get into such a rage that there'd be no stopping him from killing me. His hair and beard were bristling. You remember the way they used to bristle? Then Mamma began to cry, very loudly, and suddenly Papa, still bristling, turned round to her and said, 'For God's sake, woman, pull yourself together! It's good news she's brought us!'"

My mother was amazed. "He didn't mind?"

Aunt Alison said, "He kissed me. He'd never come within twenty feet of me in all my life. But that night he kissed me, so I suppose he didn't mind."

The others obviously hadn't heard this last part of the story before. And there was something in the way she told it that made it not a pay-off to be laughed at. Everyone was quiet for a moment, then Aunt Alison turned to Uncle Luke, laughing again, and said "Pass the salt", so the moment was over, and they all had their chance to tell their Andy Cameron stories.

Then Jason said to my mother, "Don't think, mind you, that he was all sop and honey. He was still ranting and roaring at me for pinching the best part of his river the night he died."

Every now and then I'd looked at Uncle Jonathon. He was enjoying the Andy Cameron jokes as much as anyone. No sign that Vicky was on his mind. I found myself wondering about Vicky. Wondering what she was really like. All their descriptions of her tallied. She was beautiful, she was arrogant, she was selfish, and complacent. Yet they'd all loved her. What else had she had that had made them love her? What really went on behind the bland and beautiful face? I'd have liked to know what Vicky Spencer was really like.

After they'd finished telling their Cameron stories, my mother said to Aunt Alison, "I'm glad you made Luke stay here, Alison. I always thought he'd go away somewhere. Back to England perhaps."

Aunt Alison answered, "I didn't make him stay."

Uncle Luke added, "I'd already made up my mind to stay when I asked Alison to marry me." He looked round at Uncle Jonathon, smiling. "I decided I couldn't very well spend my life in the Indian Ocean in a rowboat trying to make up my mind whether I was an Englishman or an Australian. It turned out that I was an Australian."

"What made up your mind for you?" my mother asked.

"The end of the drought. My God, Nell, you never saw

such grass as we got after that rain! It was as though nature had stepped in and decided to teach us a lesson! We'd been dragging the guts out of those paddocks for years, and it seemed as though we had been forced to spell the land to give it a chance to renew itself!" Uncle Luke stopped, as though ashamed of his enthusiasm, and he looked at Jason and Uncle Jonathon and grinned with embarrassment. "Well, anyhow, I began to get interested in raising sheep."

Jason said, "Talked our ears off, he did. Top dressing, better culling methods . . . Oh well, it's a fine thing when you've got to send your son away to get himself a Cambridge degree so that he can come back and tell you how to raise sheep when you've been doing it for thirty years."

But you could see Jason was pleased about Uncle Luke having talked their ears off.

I left Billabirra the next morning to go back to Sydney, and David drove me into Woollaby in the dirty great sports M.G. that he was having to endure until the depression was over and he could afford a new one. As we went through Cameron's Crossing he pointed to where there seemed to be some new building going on.

"Mick Dooley," he said, "starting to turn Cameron's Crossing into a city. He will in the end, too, you'll see."

The one street of Cameron's Crossing looked as though it had a long way to go. Still, it had started with one pub. Now there was a whole street of shops.

"Mick's just waiting for the depression to get itself over and done with," David said.

Prosperity is just around the corner.

After we left Cameron's Crossing we didn't talk very much. I was thinking that I'd soon be seeing Jan. I'm pretty certain David was also thinking that I'd soon be seeing Jan. I mentioned her once, casually, but he didn't bat an eyelid.

It wasn't until we'd gone another few miles that I realised I'd been trying to give him the chance to talk about that night before Polly died. Why for God's sake? What did it matter whether or not he told me about it? I'd seen them, hadn't I? I'd seen the way he and Jan had looked.

To take my mind off the way they had looked, I asked him about Snowy. I'd been meaning to ask Jason what had happened to Snowy, but somehow had never got round to it.

David said, "He died. It was just a few years ago. He was going on for eighty. One day he told Grandfather that the place was getting so full of people he couldn't hear himself think, and that he was going to move on." He turned his head. "You know about Snowy's moving on?"

I said I knew about it.

"Well, Grandfather, Grandma, Uncle Jonathon . . . everyone, tried their best to argue him out of it, but that night he saddled his horse and packed his swag and called his dog and went. The next morning we were all out searching for him, and about midday the horse came back alone. Later on we found Snowy where he'd made camp for the night. He was there beside the ashes of his fire wrapped in his blanket, and the dog was sitting beside him."

We got to Woollaby in plenty of time for my train, and then we both stood about, not knowing what to say to each other. There was nobody he could tell me to give his love to; it was no use his telling me to write, because we both knew damned well I wouldn't.

So when the train came and I'd got in, we just said good-bye, and he said, "Keep in touch, Harry," and I said I would, and then, after the train had pulled out of Woollaby station, I was miserable because I knew I should have tried to find something to talk to him about. I was feeling like that bullock one of my cousins had compared me to.

It was late at night when the train started to run into the suburbs, and I began to cheer up. In the backs of all the houses along the railway line lights were going off, and going on, and people were going to bed, and getting up, and being born, and dying, and making love, and quarrelling, and doing nothing except wait for another day. I was getting the feel of the city again.

By the time we got to Central, I was excited. I was in clover from now on. I was independent. My mother was safe at Billabirra and I didn't have to worry about her any more. I didn't have to come home and tell her I hadn't got the job. I didn't have to feel her watching me, wondering what I really thought of the road. I didn't have to watch her counting pennies, working out that if we didn't pay the rent this week, we could eat.

From now on I could do what I liked. If I didn't get a job I could go on the dole. If I did get a job navvying or something, I didn't have to worry about what she thought of it. I could paint. Whenever I wasn't working, I could live on the dole and paint, and nobody looking at me with her head on one side giving me a conscience.

I was in clover.

I couldn't wait to get back to the flat. I'd start painting that night. I knew just exactly what I wanted to do with the foothills. I'd dump my bag, wouldn't bother about unpacking. The sketches were on top. It was just a matter of getting them out and going to work.

I let myself into the flat and I turned all the lights on, and I dumped my bag, and . . .

I didn't even bother to open it to get the sketches out.

I just looked. The flat was exactly the way we'd left it in a hurry on Saturday morning. My clothes flung all over the sitting-room, an old handbag of my mother's lying on the kitchen table with its torn lining hanging out. A cockroach sitting on the sink saying "welcome home".

I had the horrors.

I'd never lived in an empty place before.

I didn't kill the cockroach because he was company. I made myself a cup of tea, but I went on having the horrors.

The trouble was it was too late to go round to Jan's place. It was midnight. She'd be in bed.

So I and the cockroach celebrated my first evening of living in clover.

CHAPTER TWENTY-ONE

THE next morning there was a letter from my mother. She must have written it before I left Billabirra. Indeed, it must have come down on the train with me. In it there was a cheque from Jason.

So much for independence.

I thought about how my mother had been the only one of the family who hadn't tried to urge me to stay at Billabirra, with the exception of Jason, of course. I thought about how she'd never tried to urge me to do anything, how she'd never tried to push herself into my mind, or make demands on me, or put over the lonely widow with an only son stunt. I thought about how we'd said good-bye when I left Billabirra, just as though we were going to meet again for lunch, and the rest of the family, an affectionate and demonstrative lot, looking on, rather puzzled, thinking that Nell and this son of hers were an odd pair and no mistake.

She didn't say much in the letter. Just that she was there at Billabirra if I wanted anything.

I didn't have to go back to the road for two more days, so I was looking forward to painting now that the daylight had blocked out the horrors. I went down to the grocer's at the corner and stocked up with provisions so that I wouldn't have to think about anything except painting; and Jan, of course.

I'd fill in the day painting until it was time for Jan to come home from work.

I got out the sketches of the foothills and sat down to let them watch me, but Jan's face kept getting in between us. Jan's face the way she'd looked that night with David. I got

the canvas ready and I cleaned my brushes and I set everything out, and then I sat down again to let the foothills
watch me. They couldn't because Jan was still there.

In the end I didn't do any painting that day, and then,
when I knew Jan would be home, I cleaned myself up and
went round to her place. She threw her arms round my neck,
and she kissed me, and she said, "Oh, I'm so glad you're
back," and everything was wonderful again. We went out
for a walk and we walked for hours, and she asked me all
about Billabirra, and all about the family, and she said she
couldn't wait to see the sketches and could she come and
watch me paint, but she didn't once mention David.

I tried again the next day, to paint, but it was no good.
The day after that I went back to the road, and all the boys
kidded me about not having been able to think up something
more original than a grandmother's funeral to get me a week
off work. Each day, when I finished with the road, I'd go
home and try to paint. Most nights Jan would come and
watch me. She'd sit there knitting, or sewing, or reading, and
I'd splash paint all over the place, but it was still no use. The
damned foothills wouldn't even look at me.

Then we came to the end of the road. It had turned out
that we had had to go up to the intersection, after all. So the
day we got to the main road, we looked back, and there was
our handiwork, and we were paid off. The foreman said
there'd no doubt be more roads.

I spent a week wandering round trying to find something
else to do, and then I went on the dole. But I still couldn't
paint.

And then, after a couple of weeks, it suddenly hit me. I
was killing cockroaches at the time. Then this thought suddenly hit me, so I left the cockroaches to do their damnedest,
and I didn't try to paint any more that day. I just waited for
Jan to come in the evening.

This thought that had come to me was that the foothills
didn't have a chance in the world of seeing me properly
while Jan was there getting in between us.

I feel I ought to make all this clear right here and now, so that nobody will think that I was doing the big self-sacrificing hero stunt.

The way I looked at it was this. I didn't have any money, and was never likely to have any. Girls wanted to get married. All girls wanted to get married. But how the devil could I ask any girl to marry me and live on a few bob a week? I'd only be putting Jan in my mother's place, that's all. Watching Jan counting pennies. I'd just broken free of all that. I was independent.

Jan came round that night, and I pretended to work for a while, and then I thought I'd better get it all off my chest. So I said, "Jan, look, you know I'm not the marrying type, don't you?"

Sensitive as a bullock.

She looked at me, surprised, and then after a bit, she said, "Aren't you, Harry?"

"The trouble with me is that I'm ambitious," I said. "I'd like to be a good painter one day."

She nodded and said she knew that.

So then I went on, "Now that Mum's settled, I'm free to live the way I want to live."

Her eyes were wide open. She was staring at me.

"If I'm going to be a good painter," I said, pulling one foot after another out of the bog, "I've got to steer clear of ties. Look, Jan, am I the sort for three-piece suites, and babies' nappies and a house on T.P.?"

She said very quietly, "No. I suppose you're not."

"I don't want to paint just in week-ends," I said. "I don't want ties, Jan."

She didn't say anything for a long time, but eventually she said, "Don't you love me, Harry?"

I said, "I don't love anybody. Except maybe myself. Not what I am now. What I might be."

Well, for God's sake, women are beyond me! I was expecting her to throw her arms round my neck and tell me this was wonderful because now she could marry my cousin David. But she didn't. She just sat there looking dismal, and, so help me, jilted.

I went on floundering round in the bog for a while, getting in deeper all the time; me, my painting, my independence, my life. Me.

Then suddenly Jan said, "Harry, I want to tell you about something. About your cousin, David Selway."

What could I do? Play innocent? Say I already knew what she was going to tell me?

I said nothing and let her talk.

"We . . . that is, I fell in love with him that night we met here at the party."

I didn't say anything.

"It was the same for him, but we knew it was ridiculous, falling for each other like that, just in a few minutes. We didn't intend to see each other again."

I wanted to say something, to help her out, to make it easier, but I was still down in the bog.

"Then the . . . the night before your grandmother died, we met by accident. In Pitt Street. Imagine! The whole population of Sydney in Pitt Street in the rush hour and we had to meet. If we'd been looking for each other, you can be certain everything would have conspired to keep us apart. But we met in Pitt Street."

Why the hell couldn't I say something?

"We spent the evening together, had dinner, went to the pictures, and then he took me home."

I know he took you home. Didn't I see him taking you home? Isn't that the whole bloody trouble?

I still didn't say anything.

She said, "We didn't see each other again." Then after a while she added, "I just thought I'd tell you."

And I said, "Sounds very romantic."

And then she asked, "Was it you who came round the corner into our street that night, just as David and I got to our gate?"

"Me!" I said. "No. Why would it have been me?"

She said, "I saw someone. I thought for a minute it was you, but I couldn't be sure because he turned and disappeared so quickly."

I said no. It wasn't me.

Jan said, "I just thought, if it was you, I'd explain why I was with David that night."

I said, trying to sound hearty, "Well, you're in love with Dave, and he's in love with you. Everything's turned out fine."

But the silly girl went on looking jilted and said, "It's you I want to be in love with, Harry."

"Want to be! How the devil can you be in love with me and Dave at the same time?"

"I was in love with you before David came, and I can be in love with you again. It's just a matter of time."

And I said, "But I don't want you to be in love with me!"

Of all the damned silly conversations!

"Look, Jan," I said, "the whole thing's worked out fine. I want to paint, and you want to marry David. No need for either of us to feel guilty about the other. It's worked out fine!"

So after a while I took Jan home, and we said good-bye at her gate, and I went back to the flat, and the minute I walked in, I knew I was going to have the horrors again.

It was hell being independent.

I didn't see Jan during the next week, and then one morning pandemonium broke out in our street because the news had just leaked through from Jan's street that Jan was going to marry the son of a squatter!

Mrs. Mulligan said she'd never been so surprised in all her life, because there she'd been walking down the street carrying the potatoes, minding her own business, when suddenly this great big rich-looking car had skidded round the corner on two wheels, and it had stopped in front of Jan's place with a noise loud enough to wake the dead, and then this very good-looking fair young man had hurtled out of the car and gone racing into Jan's house.

"A squatter!" Mrs. Mulligan said to me.

I said Fancy.

Then Mrs. Mulligan began to tell me for my own good

that if I'd stop messing about with them paints and things, girls wouldn't walk out on me and marry squatters, and it was quite a long time before I managed to get away from her.

I went back to my flat thinking that if Dave was in Sydney it would be just as well for me to be out of it. A chap I knew had a shack down at Whale Beach. He'd told me I'd be welcome any time, so I packed my painting stuff, and a toothbrush, and my swimming trunks and went down to Whale Beach.

When I got back a fortnight later, Jan and David were married and away, and forgotten by both streets, because a new couple had just moved into Mrs. Casey's top front, and Mrs. Mulligan was busily trying to find out whether they were any better than they ought to be.

I didn't enjoy the next six months very much. I worked around here and there, off and on, and I did a lot of painting.

When it got warm enough I went down to the beach, and there they all were, the same old faces, and the same old bodies rubbing themselves with coconut oil to get a tan going, but it wasn't the same somehow, without Jan there. It wouldn't have been so bad if Big 'Ead and the others hadn't been so tactful. It was their god-awful tact that kept reminding me that she wasn't there.

Someone only had to mention roast lamb, and a dreadful hush would fall on the whole Club, and so many people would rush in to try and change the subject that it would be bedlam for a couple of minutes.

So I gave up going to the beach much.

Then another chap I knew got into difficulties. He'd just got himself nicely settled with a good job in an advertising agency, with not much money but a lot of prospects, and he and his wife had decided that they could risk having a baby, and then the baby turned out to be triplets. They couldn't very well go on living with her mother with triplets, so I let the flat to them, and I packed my gear and went walkabout.

P

I wandered for a year.

I did some fruit picking, and some potato digging, and some odd jobs on a dairy farm, and anything else that turned up. If I didn't have the price of a bed I slept out, and if I couldn't earn the money for a meal, I scrounged one. I did a lot of sketching, and I stopped missing Jan. By the end of the year I was enjoying my independence, and Jan wasn't getting between me and the foothills any longer.

I decided the time had come when I could go back to Billabirra and have another go at the foothills.

I was up in New England, so I started making my way west down the mountains, and I got to Billabirra just before Christmas, and my mother said, "So you've turned up at last!" and then she said she wanted to have a look at the sketches I'd been doing, so we sat down on the verandah and I opened my swag and showed them to her.

Then other people began appearing and exclaiming and making a fuss, demanding to know where I'd been, and why hadn't I written, telling me that my mother had been wondering where on earth I was. I told them about having been waltzing matilda for a year, and it was obvious that they thought I was madder than ever.

I'd been hoping that David and Jan wouldn't be there. I'd reckoned that they would probably be living at Camerons. It turned out that they were at Billabirra after all. But I knew it was all right the moment Jan came out on to the verandah to see what all the noise was about, because she kissed me and put her arm through mine, and said she wanted to know everything I'd been doing in the last eighteen months.

I saw my mother looking at us with her head on one side, that look she used to have when she was adding up figures. And I realised that it must have been quite a surprise for her when David came back from Sydney with Jan as his wife.

Then David came up to the house, and I saw her watching him, and watching me, and watching Jan. When David and I said we were glad to see each other, and how was he and where the blazes had I been, my mother's head sat straight up and looked relaxed.

Then Jan and David dragged me off to see their son, who was six weeks old, and called Mark, and the spitting image of David.

So there were Jan and David. Another little curtain coming down, and they were living happily ever after.

I enjoyed that Christmas. The family were all back to normal again. Jason wasn't avoiding the homestead any longer. He was always popping up to the kitchen for a chat with my mother and Jan. And there was my mother back where she'd begun, back in the kitchen at Billabirra. There was no need for her to be in the kitchen, of course. The others had talked and talked at her when she first came back about how they'd tried to persuade Polly to have more help in the house.

I remember they talked about it during that family dinner the night before I left Billabirra the first time. They'd got side-tracked a bit, because Jason had insisted on telling us about Ted.

"It was about five or six years ago," he had said. "Ted arrived with his wife and the two snivellingest children you've ever seen. They didn't stay more than a couple of days. Mrs. Ted was scandalised because Polly still did her own cooking. Talk about landed gentry! You should have seen them. All the airs and graces about the place! Well, I suppose we were all a bit disgraceful, because the more they did the landed gentry caper, the more we carried on like dungaree settlers." He had turned to the others. "Weren't we disgraceful?"

They'd all roared with laughter and told stories about the things they'd done and said to shock Mrs. Ted and the two snivelling children.

Then Jason had shaken his head and said, "I'm sorry to have to tell you that we were all as glad as can be when Ted suddenly got an urgent message calling him back to Canberra. We never knew how he got the message, because it didn't come in the post or on the telephone. Carrier pigeon,

I wouldn't be surprised. Yes, I reckon Ted would be an important enough man to get a message by carrier pigeon." He'd looked round the table again, enjoying himself. "I'm told Ted's always throwing his pioneer squatter family into the conversation, hoping, of course, that none of his friends will ever come here and see what crude bushwackers we are."

After he'd finished his story, they'd remembered about Nell and the kitchen, and had begun again to tell her that nobody expected her to look after the place. They could get plenty of help, and . . .

But my mother had been adamant, and now here she was running the house with the help of Nessie. Nessie was a girl from Woollaby whose parents had been killed in an accident back in the twenties, and whom Polly had rescued from an orphanage.

At first I'd thought my mother had taken it on as a penance, but now I could see that she was enjoying it. Now it was Nell who was saying, "Nessie, I want you to run down to the storeroom," or, "Now, Nessie, I want you to run and fetch the cream."

Altogether things were going well at Billabirra. The price of wool was going up. Frank and John were looking around for wives, and David and Jan were obviously living in a world so overcrowded with enchantment that the wonder of it was spilling out all over the homestead. Some of it even spilled over me, and I felt very benign and kept telling myself that it was nice that we were all so happy.

I didn't dare to risk it for long, though. As soon as I'd got what I wanted out of the foothills, it would have to be back to Sydney and living in clover for me.

There was a radio in the front room. Jason had said at first that he wouldn't have one of those noisy things in the house, but then Mick Dooley had built a special shop that sold nothing but radios, and Jason had said that since local trade ought to be encouraged, they might as well have one of the infernal things. They could always turn it off except for the weather report and the cricket scores.

During my three weeks there, it was never turned off from
early morning until last thing at night. My mother said that
in the winter they moved it out to the kitchen.

On Boxing night we listened to Uncle Ted on the radio.
He made a speech about how prosperity was definitely round
the corner, and we could all look forward to great things.
The future had never been brighter, Uncle Ted said.

CHAPTER TWENTY-TWO

D URING the next couple of years, I always had a picture of them sitting round the radio at Billabirra. In the front room in the summer, and the kitchen in the winter, listening to how a King had died, and how another one had abdicated, and how Germany had taken over the Rhineland, and how Abyssinia had been annexed by Italy, and how Japan had occupied two Chinese provinces, and how Civil War had broken out in Spain.

My friend with the triplets had got a rise and was flush enough to move into a house, so I went back to the flat.

I got enough odd jobs to keep me going nicely, and I went on painting. Every now and then I'd have another go at the foothills, but they never would come right.

Then my mother wrote to tell me that old David Spencer had died, and I was sorry, because I'd liked him. I thought, too, about how it must be for Jason, being the only one of the first ones left.

Those were the years of the talking. Everyone talking. This one bailing you up in a corner and telling you to look at Russia, and that one taking you by the lapels and telling you that you only had to look at what Hitler had done to build up Germany, and another one saying that anyway Musso only wanted to introduce plumbing to the Abyssinians.

A couple of the boys from the beach went to join the International Brigade.

It was all very confusing. The only way we could find out anything was by reading the papers, and the papers were confused themselves, because everybody kept changing their minds about whose side we were on.

We seemed to be an awfully long way away from where it was all happening, anyway.

Uncle Ted made a speech in which he said that all war-mongers should be behind bars. Uncle Ted personally assured us that there would be no war.

I spent several weeks working on the wharves loading pig iron. It was a Japanese ship we were loading it on to.

Uncle Ted went on giving us his personal assurance that there wouldn't be a war, and when Chamberlain flew back from Munich, and made his announcement, you could have knocked me down with a feather.

I was sitting in the tram reading the paper at the time and I said aloud, "Good God, fancy Uncle Ted being right for once!"

The woman sitting next to me thought I was drunk and moved away.

Early in September of the next year, Uncle Ted said on the radio that there wouldn't be a war.

On the next Sunday I was out painting all day and I didn't get back into town until after dark. I thought I might as well get myself something to eat in town, and I walked up from Wynyard to Martin Place. As I came to the G.P.O., a fellow I knew, a radio announcer, came running down the steps. He had a couple of days' growth of beard on. He stopped when he saw me, and said, for no reason, except perhaps to explain the beard, "This is supposed to be my weekend off."

I said the G.P.O. was the last place I'd want to spend a weekend, and he said, bleakly, "It's come, Harry. It's bloody well come, after all," and then he made off up Martin Place.

I thought it was likely that all that announcing was going to his head, and I went on. Sydney seemed to be deserted. Sunday night. Everything closed. I decided I'd have to make do with a sandwich in a milk bar.

I was the only customer in the milk bar. There was a girl behind the counter reading a book and curling one curl

round and round on her forehead. She stopped long enough
to give me my sandwich and my milk shake, and then she
went back to it.

There was a little radio on the end of the counter. It was
playing music. It was playing "Deep Purple", and I was
listening to it, and thinking about how I'd wasted a perfectly
good canvas that day.

Then the music stopped, and an announcer's voice said,
"Will you please stand by for a special announcement."

I stood by, but the girl went on reading and curling her
curl.

Then I didn't have to stand by any longer, because the
announcer said that on the B.B.C. Mr. Chamberlain, the
Prime Minister of Great Britain, had just said that . . .

Well, we all know what he'd just said.

" . . . and I have to tell you that no such undertaking has
been received . . ."

The girl was still reading her book, and curling her
curl.

I finished my sandwich and milk shake, and I went over
to pay for it. I waited till the girl had come to the end of a
chapter, and when she got up to take my money there were
tears in her eyes. She smiled, embarrassed. "It's such a sad
book. I've just got to the sad bit."

I paid her, and went out, and let her get on with it.

After I'd walked for a bit, people began to appear from
all directions. Difficult to know where they'd come from.
On every street corner the newsboys were calling the
special edition. It was there in great, black letters. "War
Declared!"

People everywhere were in twos and threes. I seemed to be
the only person in the whole of Sydney who wasn't in twos
and threes. I couldn't stand going back to the flat. I wanted
someone to talk to.

All this talking that had been going on for years. People
buttonholing you and bashing your ear off about something.
Now, just when you wanted someone to bash your ear, there
wasn't a soul you knew anywhere. In the end I went into a

coffee shop which looked to be nice and crowded. If I
couldn't talk to anyone myself, at least I'd be able to hear
other people talk. I sat down at a table opposite a boy and
girl. It wasn't until after I'd sat down that I realised he was
in a blue uniform with a red stripe down the trousers.
Militia.

They didn't talk. They just sat and held hands and didn't
even look at each other.

So then I went back to the flat.

Of course, there was one thing about it. Big 'Ead, and all
the boys down on the beach, and myself got the first permanent jobs we'd had since we left school.

Six bob a day, and you should have seen me in my uniform! It was weeks before it unstiffened enough to look as
though I was in it. I always had the feeling that I was walking round and that it was walking beside me. One of Buck
Menzies' Little Blue Orchids. Laugh? You'd have killed
yourself.

While I was training I didn't get the chance to go up to
Billabirra, because on a forty-eight I'd have spent all my
leave getting there and back.

By the time the Brass had decided that at least I could get
a Wirraway into the air, and land it again, the uniform was
starting to fit, and it seemed that my courage and fortitude
were required in other climes. So I was on final leave, and
back at Billabirra in no time. I had to have a last go at those
blasted foothills.

The family, I think, were scandalised. When I got there,
very pretty in my Air Force Blue, they were all ready to have
a lovely wallow because I was the first to go, and they
couldn't believe it when I spent my whole leave painting the
foothills. My mother and Jan laughed their heads off, and
that only made things worse.

All the time I was painting, Jason sat on the stump and
watched me.

John and Frank had already enlisted and were waiting for
their call-up. Everyone was trying to tell David that it was
all very well for the rest of us to go, since we had no ties, but

that he had Jan and Mark to think of. It was obvious that David was getting restive.

On my last night everyone was very gay, and John said, "We'll meet up in Paris and make a night of it, Harry."

Paris, of course, still belonged to the French.

Then Uncle Luke threw a cloud over the proceedings by saying, "Maybe you won't get as far as Paris, John. Maybe you'll end up on some beach on the north coast."

John said, "Oh, lord, Uncle Luke, you're not going to start on that rot about the Japs."

Uncle Luke said, "They're making an awful mess of things in China."

"But that's got nothing to do with us!"

"Once they've won their war in China it could have a lot to do with us. What the Japs want is room to expand. There are teeming millions of them, and here are we, eight million of us, the population of London, rattling round in a country bigger than Europe."

John said, "Oh, I'm not saying they wouldn't like to take Australia, Uncle Luke, but I am saying they wouldn't be crazy enough to try it."

David, frowning, asked, "Why not?"

John turned to him. "Good lord, isn't it as plain as the nose on your face? Are the Japs likely to face the Royal Navy?"

Uncle Luke said, "Perhaps we shouldn't take the Royal Navy for granted, John."

John puffed out his chest and got a bit pompous and began to say that the day Australia felt she couldn't depend on the Royal Navy . . .

For a second I thought Uncle Luke was going to get into one of his glorious rages and swear like a trooper, but he didn't. He just interrupted very quietly, "That isn't what I meant, John, and you know it. What I meant is that we should be doing something about our own defence instead of hiding behind the Navy."

John was very scornful. "I can't understand you, Uncle Luke. You're supposed to be the brains of the family, and yet you can't see what's obvious to everyone who knows the slightest thing about the Near East. We've got Singapore and we've got the Royal Navy. Now would the Japs, unless they were raving mad, beat their heads against two impregnable walls like Singapore and the Royal Navy!"

I don't remember the rest of the conversation. Nothing very remarkable about it. The same sort of argument was going on round dinner-tables all over the country.

As a matter of fact, I didn't think about it again until it came back into my mind a little while later, when John just happened to be in Singapore.

The next morning I said good-bye all round and David drove me to Woollaby. It was different from our last drive to Woollaby, though, because this time Jason insisted on coming too.

He kept the conversation going all the way. He showed me all the new building Mick Dooley was doing, and I could see that Cameron's Crossing wasn't a township any longer.

"Proper scoundrel Mick is," Jason said, "but we all like him. Funny how he never got married. Quite a boy with the girls, Mick was. Dozens of nephews he's got, though. I never knew anyone with so many nephews."

When we got to Woollaby Jason said to me, "Well, Harry, I suppose you're going Home?"

I said the brass hadn't told me just exactly where we were going, but that I guessed we were going Home.

Jason nodded, and then the train came in and I left Woollaby and Billabirra.

We had another forty-eight a couple of days before we sailed, and a crowd of us collected some girls and went down to Romano's. You had to climb over kitbags and gas masks and tin hats to get in the foyer because they all wouldn't fit in the cloakroom. The band played "Hitler's Secret Weapon" and "We'll Hang Out Our Washing on the Sieg-fried Line" and the Maori Farewell.

There wasn't anybody there to whom I particularly wanted to say farewell.

We went Home.

When we got there our stomachs started doing triple somersaults because we hadn't expected falling bombs to sound like that.

CHAPTER TWENTY-THREE

PERSONAL memories play dead round about here.
I remember the letters from Billabirra, though. The nights when I couldn't sleep, I'd think about them sitting there in the kitchen at Billabirra, a lifetime away from anywhere, and a new sound and a new voice right there in the kitchen with them.

Big Ben and: "This is London. Here is the news, and this is Alvar Liddell reading it."

I thought of Jason hearing that London was in flames, and about how he'd been going to make his fortune and how Polly would ride down Piccadilly in her own carriage. I thought about how, out there, thirteen thousand miles away, the secure ground was slipping from under their feet because if there wasn't a London, there wasn't anything.

Jan wrote to say that David and Frank had gone to the Middle East.

My mother wrote to say that John was livid. After all, he'd been the first of the three to enlist and there he was still cooling his heels at Holdsworthy.

Then John wrote to ask where the hell did I think he'd ended up? In Singapore, of all places! There he was, looking forward to a bit of fun, and now here he was in the impregnable fortress of Singapore!

Well, how was Gunner Selway to know that the generals were all going to be looking the wrong way?

New places started to come into the Billabirra kitchen. The only Greeks the Selways knew were the ones who ran the fish and chip shop in Woollaby, but suddenly Frank was in Greece, and it stopped being just the place of the ancient heroes. They looked up Crete on the map, too. They heard, for the first time, of a place called Tobruk.

The shearing was over and the wool away, and they were all settling down to a miserable Christmas without the boys when they heard about another place called Pearl Harbour.

Their main interest was still centred on London.

"Suppose," my mother wrote to me, "we turn on the radio sometime, and there isn't any Big Ben?"

But there was no need to turn the radio on, for the simple reason that it was never turned off. Their lives were planned round it. It blared away with its music and its commercials and its chatter, and then they'd all stop whatever it was they were doing to listen to the news. It was blaring a popular dance number when the announcer interrupted to say the Japs had just sunk the *Prince of Wales* and the *Repulse*. It was intoning a church service when Singapore surrendered.

Poor Gunner Selway.

Then it went on blaring its various routine programmes with announcers coming in at intervals to remark in passing that the Japs had overrun Burma and Malaya, that the Dutch East Indies had fallen, that Java, Timor, Rabaul had been captured, and that finally New Guinea was invaded.

I sat in one of those new-fangled flying machines and thought about how things were getting close to home. Next stop Darwin.

How long would it take the Japs to get down to Cameron's Crossing? A couple of weeks at the rate they were moving. All that grinning and hissing was going to frighten the hell out of the sheep.

Uncle Luke wrote to say that Uncle Ted Selway had said on the radio that the time had now come when everyone must put their shoulders to the wheel.

The trouble was that there wasn't any wheel.

The only trained men were overseas. Certainly there was an armoured division, but it didn't have any armour. The militia were training with broomsticks and soaking their slouch hats in water so that they wouldn't look so new. There were a couple of obsolete training planes buzzing

about, and there were also a couple of coastal guns, but
though they banged and buzzed and rattled their loudest,
they couldn't, for the life of them, sound and look like an air
force and a coastal defence.

But they put their shoulders to the non-existent wheel, and
they painted out all the place names so that when the Japs
arrived they wouldn't know whether they were in Woolloo-
mooloo or Katoomba, and they took all the rowing-boats
and fishing-boats and dumped them inland to rot. They put
barbed-wire entanglements on all the Sydney beaches, and
in no time at all, half the infant population had scratched
itself and got blood poisoning. They had a mock battle, and,
after it, generals were bowler-hatted in all directions because
the invaders got right through the Martin Place while the
defenders were having breakfast.

The Japs were moving down across New Guinea and their
Zeros were bashing away at Darwin.

Frank was busy in Tobruk, and John was busy building a
railway for Emperor Hirohito, so David was the only one
who got home. Everyone wrote that it looked odd to see him
in jungle green.

The next letter I got was from my mother. David was
buried somewhere in the New Guinea jungle by the time it
reached me.

But on the news it said that the Japs were being pushed out
of New Guinea.

When it was all over in Europe, I went to finish my war
over Japan. I didn't have anything to do with the dropping
of Those Bombs, but I can't pretend that I'd have had a
conscience about it, at the time, if the job had fallen to me.
I, like everyone else, was only thinking about getting the
damned thing over and done with.

On VJ night, Uncle Ted made a speech at some dinner or
other, and all the papers reported it the next morning.

Uncle Ted said that everyone must thank God that it was
all over, and that they could now get back to their normal
lives. He also said that we were all safe now for all time. It
could never happen again, Uncle Ted said.

CHAPTER TWENTY-FOUR

W E went back to Sydney for demobilisation, and the day we were free men again, we all told each other that though we meant each other no harm, we hoped we'd never have to see each other's ugly mugs again.

I woke up on the first morning with a glorious sense of freedom. Nobody to tell me what to do! Not to have to listen any longer to Jonesy's grumblings; not to have to hear McKenzie talking about the women he'd had right through Britain, Malaya and Japan; not to have to feel sorry for Bluey Harris because his wife had ditched him for an American; not to have to be irritated by Jimmie Long's sniffle. Oh, it was wonderful to be free.

By lunch-time I was thinking that I might just pop into the Long Bar at the Australia in case someone should be there I could talk to. They were all there. We were so glad to see each other, you'd have thought we'd been parted for years.

I don't remember much about the next fortnight. I knew I ought to go to Billabirra to see my mother, but somehow I always missed the train. However, by the end of the fort-night I had accumulated such a hangover that the horrors of civilian life were deadened, and besides, the boys were start-ing to have consciences about their kinfolk. So we broke up the party and I went down to the beach for a couple of days' health cure before I faced Billabirra.

The beach had changed, and I didn't like it much.

Then I got back to Billabirra to find that it hadn't changed at all, except for the fact that David wasn't there; that his son was nine years old; that Jan was just a body that walked

round with nothing inside it; that Jason was an old, old man;
and that John was a walking skeleton just home from Changi.

My mother and Uncle Luke and Uncle Jonathon were all
standing around helplessly apologising for the fact that everything was still so much the same.

I wanted to tell them that I'd spent two weeks getting
drunk in Sydney because I'd been so afraid that it wouldn't
be the same. But you can't tell people things like that and
expect them to know what you're talking about.

I got out my painting things that I'd left there, and had a
go at the foothills, but it was no use. Jason came and sat on
the stump, but that was no use either. I'd lost contact with
him. I didn't feel any longer that I was sitting on a tree
stump watching myself paint.

The trouble was that I was an outsider.

They were all wrapped up in their grief over David, and
their anxiety over John, and the years were stretching ahead
of them, making circles from lambing to shearing and back
to lambing.

I was the outsider and I knew it was my fault. So I went
away.

I went back to Sydney, and I fell in with some R.A.F.
types who were ferrying transports back to England. I got
myself on board and was back in London in less than a
week.

That was when the wandering began.

I'd loved London during the war because I'd felt part of
it. But I wasn't part of the London of 1946. I was an outsider again.

The people who'd been so gay and full of courage while the
bombs dropped were glum and sunk in dreariness while they
cleaned up the mess. They were like patients enduring a
long and tiresome convalescence after shock treatment. One
felt one was intruding. One thought it best to tiptoe out of
the ward, and come back with the flowers later.

I lived in Paris for a while. There was an atmosphere of
convalescence there too, but of a different kind. You felt
that all these patients were looking at each other, and at the

doctors and nurses, in a puzzled, suspicious way, wondering
who the devil they could trust. There were lots of cheerful
patients in the wards, though. Half the American army
appeared to have returned to Paris to study something or
other. You could see them studying like mad every night on
the Champs Elysées.

Then I went to Italy, and spent a year just wandering
around looking, and wondering how the hell I'd ever had the
temerity to think myself a painter.

But habit gets the better of you in the end, so after a while
I began painting again.

I went on painting and wandering for ten years.

If you kept away from the cities you could live cheaply
enough, and you could usually earn a few lire or francs.
When the tourists started to arrive it became easier, because
there were all sorts of cafés and bars that needed English-
speaking barmen or waiters. If you couldn't get a work
permit, you could always put an insane gleam in your eye,
and then the tourists would all tell each other that you were
a mad painter, and they'd come and ask you to do a picture
of the beach, or the port, or the square.

After ten years I ended up in Spain. Until then I'd been
painting for exercise. Alien scenes on alien canvas. Mountains, seaports, villages, churches, chalets in the snow and
vineyards in the sun. Then, in Spain, I began to get a feeling
of contact. The landscape began to feel familiar. It had that
hostile, aggressive, lean look that the rest of plump, tamed
Europe lacked. It had that feeling, too, of sun-roasted space.

The first thing I did in Spain was to get out the sketches of
the foothills, and with Spain all round me I started to paint,
and Jason was sitting on a tree stump watching me.

For the first time, the foothills came right.

I stayed in Spain for three years. Then one day a party of
tourists came to look at the church. I was working a couple
of hundred yards along the road. I was trying to put a
Spanish landscape on canvas, but I was thinking about the
dust, and the blowflies, and the heat, and the part of the
river you could see from the verandah of the Dooleys' pub.

I heard the tourists talking as they came out of the church and turned back towards the village. I thought they'd all gone, until I became aware that someone was breathing down the back of my neck.

I began to reckon how many pesetas I could ask for a study of the church.

After a while, the tourist, an Englishman, asked, "Have you got any more canvases?"

I told him I had a roomful back at the *residencia*, and he said he'd like to see them.

I showed him what I had, and kept the foothills till last. It turned out that he was a dealer. He wanted to buy the foothills, but I wouldn't sell. So in the end he took half a dozen other things back to London with him.

I had a letter from him six months later, asking for some more, so I thought it was time to pack my things and stop trying to escape.

I found that London had cheered up tremendously. The scars were healed, and the patient had made a full recovery. It was mid-winter, but the lights were on again, and everything was back to normal. The food was still terrible, but there was plenty of it, and two Londoners still automatically formed a queue, but it was good to be back again.

At the hotel the manager scowled at me when he found out I was an Australian. The porter looked, for a moment, as though he was going to throw the tip at me, but then he thought better of it.

Reading my paper the next morning at breakfast I first came across the name Meckiff, and everything became clear.

Once, early in the war, a chap said to me in the mess, "The trouble with you Australians is that you don't treat cricket as a game. You take it too seriously."

Well, I wouldn't be surprised if he was right, but I do know that for the rest of my first day in London I passed myself off as a French-Italian-Spaniard. On my way to the gallery in the bus, I sat next to an elderly schoolboy with a large white moustache and no hair. He was reading the cricket reports and looking as though he was going to burst. I didn't dare to open my mouth to tell the conductress where I wanted to go in case my accent gave me away.

My friend at the gallery told me he was prepared to offer me a show. I was terrified of that. I knew the best stuff I'd done was Australian, and for me to follow Nolan and Drysdale in London was pretty cheeky. I also knew, however, that it would be most eccentric of me to turn the offer down. So it was arranged that I'd have a show in the spring.

London seemed to be full of Australians. You ran into them everywhere. Someone once likened the post-war American in Europe to a sad-eyed Spaniel sitting up and begging to be loved. The Australian is a dog of a different breed . . . a sort of Irish-Scotch-Welsh-English Terrier-cum-Setter. And it never occurs to him that he isn't loved. He comes bounding into the kennels of his ancestors with his paws splayed everywhere, face a-grin, tail a-wagging, bark a-barking, ready to shower everyone with his devotion and affection and to show off all the clever tricks he's learned. "Look, Mum! I'm home!" It's a long time before he wakes up to the fact that the breed is not acceptable at Cruft's.

During the weeks before my show all the Australians I met were either at the "Look, Mum, I'm home" stage, or at the puzzled, aggressive "I can't understand why Mum doesn't love me" stage. No sitting up and begging.

I spent those weeks feeling rather like the filling in a sandwich. On one side cricket-inspired distrust, and on the other side Mother-complex-gone-wrong heartburning.

When the time came for my show, however, it turned out that either the critics didn't read the cricketing journalists or that time had healed the breach, because the thing didn't go off at all badly. They liked the foothills.

I was in the gallery one day, because I was still naïve enough to like wandering in to hear comments. I felt safe in the knowledge that nobody would recognise me as the artist, because I look so much more like what they call a sheep farmer, and I was hanging about, all ears, when I noticed four extremely well-dressed visitors. They were standing in front of the foothills, and I edged closer to hear what they were saying.

Then I realised that they were fellow countrymen. They weren't at any stage of the Mum complex for the simple reason that they were trying very hard to pretend they weren't Australians at all. The antipodean vowels somehow sounded so much worse when they unexpectedly popped out from among the so carefully cultivated Mayfair ones.

It's funny how you become accent-conscious in England. You ask a perfect stranger the way, or you talk about the weather to someone who happens to be near you at a cocktail party, and before you've got five words out, they'll say, "You're an Australian, aren't you? I recognise the accent." Or some cockney waitress, or some Lancashire bus conductor will say, "You're an Australian. I can hear the twang!"

At first it seems like sheer bad manners, but you get used to it after a while. Maybe it's that you get less thin-skinned.

While I was trying to decide whether or not I dared to edge closer to my elegant countrymen, a voice beside me said, "Hullo, Uncle Harry."

Uncle Harry! Me? Somebody's uncle?

I turned round, and standing at my elbow were a good-looking boy, and an even better-looking girl. I must have looked as astounded and suspicious as I felt, because they both laughed, and the boy said, "It's all right, Uncle Harry. I'm Mark. Mark Selway."

Mark Selway. He was Jan's son.

He wasn't trying to cover up the vowels, and, indeed, seemed unaware that there was such a thing as a Mum complex. I liked the look of him.

Then he introduced his wife, and her name was Christine, and to say that she was beautiful was putting it mildly.

"What are you doing here?" I asked him.

He explained that he'd been over for two years at a School of Animal Husbandry at Cambridge. Animal Husbandry! I ask you! How scientific can you get!

He was a nice boy, a thinner, taller edition of David. He looked a little like Jan too.

I said, "Let's get away from here where we can talk. Let's go and have a drink." I'd forgotten that it was the middle of the afternoon and that there were licensing laws. They both reminded me that it would have to be tea, and then Mark added, "If we're going, let's go quickly."

I didn't know what he meant. "Quickly?"

He had his back to our countrymen, but he gestured with his head and said, "I'm not strong enough to cope."

"Do you know them?" I asked. I was thinking, of course, that they looked rich enough to buy something.

Mark said, "Come on," but it was too late because the quartet had been looking at Mark all the time we'd been talking, and the two men had had a conference, and now they were bearing down on us.

The leading one put his hand on Mark's shoulder, and said, "Mark Selway! Fancy meeting you here!" Then Mark had no choice but to introduce his wife and me to Mr. and Mrs. Tom Dooley, and Mr. and Mrs. Dan Dooley.

First the Dooleys twittered over Christine and then they twittered over me. Vowels went slithering and sliding in all directions.

Mrs. Dan Dooley wanted me to settle an argument for them. Was that big picture a painting of the foothills beyond Cameron's Crossing?

When I said it was, Mr. and Mrs. Tom beamed triumphantly at Mr. and Mrs. Dan, who'd obviously been the doubters, and then all four of them beamed on me as though they expected me to congratulate them on their perception.

Then Mr. Tom cleared his throat and became Chairman of the Board, and the vowels came thick and fast.

Mr. Tom said that although he hadn't yet been in touch with his Uncle Mick—he wanted me to be quite clear about that—he wanted me to understand that what he was saying was not meant, in any way, to commit Uncle Mick to anything—but what he meant to say was that, although he hadn't yet been in touch with his Uncle Mick, he had a pretty good idea that when he did get in touch with his

Uncle Mick, his Uncle Mick would, in all probability, be prepared to buy the foothills . . .

I broke in to say that I regretted that the foothills were already sold, but Mr. Tom didn't let me get it out. He put his hand on my shoulder and said, "I can just see that picture hanging in the saloon bar of the Cameron's Crossing Hotel. Can't you see it, Mark? Don't you think it'd look right on that wall? Just the right size and everything."

When I finally got through to murmur my regrets, the Dooleys were very disappointed indeed, but then Mrs. Dan cheered up and said perhaps I'd do another picture for Uncle Mick to hang in the bar, and I said perhaps I would, and then the other three cheered up too, and invited us to drop in later for a drink at their hotel. They looked very relieved when we said we had another appointment. I expect they thought I was pretty scruffy to be seen around a civilised hotel.

After they'd gone, Mark said, "You won't recognise Cameron's Crossing when you see it again."

I said that it sounded as though Uncle Mick was quite a power, and Mark said, "He keeps the whole family as far as I can see. He sends them all to the best schools, and on trips round the world, and he buys them mansions with swimming pools, and all they have to do to earn their keep is sit on boards."

Then I took Mark and Christine out to tea, and I must say I regretted that Big 'Ead and the boys weren't around to see Harry Brandon going out to tea at four o'clock in the afternoon.

My correspondence had been rather a hit and miss affair during the last years. I'd wandered round Europe so much that I'd never established any permanent address. I wrote to my mother and sent her cards to tell her where I was and how I was, but since I never knew whether I was going to stay in one place for six minutes or six months, it wasn't much use going into details. I expect there are letters still waiting for me, poste restante, in cities all over Europe. Some letters did catch up with me early in the piece, of

course. That's how I knew that Aunt Alison, Mark's grandmother, had died about five or six years ago, and that Frank
and John were now married and producing families at an
alarming rate.

I should have stopped in Barcelona on my way back to
London. I had known there'd be letters waiting for me in
Barcelona, but I had deliberately avoided collecting them.

It wasn't until I met Mark in the gallery that I realised
why I hadn't collected them. The old man, Jason, was over
a hundred years old, and even legends don't live for ever.
I hadn't wanted to read on an air mail flimsy that Jason was
dead.

It turned out that he was still very much alive. I didn't
ask Mark, because I was still trying to work my way round
to it when he came out with, "Grandpa's as spry as a
cricket!"

That was all right then. Now I could drink tea.

Mark said, "He gets the family mixed up sometimes,
particularly Uncle John's and Uncle Frank's offspring, and
occasionally he goes off into a world of his own and orders
someone to pack rations for him because he's going off for a
couple of weeks to inspect the fences, or comes ranting into
the house threatening to play merry hell with Andy Cameron
next time he meets him." Mark laughed. "Auntie Nell says
he only does it to show off. She says he's more mentally alert
than anyone else in the family."

I said I wouldn't be surprised if my mother was right, and
then we settled down to all the news.

I kept watching Christine, wondering how she was going
to fit into life at Billabirra. I decided she'd weather it all
right. She had a sense of humour, and that was a relief,
because from what I'd seen of London youth in coffee bars,
I'd begun seriously to wonder whether humour was one of
the things that had got cleared away with the bomb debris.
Anyway, the important thing was that she and Mark were
obviously very much in love and very well suited. I thought
Jan would like Christine. I didn't let myself think about Jan
very much.

Mark and Christine were leaving for Australia in ten days, and we spent most of the evenings together. We saw so many shows that I was beginning to sag at the knees after a week, because London theatres aren't designed for characters with long legs. I went down to Tilbury to see them off, and then afterwards I came back to London. It was rather like that time I went back to the empty flat in Sydney.

I think I'd enjoyed being somebody's Uncle Harry.

Mark's last words to me were, "When are you coming home, Uncle Harry?" and I'd been caught on the hop. All I could think to say was that I'd spent nearly twenty years in this part of the world and that home was where you'd spent nearly twenty years.

I wandered round London all the afternoon. The sun was shining for once, the window boxes were gay, and St. James's Park was as pretty as a picture, and everything was as neat as can be.

I began to think about how home is where you've spent nearly twenty years. All right. That meant that home was three or four R.A.F. stations, and a lot of villages all over France, and Italy, and Austria, and Spain, and a lot of mean little *pensions* in Paris, and Rome, and Copenhagen, and Amsterdam, and Florence, and Barcelona, and Cannes, and . . .

I wandered into a pub in St. Martins' Lane just after opening time. I went to the bar, and then tried to shy away because there was a professional Australian at the bar and he was bawling at the top of his voice, "All right, mate, give us a pint of wallop and make it snappy!" The barman appeared to be used to him because he said, "Coming up, Mr. Moran," in a mild, forgiving voice.

I couldn't get away, because another barman asked for my order before I'd properly got the lie of the land. I made up my mind to drink fast and get out.

Mr. Moran got his pint of wallop, and all the time he was drinking he kept up a running commentary on its bloodiness. "We wouldn't give it to the pigs at home," he said. "Flaming terrible beer!" he said.

Gents in bowler hats were carefully reading their papers. The word "pigs" struck a distant chord.

I was drinking whisky because I'd decided I'd better get drunk that night. I was wishing I had a paper to read, because the trouble was that standing at the bar I could see Mr. Moran in the mirror, and he was looking at me. All the chairs away from the bar were occupied by the bowler-hatted gentry.

Suddenly Mr. Moran slammed his mug on the bar and said, "I've got it! You're Harry Brandon!"

I gulped down the last of the drink, and started to move.

"I saw your picture in the paper this morning! I wondered then if you were the same one! Now I look at you I can see you are! Well, spare me days!"

I was trying to get away, but two portly gentlemen were trying to get to the bar. There was a bit of a scrimmage.

"Don't you remember me?" Mr. Moran bawled, pushing his way between them. "I'm Rory Moran! At school! Don't you remember?"

Pigs. Rory Moran. The summer Mother and I had lived in the cottage on the coast. Rory Moran. It hadn't registered, because in the old days the accent had been on the first syllable of Moran, and now it was on the last. He didn't smell of pigs any more. He'd been beautiful then, now he was just plain good-looking. Rory Moran. I heard old Pye's voice, "Use your imagination, Brandon!" I heard Rory's eleven-year-old voice: "Beside the lake, beneath the trees . . ." I could hear the locusts and feel the heat. I could see the Moreton Bay Figs going plop on the playground.

He dragged me along the bar away from the portly types, and suddenly his voice changed, and he stopped showing off, and he sounded just like any other human being.

"Imagine meeting like this," he said.

"What are you doing in London?" I asked.

"Working on and off. I've been here five years."

"What kind of work?"

"I'm an actor!" He grinned. "Don't tell me you never

heard of me at home. Good lord, you couldn't turn on the radio without hearing me!"

I explained that I'd been away since 1940.

His mug and my glass were empty, so the professional Australian act started again. "Eh, mate, same again, and make it snappy. You got a couple of thirsty schoolboys here!"

I had to ask, "What's the boy from Woop Woop act in aid of?"

He grinned again. "It's the B.B.C. idea of an Australian," he said. "Got to play up to them, bless their hearts." He looked round. "You never know when there might be a producer about. They're doing a lot of Australian stuff these days."

Then he saw someone with a beard who looked as though he might be a producer, so the voice got loud again, and the act went on again. I bought a drink and gulped mine down and said I was late for an appointment.

I walked across through Leicester Square, and through Piccadilly Circus and along Piccadilly. I'd forgotten about getting drunk.

"Use your imagination, Brandon."

I wandered lonely as a cloud. Rory's voice. That's when it had all begun.

The daffodils were out in Hyde Park. Everything was neat and pretty. Plump and pretty.

I remembered Pye's homesick face.

Uncle Luke. "Of which country am I an expatriate?"

Home was where you'd spent nearly twenty years.

A slab of gold eight feet high. You tear up your roots and you look for gold.

Where, in the end, are your roots?

A slab of gold eight feet high.

I booked a seat on the plane for the end of the week.

CHAPTER TWENTY-FIVE

I T was autumn in Sydney. You wouldn't have known it
except for the slight chill in the air. No leaves to sweep
up, to burn. No melancholy feeling that a year was dying.
The years don't die, any more than they are suddenly resur-
rected six months later. The years stay green and glower at
you and say, "You're going to die, but I'm not!" Aggressive. Fighting you every inch of the way. Out in the bush
everything just stays green until it's time for the wattle.

Thomas Wolfe had warned me that you can't go home
again.

I saw the buildings that had been pulled down, and the
new ones that had been built. I heard the tongues of Europe
everywhere. You could eat the food of Europe and see the
faces of Europe. There was a new character called "A New
Australian". He was every eighth person you saw.

In the foyer of the Australia I saw my Uncle Ted Selway
for the first time.

He didn't see me, of course. He was surrounded by re-
porters, and newsreel and television cameras, and microphones. He'd just come back from some sort of mission
abroad. He looked on top of the world.

He was saying into the microphones that he was very glad
to be home. And then the interviewer said: "Ladies and
gentlemen you have just been listening to Sir Edward
Selway . . ."

I was glad Sir Edward was glad to be home.

I got to Billabirra in the middle of the night. It cost me
the earth to get out there from Woollaby in a hire car, but

I was impatient to finish the journey back, in spite of what Thomas Wolfe had told me.

Everything was in darkness, and I was just preparing to doss down somewhere on the verandah, when a light went on, and my mother appeared, blinking and clutching a dressing-gown round her.

"So it's you!"

I said yes, it was me.

"Did you bring all the cuttings? What the critics said?"

I said I had.

"Good. Come on. I'll get you something to eat."

My mother was an old woman. She was in her seventies. Then I realised that, after all, I was a middle-aged man. The grey in my hair must have been a shock to her, too. I wanted to apologise for those postcards that had said: "Am here. Am well."

We talked till the rooster began to set up a racket down in the fowl run, and then my mother made up a bed for me on a stretcher on the back verandah, and I went to sleep.

In the morning, when I went into the kitchen, only Jan was there.

She said, "So you're back," and I said yes I was back, and then she came over and kissed me and said she was glad I was back and had I brought the cuttings of what the critics had said. I told her I had, and then I told her about Mark and Christine, and how she was going to love Christine, and she made a wry little face and said, "Ooh, Harry, I wish there was some other word for mother-in-law." I told her about how I'd liked being called Uncle Harry by her son. Then I told her that I was sick of not having any ties, and that I'd be glad if she'd marry me.

And she said, "Really, Harry, before breakfast! You haven't got an ounce of romance in you."

But I knew it was all right by the way she said it.

Then Uncle Jonathon and Uncle Luke came in, and Uncle Luke sat down and began to roll himself a cigarette, spilling the tobacco, and I wanted to kick myself for not having taken his allowance and helped him to salve his conscience.

Jason was the one I was afraid to meet. He'd been an old, old man fifteen years ago. I expected a withered centenarian. How old was he? Well over a hundred. A hundred and three.

What bounced into the kitchen was a very active old gentleman with a smooth, pink face like a baby's. His eyes were enjoying themselves.

He said, "I've been outside waiting for you!"

I said, "O.K. I'm coming."

Uncle Jonathon said, "Let him have his breakfast, Dad."

But I didn't wait for breakfast. I went out with Jason, and he'd set up all the gear I'd left behind me, and there was everything waiting for me.

He said, "You know, I think you'd turn out a much better artist if you'd take my advice and paint The Bend."

So I said, "All right. I'll paint The Bend."

And he sat on the tree stump and watched me.

After a while he said, "So you got back home after all," and I said, "Yes, I got back home."

And after that I painted and sat on the tree stump and watched myself paint.